I STILL HEAR HER

CALLING

A Novel

By

Ruth Benjamin

(Written Under the Pen-Name
Ruth Soroson)

With thanks to Nicole Heiman, organiser of Community Environmental Education Project (South Africa) and a volunteer at the Treasure Oil Spill, for her personal account.

Previously published in 2010 by Raider Publishing.
Under the pen-name Ruth Soroson

Dedicated to: My Family

Create Space Independent Publishing Platform

2013

INTRODUCTION

"We don't have any mercy," announced the muffled voice on the phone. "We did not have mercy on your wife, and we won't have mercy on your parents-in-law and on your daughter, and even on you... Andrew Sneddon."

"My-my wife?" stammered Andrew. He had just finished eating with Andy, his daughter, and the two were watching a video they had chosen together at the video shop, a Walt Disney fantasia that had the child totally engrossed.

He felt his hand becoming wet and sticky on the phone. "My-my wife," he repeated.

"Your late wife," the voice whispered. There was a click as the phone went dead.

Even the fantasia would not replace the dread the phone call had injected into his mind. That was surely some crank caller. Who would want to harm his wife? Who would want to harm his family? What had he really done to anyone?

His wife had gone to her meeting in a nearby town. She had gone every week. In fact, she should be nearly there. He reached for his cellular phone and pressed the button, which would dial her number.

"The number you have dialled is unavailable... Please try again later."

She must have forgotten to switch on her phone, or perhaps she had already arrived at her meeting and switched it off. However, it was too early. She would have to be on the road. The uneasiness deepened, like a knife turning in his stomach. Maybe she had

—

forgotten to charge the battery. Maybe the signal was not picked up well in that area. He found himself calling her again and again but without effect.

"Daddy, come and watch this," said Andy, her blue eyes wide with excitement. "A dancing bear with all the others dancing around him. Can we see the bears at the zoo again, Daddy? Can you and I and Mummy go next week?"

"I am sure we can make it," said her father a little distractedly. "You and I will have fun together."

"And Mummy?" asked Andy quickly. "Mummy will come with us, won't she?"

"Of course she will," said Andrew a little too sharply. "Absolutely!"

However, the child, too wrapped up in the movie, did not notice his hesitation.

Once more, he dialled the number knowing the response would be the same. Nervously, he poured himself a drink. Why was he worried about a crank call?

The landline rang shrilly and he picked up the call. The voice at the other end was official, serious and sympathetic. "Mr. Sneddon," it was saying, "Mr. Sneddon, there has been an accident."

"My-my wife..." stammered Andrew.

"I am sorry," said the police captain. "They are cutting her out of the car at the moment. She went over the edge at High Point."

"She is...? She is... dead?" stammered Andrew.

"There are some signs of life," said the man sympathetically, "but the paramedics seem to be holding out very little hope of getting her out of there alive."

"I will come down there," said Andrew, "my daughter and I."

"How old is your daughter, Mr. Sneddon?" asked the policeman.

"She is nearly six," he whispered... A child, orphaned from her mother at age six. He felt as if his heart would burst out of his chest, it was beating so rapidly and, so it seemed, erratically.

"Don't bring her," said the policeman. "Are there relatives she can go to?"

"My wife's parents," he said breathlessly.

"Then I will meet you at the scene of the accident in, say, twenty minutes," said the policeman, going on to give the details of the exact location.

"But why to Granny and Grandpa?" asked Andy.

"I have been called to do some urgent work," he said, trying to pacify his daughter. "Look, take the film with you and you can show them. They would love it."

"I heard you say something about an accident," said Andy anxiously. "Has Mummy had an accident? Is she hurt?"

"I have to go and see, my little one," said her father, knowing that it was not easy to hide things from her. "But you must go and stay with Granny and Grandpa. I am sure she is all right," he lied.

Andy seemed to have withdrawn into herself. Her child's sixth sense told her that something was desperately wrong. He had not been too careful with his words either, but he had to hurry. Perhaps it would be the last time he would see Tracy alive. Perhaps by this time she was no longer alive.

As he came to the place where the car had gone over the edge he knew there was no way she could have survived. His head felt as if it

—

7

would burst into a thousand pieces as he started to climb down the embankment.

He could see the car was there, right down at the bottom; the car surrounded by dozens of people. An ambulance driver who had had to use a four wheel drive vehicle to get there and to assist the Jaws of Life in prizing open the car to let out the victim was there. A policeman seemed to know instinctively that he was Andrew and he climbed up halfway to meet him.

At that moment Andrew looked past and saw the Jaws of Life finally prise open the car as the paramedics rushed in. He quickened his pace, almost breaking into an involuntary run down the steep path.

She was not dead, but the policeman was right; she probably would be soon.

Her beautiful face, framed by blood-soaked dark curls was relatively untouched, but that was all. Her head was gashed open and her limbs fell at strange angles to her body, like a rag doll that had been thrown down the stairs by a spoilt child.

CHAPTER 1

She was in a desert, trying to cross the parched land. The sand was hot, and the sun beat down mercilessly. Oh, why was it so hot, and why was she so thirsty? *Surely there must be water somewhere. Surely there must be an oasis.*

Yes, yes, she could see it. There it was. She could see it now quite clearly, a few tall palm trees and a lake of sparkling, cool water. She would soon reach it, soon be there, and soon be able to drink her fill from the refreshing water. However, as she approached, the oasis seemed to be distancing itself, retreating further and further away, tantalising her and increasing her thirst at the opportunity of it being quenched so soon. She needed something to break the heat.. Perhaps she would even be able to swim.

That is what she needed, a nice cool swim. At the moment, all she felt was hot and dry. Her lips felt as if they would crack into pieces if she did not find liquid to wet them. *Oh, for some water! Oh, for some cold, icy water!*

The sun just continued to bear down. She was so weak, and so tired. She was in pain. Everything was sore and heavy.

She seemed to have fallen asleep, but somehow she had arrived at the oasis and was lying by the cool water. Someone seemed to be sponging her face, wetting her lips. Desperately she tried to suck some of the water from the sponge, but she was not going to be allowed to do that because it seemed to be wrenched away from her grasping mouth.

No water; definitely no water at all. The coolness seemed to be wearing off and she was so hot, and so parched.

She could hear a river nearby. She could hear the rush of flowing water. Perhaps she could reach that, but then she realised that the rushing sound had been with her all the time. It seemed to have been there for an eternity, together with a steady beeping, which seemed to become faster as time went on.

She had to get to the water. She was burning hot, and so thirsty.

Ouch! She had been bitten by something. In fact, she had been quite regularly bitten by that something. It was worse than a bee, more like a wasp. No, the sting was hard, long and sharp, almost like a needle. She knew that these stings would put her back into oblivion. Perhaps it was a snake, yes, some kind of poisonous narcotic snake. Yes, that was more like it, some sort of desert snake.

From somewhere far away she heard a disembodied voice.

"Her temperature is not dropping. I think we have some serious sepsis. We will have to consider another operation. I don't know if we will be able to save her this time. We seem to be fighting a losing battle."

"I never give up on a patient," said another disembodied voice.

"I didn't say we should give up," said the other voice. It seemed to be a woman's voice. "I just think we need to devote our time to someone who has a better prognosis. This one will be no more than a vegetable."

"We don't know that for sure," said the first voice sternly. "I have seen brain scans that I would have said were of dead men. The people have recovered. They are useful, working citizens. They have recovered completely."

"Completely?" asked the female voice in surprise.

"Completely," said the man flatly. "Some have held high academic positions and have returned to their work within two years."

"Then perhaps her husband was too impulsive," said the woman.

"I can understand his point," said the man. "He had to get on with his life. He had to use these rare moments of consciousness to free himself."

"Consciousness!" exclaimed the woman. "You call that consciousness?"

"Didn't you see the EEG?" asked the doctor.

"Yes I did," said the nurse, "but the scan was still the scan of a dead person."

"It has improved," said the doctor.

"Not much, and too late," said the woman. "This infection will take her away. No one can tolerate this kind of body temperature."

"You are sponging her regularly, Sister?" he asked. His

voice was concerned.

"Regularly, Doctor, but it has an effect for barely ten minutes."

"Then have it done every ten minutes," said the doctor, irritably. "I have to have this temperature kept down."

"She keeps asking for water," said the sister.

"Her kidneys are hardly functioning," said the man. "There is no way that she can be allowed to drink."

She drifted off, too tired to concentrate on the disjointed words coming through to her. Oh, why was she so hot? When would she get through this desert...? Why was she so thirsty? Why was she in so much pain? She could not hold on any longer. It was far too much.

Suddenly, she found herself being plummeted into a tunnel. It was filled with a dark mist and seemed to go on forever. She felt hot and then a deathly icy cold. Then, very slowly, the mist became luminous, and she began to feel cool, comfortable, and intensely at peace. All the pain, the heat, the icy coldness and the intense thirst had left her. It seemed as if she was floating, weightlessly through the tunnel towards a radiant light at the end of it. It seemed to draw her with an overpowering strength. She floated on and on as if drifting through many worlds. This was what she needed. This was the kind of peace she had been searching for all her life. This was complete fulfilment. This was intense joy. This was where she belonged.

But there was a pull from another direction. Slowly, she

became aware of a sound behind her. It was a voice, the delicate voice of a child; a little girl's voice, calling her back. But the magnetic power of the light was too strong and irresistibly she felt herself being drawn closer and closer.

The child's voice became more insistent, more desperate, and, when it whispered 'mummy', the spell was suddenly broken. Again, the 'mummy'; this time, with a question mark.

She turned to face the child, at the same time turning her back on the radiant light, but she could see only a small, vague shadow. There was no more voice.

She turned once more to the radiance, but that, too, was gone. The mist began to fade and she was left in total darkness.

"She's back again," said a young nurse, with obvious excitement. "Look at the machines. They are reacting differently now."

"Nonsense," began the older nurse. "She's gone, definitely gone."

"But look," said the young nurse, "Look at that!"

However, she did not have to say much. The machines themselves registered life. There was definitely an improvement, a marked improvement. In fact, the readings that the machines were giving were better than they had been for weeks, in fact, for months.

"Oh well, I suppose miracles do happen sometimes," admitted the older sister. "But she will be a vegetable. She will recognise no one. Maybe, in a year or two, she might be able

---

13

to recognise one or two of her relatives or friends, and maybe even say a word or two, but that is all."

Their voices faded, and she found herself in a cool oasis, and began to drink thirstily.

It was eight weeks later that she briefly registered some kind of consciousness and with it a terrible confusion about where she was and what had happened. In fact, the confusion even extended to her identity. She withdrew once more into unconsciousness.

*   *   *

There was far too much agony for a human being to bear. If only something could stop it. She tried to cry out but no sound would come. She began screaming in her head, screams that seemed to wrack her whole body, but, at the same time, she was aware that she was not moving and the screams were trapped within her own dimensions. Then there was the pain; how could she bear the pain? It seemed to be eating its way relentlessly into her body and mind.

She heard someone coming into her room, and recognised the footsteps of the nurse who usually attended to her. She felt the bed covers being pulled back, a fierce, cool rubbing on her leg and the stab of the injection needle. The pain started to lessen and gradually disappear as she found herself floating off. Just before she slept she felt her mind groping towards a picture. It was a picture that filled her with terror, a glimpse of a face in her rear-view mirror and of a red car following a little too closely behind her. Then her mind became confused as she saw her car going relentlessly towards the slope, heard the sound of a helicopter, and then the strange whirring of the Jaws of Life....

She felt, rather than heard, someone else coming into the room, someone who did not belong there. He was moving very furtively around her bed towards the machines next to her. The impression of the red car and the terrifying eyes seemed to engulf her. She felt her heart running cold and her skin crawling with terror. Somehow she knew that this presence was not a good one. She tried to scream but it again remained trapped within her body. She felt him lean slightly over the bed until he could reach the plug into which all her life support machines were plugged. She could feel his mildly foetid breath on her face and his stare boring through her eyelids.

Instinctively, she tried to hold her breath but the ventilator continued to breathe for her. However, for some reason, the machine rang a warning bell. As the nurse rushed into the room the intruder slipped out of the door and muttered an apology about the wrong ward and section.

Who was this? Had she imagined it? However, there was nothing she could do, no way of communicating her terror.

Tracy's parents took turns in spending time with their daughter, especially her mother , spending several days at a time in Pretoria, close to the hospital.

Her father would often drive over after work and spend many hours reading by her side.

When Tracy suddenly opened her eyes three months later, the nurse retreated in surprise, eventually regaining her poise and running to fetch the doctor.

When the doctor arrived it was clear that Tracy was not only awake, but that her mind seemed to be functioning well.

"Andy, where's my Andy?" she whispered. "What has happened to all of us?"

"There was an accident," said the doctor, "a terrible accident. We thought that there was no hope that you would ever wake up."

"I heard you saying that," said Tracy. "There was a nurse who kept saying I would be all right. She gave me a lot of encouragement."

"You heard that?" asked the doctor, aghast.

"Yes, I did, though I am sure I was sleeping a lot of the time. I don't remember everything. But where are Andrew and my Andy? I want to see them."

"They are gone," said the doctor quietly.

It was as if someone had turned off a light as she turned her head away and, once more, seemed to decline into an altered state of consciousness.

"I am sure she thought from your words that they had both died in the accident," said the nurse. "That is why she has retreated from us once again. They were not even in the car."

"For her, they are dead," said the doctor quietly. "I hear they have left the country without a trace. I was talking to Tracy's mother. She is frantic about the child. She is the grandmother."

"You mean he just abandoned her?"

"Well, you know that the divorce went through when she had only a semblance of consciousness. He paid a whopping big sum to support her in comfort for the rest of her life. And, of course, the insurance also paid out. She is not abandoned."

"I don't mean financially," said the nurse, a little haughtily. "They have abandoned her."

"They abandoned a vegetable," the doctor insisted.

"This was a vegetable that spoke to you now?"

"No, definitely not! I have no idea how she managed to recover to that point. It goes against all her head injuries, all her scans. It is some kind of miracle. What a pity they left, and that he now has to bring up the child alone."

"He won't be alone for long," said the nurse, wistfully. "He is incredibly good looking."

"He's gone," said the doctor, with a laugh. "Sorry you lost your chance." His voice had a trace of bitterness.

Once more, the man slipped past the sisters on duty and made his way to Tracy's ward. He hesitated when he saw someone was there. It was a young woman, probably one of her friends, maybe even a nurse. She had a small book with her and she was sitting by the bed reading very softly. Well, she would not be long, he was sure. He remained in the passage as unobtrusively as possible, after an hour deciding that he would have to deal with Tracy on another occasion. There was no way she could be allowed to remain alive!

It was the doctor who eventually told Tracy the details of what had happened. He was standing at her bedside assessing her condition when again she suddenly woke up.

"You are awake!" he exclaimed in delight.

Tracy just stared at him for several seconds. "There are so many questions I want to ask you, and maybe I will ask you," she said slowly, shutting her eyes and opening them again. "So many questions I have been asking in my head. Though, of course, no one has heard the questions, because I say them in my head and, of course, no one hears."

"I am hearing now," said the doctor.

She was silent for a few minutes. "Please tell me about the accident. How did Andy and Andrew die? Were they killed immediately or did they suffer very much?"

The doctor looked at her questioningly. "They are not dead," he said at last. "They are gone."

"That's what they said," said Tracy. "They are just gone?" she questioned as a smile spread across her face. "My baby is not dead? She is just gone? "

"Yes," said the doctor gently. "Andrew divorced you and took Andrea away. We don't know where they are."

"But she is not dead," she repeated. "She didn't suffer."

———

"Other than severe mother deprivation, no, she did not suffer. From what I have heard, they were not in the car with you."

However, Tracy's relief was too great to realise the significance of what the doctor was saying. Or did she? The child, who she thought was dead, was alive. Of course she would be happy.

"I will find her," she said after a long silence. "Whatever it takes, I will find her."

Quite suddenly, she fell asleep.

*   *   *

"Mum, I don't think I am ever going to walk again. I am just going to give up. It is too hard. My legs just don't work. I can't take it. "

She started to cry, the strange cry that had only come with the accident. "I will never walk. I will just fall. I am afraid. I am so afraid."

"But they let you hold on the bars, don't they?" asked her mother. "You are holding the bars so nothing can happen to you. You can't fall. And you can't fall in the water, either. I see that you are almost walking there. Your legs are moving very well. I am really happy about it."

"But, Mum, that is in the water and, is much easier because you are sort of floating. But, on the ground, I will never be able to do it, not ever. I am sure I will be in this

19

wheelchair forever."

Somewhat against her nature, her mother tried not to push too much. "What does the physiotherapist say?" she asked.

"Mum, you heard her. She says I have to work at it, work hard at it, and I have to do these exercises every day."

"And you don't really," said her mother resignedly.

"Well, I try, but my legs ache and ache. You have no idea how painful it is to try to walk. You have no idea what it is like, not just from the steel pins that are there, but also from my muscles. They must have become shorter or something from being in bed for so many months. They just don't seem to stretch enough for being able to walk. Maybe I am just a coward."

"A coward you most definitely are not!" exclaimed her mother. "You have no idea how much you fought to live, no idea at all. All the doctors, all the nurses, every one of the staff was amazed. They could not believe it."

"But it was all for nothing," she whispered.

"Nothing?" asked her mother sharply. "What do you mean nothing?" Her face looked blanched, and her eyes were wild and frightened.

"Well," said her daughter bitterly. "I fought for the sake of my baby, my little girl. No one has been able to find her. I want my baby back. I want my baby back." She dissolved into uncontrollable tears.

"Tracy," said her mother, trying to speak through her own

tears. "Tracy, please listen to me. You will get married again; you will have other children, many other children. You will have another baby, a boy, a girl, two boys, two girls."

"But I want Andy!" she screamed. "I want her! I want her! I want her! And she wants me. I know she wants me. I hear her calling. I still hear her calling! She is calling, 'Mummy, Mummy'. She is calling me!"

"My darling daughter, I know you miss her, and I am sure she is missing you and calling you. I am quite sure of that." Her mother started to cry, bearing in mind the image of her granddaughter. "It is difficult for me, too." She sniffed.

"But then why did you let her go?" whispered Tracy.

"I have answered that before," said her mother, still sobbing. "He just took her. He divorced you, and then just took her."

"But why did you let him? Why didn't you just stop him? You are such a strong person. Why didn't you do something?"

"He went so quickly. He was gone before I realised it, before I could really find out where he was going. They were both gone. We tried to find out, but there was no way, no way at all."

"But why didn't you tell me? Why didn't you let me know? I could have stopped all this."

"You were on machines, all kinds of machines. They said you would never recover, never get your mind back, and never be yourself."

"But then how could he have divorced me? How could he have divorced me without my knowing? How did he do that?"

"I am not sure, my darling," said her mother, knowing she had said this so many times before. "It just kind of happened. He paid a lot of money to a lawyer and, somehow, organised it. It was just done."

*   *   *

Weeks turned into months and Tracy improved slowly and steadily. There were, of course, setbacks. There were days when everyone seemed to despair, days when Tracy seemed to lose her ability to remember even simple things.

At times, losing patience, her mother would 'tackle' the doctors, hoping for answers.

"Will my daughter ever be herself again? Will she function as she used to, be able to read a book, be able to walk and talk without any effort as she used to? I mean, she can't be like this for the rest of her life. What are we going to do with her? Will she ever get married? Will she be able to get married, to ever care for a husband and family?"

The doctor turned to the mother with a serious expression.

"We have absolutely no way of knowing," he said soberly. "It is a miracle she is alive at all, and, more than alive, she can communicate with us. That itself is a miracle. We don't know how much more we can expect. It will take time, months at least, maybe even years. We don't know at all what she will be like in three years' time. I would have said two months ago that she was finished with this world, but she isn't at all. She is gaining ground every day."

"Not fast enough," said her mother impatiently. She turned to her daughter. "Now, Tracy," she said in an irritated voice, "Tracy, you must try to concentrate. Try reading to me. Don't just stare at the words. Concentrate! I am getting really annoyed with your laziness. The doctor was right. You are nothing but a vegetable!"

Tracy was crying, and the doctor rushed over.

"Mrs. Berns, I don't want you to speak to your daughter like that. Do you think she can help what she is not yet able to do?" His eyes blazed angrily.

"Well, as soon as she comes home, we will start her on an intensive programme of work," said Mrs. Berns. "I will show you that I am not having a backward daughter. She will learn to be a useful citizen, even if I have to break every bone in her body."

"We have just fixed those," said the doctor grimly.

"Not enough; you have not done enough," said Mrs. Berns, beginning to sob. "I don't know why all this has happened to me. Look what misfortune I have, my once-beautiful daughter now reduced to nothing!"

For the next four months this scene repeated itself regularly.

However, one day, the message was different.

"We have to make some decisions now," said the doctor. "We could send Tracy home to you, and you could engage a nurse to look after her, and she could come for daily physiotherapy, occupational therapy and the various other therapies she needs."

He saw that Mrs. Berns looked somewhat put out by the suggestion.

"Maybe she could just come home and be herself. I can use my own kind of persuasion to get her to do things. She can do odd jobs around the house, or maybe, during the day, she can work at the Sheltered Employment Institute. They cater for people who are either born retarded or somehow become so. I am beginning to accept that Tracy will never be normal, never be able to read or write again, never be able to walk very far, and will have her face pulled downward to one side. Maybe she just needs to rest. She has had enough of all these therapies."

"But you were pushing her to do all these things," said the doctor. "My nurses have heard it, also, and have been quite distressed by it."

"It is just a mother's frustration at wanting things to be different." She sighed. "But, basically, I have accepted that they won't be. Today, she asked me the same question at least six times, and went on and on about the subject. If she gets on one track, you just can't get her off. I can't take these things anymore. I myself am becoming a nervous wreck!"

"I have spoken to your husband, and he has agreed to the

other alternative," said the doctor.

"Well, he really does not have the ultimate say," said Mrs. Berns, a little rudely. "It is what I decide that counts."

The doctor went on, making no comment on her last statement. In many ways, the situation had become obvious to anyone who happened to notice.

"There is a rehabilitation centre in the Cape, about sixty kilometres from Cape Town itself. They have produced very good results in cases like these. We at the hospital have decided that it would be to best place for her to go."

"If you are going to institutionalise her, can't she go to a place nearer home so that we can visit her on weekends? I mean, they have homes here for the mentally handicapped, and the conditions seem to be fairly good for people who don't really care about their surroundings."

"This is not a home to place Tracy," explained the doctor patiently. "This is a residential rehabilitation centre where she will get all her therapies, and where we hope to see her improve to what she was before."

"Doctor, you have got to be honest with me. We all know she was almost a vegetable and, now that she has improved to this point, we must all be grateful. I am not expecting her to be different. I know she is not able to do things and that she does not really understand what we are all saying. At least she is alive."

"Give it a chance in Cape Town," said the doctor. "The medical insurance will cover it quite adequately."

"How long will it be, Doctor?" she asked.

"Between eighteen months and two years," said the doctor.

Mrs. Berns gave a gasp. "And then?" she asked.

"And then, hopefully, she will be more herself. Hopefully, we will see the old Tracy again."

"Can't she stay here, in this hospital?"

"I am afraid we have done all we can for her. This is an acute hospital, and we have stabilised her, and, may we say it, actually saved her life. I thought on a few occasions that we had lost her, especially in the first few weeks when she had septicaemia."

Mrs. Berns shuddered. "You really think that, in this place, there will be an improvement?"

"Yes, I do."

"Then we should send her there. We will keep in telephone contact, and we have relatives in Cape Town who can visit her regularly. When would she be going? Does she know?"

"As much as she can really know anything," said the doctor, "though there are times where she seems to be quite clear with us. I have been, on some occasions, quite surprised."

"How will she get there?"

"We will send her down by train with an escort, and the centre will pick her up at the station. I will let them know they should contact you as soon as she arrives."

CHAPTER 2

For the next several months, Tracy's memories were vague and disjointed.

She remembered part of the train ride and the coupe' she shared with some kind of health worker who she knew was in charge of her, and she remembered the seemingly endless ride to the Home.

The Crawley Centre was housed in an old Cape Dutch gabled mansion that spread itself over the centre of nine acres of land, which had been used to cultivate magnificent gardens.

It was definitely not a hospital in that patients were not in wards surrounded by machines, heavy drips, nurses in white starched uniforms and doctors wearing stethoscopes.

In many ways, it was like a home, or even a boarding house or residential hotel. Each patient had his or her own room with a shared bathroom and shared lounges with the TV invariably running. It was a pleasant enough house with open air, good food, and healthy living.

There was a gym, under the supervision of four physiotherapists, extensive occupational therapy facilities and small conference rooms for group psychotherapy.

Tracy seemed to accept her surroundings as part of her life, a shadow amongst forty shadowy figures residing in the centre, all recovering from similar accidents and traumas.

Like the majority of those around her she spent most of her waking hours in a wheelchair, though there were painful strenuous times when she would have to try to walk and to exercise her legs.

She made friends with the other patients knowing that some of them too, lived in and out of a haze. At times, she would find herself trembling from fear for reasons she could not remember. At other times, she would find herself crying uncontrollably, calling for Andy and sometimes, also for Andrew.

A particular day stood out in her memory, accentuating the terror that sometimes threatened to engulf her.

"I will take you for a walk," said Patricia, one of her fellow patients who was doing very well and had improved beyond anyone's expectations. "I will ask the sister in charge and take you out in the wheelchair."

Tracy nodded gratefully. She was tired of sitting with the other patients in the veranda overlooking the vast gardens. She wanted to be out, to be pushed along the paths. Would she, one day, actually be able to walk on her own? True, she was able to go a short distance on crutches, but this was very slow and they hurt her arms.

She looked up at Patricia. "Please, Pat. Please do that." She had been with Pat before, and had really enjoyed the comparative freedom of just 'walking'.

They soon collected her wheelchair from her room and she

got into it, with Patricia holding it steady for her. Ten minutes later, they were taking a delightful walk along the path.

Patricia, though having a remarkable recovery, still felt a little unsteady in her walking, and having to push a wheelchair made her feel easier and far more confident. She had found a willing partner in Tracy, who would never refuse a walk. Tracy could still not communicate well, and Patricia chatted happily.

They came to a sheltered spot and seeing they were on a slight incline, Tracy felt with her hand for the brake of the wheelchair, but somehow she could not find it. "Help me, Pat," she said. "My brake has gone."

Pat turned to look at it and noticed that the position had been shifted. She was just about to push it when something made her realise that the cable was about to snap. "Hey, this isn't strong enough," she began, and then gave a gasp of horror. "You know, someone has been at this with a knife, a really sharp knife."

Tracy frowned. "Why?" she asked.

"Well, that would make the brakes fail suddenly, badly."

"But why would someone do that?" asked Tracy.

"It is dangerous, very dangerous," Patricia continued. "I mean, if you had been with the others on a slope, you might have gone out of control."

"Out of control," echoed Tracy, her voice suddenly becoming full of fear. For a few seconds, her mind flashed back to a red car following her and those eyes.... She felt a rising panic. "Take me back," she said. "Take me back quickly. Now!"

"I was going to do that," said Patricia. "But maybe we could just do a bit more walking. We won't stop. We won't need the brake. "

"Please take me back now," said Tracy, sounding quite terrified.

Sensitive to her mood, Patricia concurred. She herself had been a little shaken to see the brake tampered with. They reported it as soon as soon as they got back. The staff showed only a faint hint of concern, with a request for transport to take it in for repairs. Did they not see the danger of the situation? Did they not believe them? The brakes were definitely tampered with. Did they perhaps think that they had done it themselves?

Tracy was duly given another wheelchair with 'perfect' brakes, and, at least on the matron's side, the incident was forgotten.

Tracy was phoned regularly by her family and visited by her cousins. As she got better, they began to take her out for drives. Again these memories were vague....

Why did the sun always make her feel so drowsy? She found herself dozing off in the chair that had been placed for her by her caring cousins. Yet, how comfortable she felt. It was wonderful to hear the soft swish of the waves as they threw their shining foam onto the beach. The air was so fresh and clean. Even the vague smell of seaweed and fish was

---

pleasant to her, blending into the atmosphere.

She must have dozed off, because she awoke to find herself facing several dozen black and white penguins who had obviously been watching her. How delightful, three rows of friendly 'flippered' creatures standing upright as if they had paused on their morning walk to investigate and greet the stranger.

She called 'hello' and they did not move away, and though they did not actually move closer their bodies seemed to draw closer. Was she dreaming? Did penguins really behave like that? Surely penguins were wild birds and surely they were taller.

Her cousins, Robert and Tammy, were standing behind her watching them. "Penguins?" Tracy queried.

"Yes," said Tammy. "Jackass Penguins."

"That's a bit rude," commented Tracy. "They look very clever."

"No, that is really what they are called, the African Jackass Penguin. There are many on the islands off the coast. Boulders is one of their favourite places, and they have become quite tame."

"I love them," she said, stretching out her hands. "I just love them. I could watch them all day. I just love them."

"Well, you can look at them for a few more minutes, and then we have to take you back to the convalescent home. The matron said that you must not stay out too long, and I am sure we have already stayed too long, and there was the drive here, also."

"I love them," continued Tracy. "I just love them. Andy would love them. I must bring Andy one day." Her cousins were at a loss for words.

Except for a slight shifting of their feet, the birds did not move.

"Why don't they run away?" she asked, simply.

"They don't," her cousin said, "unless they are really frightened."

"What could frighten them?" asked Tracy.

"Well, apart from sharks and seals and things, there was a dreadful oil spill about a year ago from the sinking of the Apollo Sea. The oil soaked all the penguins around the Cape. Many thousands of oil-covered penguins were rescued and cleaned. Apparently, less than half the birds actually survived; those that did were returned to their homes and, hopefully, will carry on breeding. I am not sure if these penguins were affected. I am not even sure if it came close to this area. We were in Natal at the time."

Tammy wondered how much Tracy had understood but the dejected expression on her face seemed to indicate that she did.

"That is terrible," said Tracy, seeming to withdraw into herself. "Perhaps we should go now."

She remained withdrawn and sad during her trip back in the car until they were a few kilometres away from the home, when she seemed to recover.

"Can we go there again?" she asked. "Can we go and visit the penguins again?"

"Yes, of course," said Robert graciously. "We can fetch you in two weeks' time. I will speak to the matron about it."

Thereafter, followed several visits and Tracy seemed to enjoy her communication with the penguins more than anything else.

Month after month passed and, slowly, the haze that had seemed to be clouding Tracy's brain began to clear, first in patches, and then altogether so that by the end of the year, she was managing to do things that she had earlier despaired of. People and things began to have meaning, and she was able to laugh and joke with them.

Her reading and writing improved steadily, and she was

able to write home in a somewhat childish handwriting, quite unlike her own had been.

She appreciated the letters she received, especially from her father, who wrote twice a week. Her mother's letters, at times, tended to be somewhat critical.

She was still not ready for discharge, however, and it was around this time that a new element entered her life, or, rather, an element she had been constantly aware of, but was becoming aware of it anew, an element of fear....

It was about 7:40 p.m. one evening that she arrived, at the door of her room and she unlocked and opened it, reaching for the light switch. It clicked, but the light would not go on. She walked further into the room and switched on the bedside light switch. This, too, only clicked. Surely both lights could not be off, or maybe there was something happening with the electricity in the home?

She went back into the passage. The light was on, as it always was, but perhaps that was a different circuit.

She looked through the fanlight at the top of the doors of both her neighbours. Their lights were on. She wondered if either of them possessed a torch, or even a candle. She couldn't see much by the hall light and it was most irritating not to have a light in the room. Not many staff seemed to be around at this time and she did not want to really bother them.

She tried her first neighbour unsuccessfully, but had more luck with the second, and she came back and shone the torch onto the ceiling light. There was no bulb in it. *Strange!* She shone the torch on her bedside lamp. This, too, had no bulb. How could light bulbs just disappear? Her door had been locked. Why had they been removed? Now she had to try to borrow a bulb, otherwise her room would be in darkness.

She spent about twenty minutes finding someone who possessed a spare bulb, and she brought it back to her room, standing somewhat unsteadily on her chair in order to place it in the socket.

She walked over to her light switch and switched it on. *Zabang!* There was an explosion within the bulb as it burst.

Aware of the crunching of glass slivers beneath her feet, she tiptoed to the place she had left the torch and shone it around the room. There were tiny splinters of glass everywhere, all over her carpet, her bed, her stool, everywhere.

Several of the residents, hearing the explosion, had come to her door and they stared in horror at the scene.

"You must have twisted the wires when you removed the old bulb," said one of them. "It can be quite dangerous."

Tracy was about to say that she had not removed the bulb, neither of the bulbs, when she checked herself, not quite knowing the reason.

Doreen, her next-door neighbour, spoke. "You had better come and sleep in my room. You can't stay in here with all that glass. You need a vacuum cleaner to get all that out, and we can't get one till tomorrow. Even so, we had better tell the matron tonight."

Tracy reluctantly agreed. What else could she do? It would be totally impossible to stay in the room. Apart from that, she herself felt emotionally bruised, shattered and tired.

Who had turned the bulbs around in their sockets until the wires were twisted and then removed them, especially as her door had been locked and only she had the key?

The sister on duty, realising something was wrong, came rushing in.

"Surely you know you must not do your own electrical repair work."

"But I didn't; I always replace globes. But I didn't even take these out. They were gone."

"We understand our memory is still not that it should be," said the sister warningly. "But look at what you did. You could have put the whole place on fire. And look at this," she said, pointing at some naked wires. "Anyone could have touched these wires and killed themselves instantly! What did you think you were doing?" Her voice rose in anger.

"I'm sorry," Tracy said resignedly. Maybe she was really going crazy. She knew she had not touched any of the wires, but the matron was in no mood to believe her.

Time passed, and Tracy became, once more, the attractive young lady she had been before the accident.

Apart from some of the art classes she had enjoyed she felt that her only bright spots had been her visits to Boulders, her only true friends, the penguins. Even her cousins began to become irritable with her especially as she had found the need to ask questions continuously. Why did everyone have to treat her as a child? True, she had been very badly hurt, and had spent a couple of years recovering. However, she had recovered completely, except, of course, that she had to concentrate harder on things she was doing, and for a very slight limp that showed only if she was very exhausted. The slight distortion of her face had gone completely.

*   *   *

It was early evening. The sun was just beginning to yearn towards the western horizon where it would light up other lands and other peoples. Except for the terrible ache in her heart for her child, Andy, Tracy was feeling fairly at peace.

She could say, now, that she had truly recovered. Her thinking was sharp. Her walking and even her running was good; her writing, though different to what it had been was quite mature looking.

She knew she had, in many ways, changed, become softer, more sensitive to others and more aware of her surroundings. She knew that the time for her discharge was close and she looked forward to it.

She decided to go for a walk on her own before it got completely dark and ten minutes later found her walking along a leafy path. She had been wheeled so many times along this path, especially with Patricia, who had long ago been discharged and taken up the threads of her life again. How wonderful it was to be walking at such a swift pace.

The slight breeze was blowing through her long dark hair that had lengthened considerably whilst she was ill. Even that made her look different.

She was suddenly aware of a faint rustle on the side of the path and she turned to see the terrifying sight of a cobra or was it a ringhals rearing its head, trying to force her to acknowledge it and submit herself as prey. Terrified, she flew back along the road towards the home, arriving at the matron's door to report the snake.

"We don't get those snakes in these parts," was her only curt comment. "You must have been imagining things. But I suppose we will investigate. It was probably a harmless mole snake."

"It definitely wasn't," said Tracy, still out of breath. "That was something very dangerous." Trembling, she returned to her room.

Thankful to be back inside, but disturbed by the matron's reply, she decided to report it to the security man at the gate first thing in the morning.

The next day found her on her usual morning walk down towards the gate. This time, she stuck to the road, not wanting to encounter any kind of snake. She approached the gate and went through it, mentioning to the security guard that she had seen a cobra. He frowned. It was not possible, he was sure. However, in his contact with her, he had come to have a certain respect for her, and reassured her that they would look for it.

"Can I go and stand on the road outside the gate?" she asked. She just needed to know exactly where she was. She just needed to stand outside the home and look in. "I just feel I have been here too long," she said. "Please tell me what is around us, where we are exactly in relation to everything."

"Well, Miss," he said, taking her literally, "over to the right of us in that direction is the train. It is the main line from Cape Town to Johannesburg. In fact, there is a small station there. The train doesn't always stop there, but the very last train does, the one at 11:15 p.m. At that time, you can hear the train quite clearly, because everything else is so quiet. But you can't get to the station directly, because there is a lake there. You have to go around it. To our left, over in that direction, are the mountains. Have a look. You can see them from here."

She looked with longing to the mountains. If only she could be free to go wherever she liked, to be who she liked, free to find Andy; free to be herself.

She walked a few metres along the road and stood looking around her. The scenery was beautiful, the mountains majestic.

Suddenly she heard a car coming along the road and realised that the driver must be going at a tremendous speed. The security guard called to her to get out of the way, but she wasn't on the road, was she? She was on the grassy pavement. However, the car was coming straight for her, and she instinctively jumped out of the way. She was trembling when the guard once more called to her and she saw that the car had made a U turn and, once more, headed in her direction. She ran towards the bushes as the driver went over the place she had been standing in not a second before. The car went speeding off into the distance.

"That car came straight for you... twice!" said the security guard, visibly shaken. "It was too fast. I am sorry I did not take his number. I was too shocked. I never expected him to come back. He was going right for you. Please go inside. I am really not allowed to let you out of here, but I have kept an eye on you, haven't I?"

Reassuring him, she went inside. This time she did not report anything. Who would believe her, anyway?

Later that day, a note was pushed under her door. 'We

---

will get you' was all it said. She thrust it into her pocket. She would have to speak to the doctor straight away. She could not stay here. There was no way she could stay at Crawley Centre.

The doctor however, was going to a meeting and could not see her till late afternoon. She had to be satisfied with that, but she could not stay here, she knew she could not stay here. Someone was after her and now she had written proof.

"I would like to go home," she said to the doctor when she finally saw him. "I feel I am

so much better and I am ready to, and would love to go home."

"You are up for discharge in the next few weeks," said the doctor with a smile. "I just want the social worker to make the final arrangements. You have improved beyond anyone's expectations or imagination."

"Thank you," she said, returning his smile. He had always been a wonderful caring doctor. Perhaps he would understand why she needed to leave. "Doctor," she said, "I need to leave right away. It has become dangerous for me here. Someone is trying to kill me."

The doctor's expression changed and in a very serious tone he corrected her, "No one is trying to kill you. We have not heard you say things like this for many months, Tracy. I am very distressed about it. I will have to call in a psychiatrist. I had thought that these paranoid delusions were simply part of the after effects of the accident. I had not expected them to rise again when you were better. We can't let you go home."

"But I am better. I am definitely better," she almost screamed. "There is no doubt that I am better. I have been able to read books, write letters, go for walks, and carry on conversations, all of which I could not do before. I am really better."

"And these paranoid ideas?" he questioned.

"Doctor, there is someone trying to kill me. Look, I even got this note, this threatening note." More confidently, she felt inside her pocket, only to come up with some rather worse for wear tissues.

"Tracy, you are not well yet," said the doctor finally. "Let's give it a few months more, shall we? We can't go wrong."

"I can't...." she began. She was going to ask him to speak to the security guard, but she knew that he should not have let her outside the gate, and she would get him into trouble, perhaps fired. "Also, I have to find my child, Andy."

"Listen," he said. "I want you to go home as much as you do. I have been watching your progress with a great deal of pride, real pride. You see, except for these paranoid thoughts of yours, you are ready to do anything, absolutely anything. You can go back and study if you want. I would support that. I just want to see you well. Please, Tracy."

"But you don't understand the danger," stammered Tracy.

"For that reason, I am keeping you here," said the doctor firmly. "When a person is not related to reality, they are in

---

42

danger."

"But the danger is real," she insisted. "Look at the car accident."

He looked at her in genuine surprise. "That was an accident," he said." Unfortunately, car accidents happen. I mean... Look at all the other patients in this home. They have all been in either motorbike or car accidents, and do any of them blame anyone else in the sense that they think it was done on purpose?"

"Do you think that, in my case, it was done on purpose," asked Tracy?

"No, of course I don't," said the doctor. "These things are never done on purpose. Someone just got too close to you; that's all. It was not done on purpose at all."

"You mean I really was hit off the road? I didn't just lose control and swerve?"

"Not according to what I read," said the doctor. "As far as I remember, they were trying to rule out suicide, and there were definite marks of a red car having bumped you, at least as far as I know."

The words seemed to explode in Tracy's brain. There was a red car. The eyes were real. That face was real. There was someone who was intent on killing her. No one believed this. She could turn to no one. Months, still, in Crawley Centre? She could not take it.

Tracy returned to her room, desperate. Was it all worth it? She would never get away, never find Andy. She had fought for nothing. Nothing in her life would ever come right. They would find her and kill her, or she really would go crazy. What was the use?

*   *   *

It was dark and cold. Tracy shivered as she tightened the thin jacket around her, hoping it would give even the illusion of warmth. She had not known it would be so cold. The wind stung her face with its icy breath, and made her hands numb and sore. She tried to rub them, but that increased the pain.

She felt again in her pocket. The money for her ticket was there, and a little extra money that she still had left over from what she had saved of her pocket money, almost from the time she had arrived. There was also the money she had originally brought with her, which she had only partly handed in, even, at that stage, feeling that she might need it.

She had to get away. Life had become too dangerous, too terrifying, and the doctor and the nurses did not seem to understand. All they were interested in was for her to see a psychiatrist because she was 'imagining' she was in constant danger.

She looked behind her at the large imposing mansion and sprawling outbuildings, which she had fled. She had been relatively happy there not so long ago. She had realised she was making a slow but steady recovery and was prepared to stay there, until her life had become fraught with terror.

The cold wind was penetrating, making her very bones ache, but it could not match the ache in her heart as she realised she was no nearer to finding her daughter.

She felt the tears starting and falling down her cheeks, strangely warming before they too turned sharply chilled.

Less than three hours ago, she had been at the point of ending her life. She had had all the tablets ready. All she had to do was to swallow them. Her mind had been made up. She had written two suicide notes. She had had no intention of surviving. Nothing would work out, nothing!

Then, from the deep recesses of her heart and mind, a child's voice, Andy's voice, had called out, called her back to this world... Mummy... Mummy...

She paused as she realised that she had not brought the suicide notes with her, nor had she destroyed them. They would be found.

Would they come after her? Would they try to stop her? Would they not see that they had driven her too far? Maybe death was the only way.

There were things one could not run away from. It had been more than two years since she had heard anything about Andy. Andy would have forgotten her. Maybe Andrew had even married again and Andy had a new mother. She would forget that her real mother had ever existed.

She slowed down. The lake ran almost alongside the path on which she was running. Why not? Perhaps that was better than tablets. Why catch a train? Why be constantly hounded by the people? She would never get away, never! She would never find Andy, never, ever!

She changed direction and in the light of the half moon, she saw the waters beckoning her with their sinister, shining blackness. Death! That would be preferable! Death, with its welcoming icy fingers.

She got to the water's edge and stood looking at the river. In a sense she felt even colder. In another sense, all feeling had gone. It would soon be over. She walked along the edge, and suddenly her feet caught on some kind of root and she felt herself falling. Survival instinct made her break her fall, clutching on to the bushes, scrambling, crawling away from the deathly lake, which had opened its mouth to claim its prey.

She felt again in her pocket. The money was still there, money she had hidden away. Had she, all along, not trusted them completely? Or had her father not trusted them completely as he slipped it into her hand the day before she left the first hospital? She could not remember exactly, but surely he had said something about her keeping it with her. Memories of these days were not clear at all.

She stood up, smoothing out her hair. She had somehow in her fall, lost the velvet bow she had been wearing. What was a velvet bow? Perhaps, if she lived, she would get another one. The ache in her heart grew stronger. What would her family say? What would her father say? Would he be told that she was missing, believed dead? For one crazy minute, she thought of somehow phoning him. However, he, too, would surely not believe her. He might call the police, call the doctors to come and fetch her. She had to speak to him face to face.

She had written home about the things that had happened to her but they had not responded to any of that. Had they, too, not believed her? Had they, too, decided it was part of her accident and recovery?

She turned her steps again towards the river. She could swim, yes, but then she had heard people were constantly worried about river vegetation that pulled a person down, sucking them beneath the water.

Was that her answer?

She looked at her watch. It was almost 10:30 p.m. Hadn't

the security guard had told her that the train to Johannesburg would be passing through in about forty-five minutes? Perhaps she could catch it! She had no idea how close or far away she was.

He had not mentioned that, but he had mentioned that this train stopped at this station, and he had indicated the direction.

Putting everything else out of her mind, she ran towards the station. If the station was not far and she was going in the right direction, she would wait for the train. She wished she had brought something warmer.

It was quite early the next morning that they came to look for her. They had read the suicide notes with a great deal of anxiety and anger. They had started to search the house and then the grounds, going further and further afield.

It was about 10 a.m. when they found a place on the bank of the lake where someone had obviously struggled with themselves before they had met their death in the waters. The velvet bow, caught on some twigs near the water gave testimony as to what had happened.

After looking up and down the river, they had all walked back, entered the centre and closed the gates. The police had to be contacted and the family informed. It was a pity that they had not thought to call the psychiatrist sooner. The young lady had been more disturbed than they had thought.

CHAPTER 3

As she ran, Tracy's mind kept flashing back to the day, or rather the evening she had first met Andrew, which seemed like a whole lifetime ago.

"Tracy, Tracy, please come help me lay the table for the guests. We have eight of them and I want things to be exactly right. I managed to get these special serviettes, and I spent an hour and a half looking for just the right starter. You are so artistic, Tracy. Just see if you can make those special shapes for me. And take the silverware from the drawer on the right-hand side. Mrs. Tilsey is coming, and she must see what good cutlery we have. And, oh Tracy, do something about your hair. You can't possibly let my friends see you like that. They will think we just have no taste at all, none at all! I want you to look really nice. After all, I have invited the Snedden boy."

"What is he like, Ma?" asked Tracy, not at all sure she would like to meet him.

"Oh, I am sure he is presentable enough," her mother went on. "But what you must look at, is the fact that he is an up and coming accountant and has already made himself a lot of money, and has many investments and shares in big companies. And, Tracy, please try to look nice for your mother and father's sake, and take off those awful denim jeans. After all, this is to be a semi-formal party. I suggest you

---

wear that off-shoulder dress that your Aunt Bessie bought for you, and you can borrow my pearls, as long as you give them back. The meal should be outstanding, though I say it myself. It isn't often that we can get fresh lobster in these parts. We will have that with pineapple and celery followed by chicken and cheese soufflé, and baked potatoes, peas and..."

"Okay, Mum, sounds good," said Tracy. "But do I have to wear that dress? Can't I wear something a bit more casual?"

"No, you can't, Tracy. I want you to look your best. And you look really marvellous in that dress. You are nineteen now, and you have to realise that you are no longer a child, and you can't dress like one of these cheap teenagers."

Tracy gave a sigh. "I think I've put on weight, maybe it won't fit," she said hopefully.

"I'm sure it will fit," said her mother. "And, now that you mention it, I wish you would stop buying chocolates and potato chips, and all that bubblegum. I am so ashamed to see my daughter chewing all the time. I want you to be a lady. You must think of getting married in the next few years."

"There was George," said Tracy slowly.

"George!" said her mother. "George! His parents are nobodies. They exist on a salary that hardly covers their expenses, which aren't that great, I am sure. Their house is tiny and their furniture is old. How could we possibly have anything to do with them? How could we introduce them to our friends as the parents of our son-in-law, the grandparents of our grandchildren? People who are simply nothing!

"And flowers, Tracy," said her mother, changing the subject. "Oh, you are so artistic. Please go into the garden and get some flowers to make an arrangement for me. Mind you, I don't want one of your modern arrangements. The last one you made was all branch and hardly any flowers. I had to hide it. This time, I only want flowers done in the way the florists do it. And Tracy, please stand up straight. You look like the hunchback of Notre Dame when you do that. I don't know where you got that posture from. You are always slouching; you are not walking correctly. Take little steps; I wish you would wear your high heels. I don't know why you are so sloppy. It is just all your sloppy friends who influence you.

"Now, Tracy, don't just stand there. Think what I want you to do next. Come on, use your brain. You are supposed to have one, even though I find you incredibly lacking in common sense. And to think you want to go to college to study. You wouldn't be able to keep up with the class. School is different. You did well there – but college! And anyway, rich young men don't really want a girl with too much education. And it does seem to be that the more educated you are in many instances, the less you earn, unless you find a really successful doctor who isn't too soft and too dedicated to his patients. But that's not the kind of person you would choose," she ended in disgust.

Tracy did not reply. It was no good arguing with her mother. She would have to wear what her mother 'ordered'.

She knew that if she wore anything else, the evening would be full of jibes and grimaces from her as to how odd and strange she was looking.

From a very young age she realised that if she didn't wear exactly what her mother wanted, she would make biting comments until she did. From the age of seven, she had learnt to ask, "What shall I wear today?"

Her mother had responded by telling her friends that her daughter was so dependent on her that she even had to ask her daily what to wear.

It was only in the last year that she had earned a bit of money part time and had chosen her own clothes, but she had had to suffer the constant jibes about them.

"Where is your father?" asked her mother. "He knows there is a dinner party tonight, and I asked him to come home straight from the office. I told him to terminate any conversation he was having and to get into his car right away. He isn't here." She looked at her watch, and, at that moment, a key turned in the lock.

A tired Mr. Berns, her father, walked slowly into the house, trying to make a beeline for the sofa where he could relax with his paper for ten minutes.

"Thomas," his wife said. "Tom, how could you? Here I have been slaving away getting the dinner party ready, and you want to sit down and busy yourself with the paper. Will you please go out right away and get the drinks? I have ordered them from the bottle store. They should have delivered them by now, but they are not here yet."

"I am sure they are coming," he said, looking longingly at the sofa and fingering his newspaper.

"I am sure they are coming," said Mrs. Berns, giving a fairly good imitation of his tone, except that she had turned it into a whine. "You are too lazy. You sit in your office all day chatting to the secretaries and to the people beneath you, and you won't even help your hard-working wife. And the Tilseys' are coming, and, we hope, Tracy's future husband."

"You like him, my girl?" he asked, smiling at his daughter.

"I haven't met him yet, Dad," she said.

"Stop talking to your father and let him get on with what he has to do."

Mrs. Berns' voice rose angrily. "You are always being cheeky to your mother!"

Mr. Berns put down his briefcase, took out his car keys, and left. They heard his car drive away.

Five minutes later, there was a clink of glass and a ring at the door. The drinks had been delivered from the shop.

"Never mind," said Mrs. Berns to Tracy. "Your father will be back when he finds the drinks have been delivered. I hope he hurries and doesn't speak to anyone he meets. I have a lot of jobs for him to do."

The dinner party was not as bad as Tracy had expected. Andrew Snedden had been a very special person, not at all as she expected, and some of the other guests had been quite interesting. She had been fascinated whilst listening to Mr.

53

and Mrs. Tilsey, both lawyers. For some reason, her mother had cut short her conversation with them. The food had been good, too. Her mother definitely was an outstanding cook.

She shuddered, however, as the last guest left, knowing that for the next two hours at least, there would be the party post mortem. There would also be a massive number of dishes to wash. She would love to have washed them alone, putting on her radio to listen to music whilst she worked. Occasionally she had done this and had enjoyed it. She offered to do it now.

"No you won't, Tracy. You leave greasy stains on them," said her mother. "We will all do them together." Tension was already mounting. "And your father will help."

Mr. Berns walked into the room.

"Can I help, dear?" he asked.

"Can you help!" she exclaimed. "Do you think you are going to charm me in that way, after what you did?"

He looked at her in genuine surprise. Surely he was used to this already.

"I was terribly ashamed of you," she said, "telling all those Garfield jokes. How babyish, how puerile, infantile and childish; a man with a so-called brain like yours. I know everyone pretended to laugh, but you could see how embarrassed they were. Oh how you shamed us all! And that tie you wore! You know how I hate it. It was in such poor taste. I know Tracy gave it to you, but she chose it herself, and you should have left it as a memento in your cupboard. I can just imagine what everyone is saying about it now. Oh, aren't you ashamed of yourself?"

Mr. Berns made a move to go out of the kitchen.

"Now don't go," his wife said. "Stand up like a man and listen to your faults. Don't sneak away like the mangy cur that you are. Oh, they are laughing at you, sniggering in their expensive homes, gossiping about what I have to put up with. What kind of man are you? I rue the day I ever accepted your proposal of marriage. I didn't realise what inferior quality I had married. Or maybe I did, and I thought I could mould and shape you into a decent human being. But look what you are... Arrgh!"

Tracy knew this would carry on for hours. She knew that if either of them left the room to go to bed, her mother would follow them, forcibly waking them up through the night to listen to her. There was no way to shut her out. She didn't believe anyone in the house should keep secrets away from her and she kept all the keys. What was the use?

Two hours later Tracy sank, exhausted, into bed, very conscious that the way she sat, the way she talked, the way she ate, had all come under fire. Even her interest in the Tilseys' had been destroyed. Her mother had told her that the Tilseys' had remarked about what an impudent, flippant girl she was.

She was exhausted, but sleep would not come. One day, she would leave home, but her mother kept telling her she wouldn't last a day without her, that she would come

---

55

crawling home, begging for forgiveness. No – she would remain at home, till a rich man would come and claim her hand. No one else would do. All friends of either sex had been successfully banished by her mother.

Would she ever be able to hold her own opinion? She had been speaking to Andrew, the Snedden boy and had commented on some political factor. Her mother had looked at her darkly. "Now, now Tracy. You don't know much about that, and that isn't your opinion at all." Andrew had stared at her, open mouthed.

She could not sleep. Her mother's monotonous, sometimes ranting voice went on and on in the room next to hers and then she heard the sound of crying as her mother bemoaned her fate at having to give up her life for a husband and daughter who shamed and embarrassed her at every turn. Tracy felt overwhelmed with guilt.

However, why would she be feeling guilty? She realised that this was a response she had developed over the years, a response that had become second nature to her. When her mother cried about her sad 'lot', with her husband and daughter, she would feel overwhelmingly guilty that it was her fault. Why it was her fault, or in what way it was her fault, she had never really tried to discover. If she had ever tried, she had given up years ago.

She tossed and turned in her bed, and, suddenly, a thought came to her about Andrew Snedden. He was nice, she had to admit that, and he, at least, had seemed to understand her. He had been to college and had spoken to her about it. Perhaps, if her mother was so keen for her to marry him, something could be organised there. At least she would be getting away from home.

She was awakened by her mother sharply drawing the curtains of her room, allowing the sunlight to shine in with all its brilliance. It hurt her eyes. She rubbed them and looked up.

"Come on, come on," Mrs. Berns said. "Don't waste the sunshine on this beautiful morning. Let us get up and start to do our duty."

She gave a sigh. If only she could have stayed in bed another hour, but it wasn't worth it. She wouldn't be allowed to rest.

She looked at the clock. Had she slept three hours? Four hours? To her surprise, she saw it registered 9 a.m. That wasn't too bad.

"He has been on the phone twice already," her mother said, smiling at her. "We have had quite a nice chat."

"Who?" asked Tracy, genuinely puzzled.

"Why, Andrew Snedden, of course," she said. "Who else?"

It was Tracy's turn to smile.

Her mother went on, "And we have agreed that you should make a late application to college. I am sure they will accept you. They are only three weeks into the semester. I am sure you will catch up. You do have some sort of a good brain and quite good school-leaving marks. I am sure one could pay the late entry penalty and persuade the college to take you."

Tracy was staring at her, her eyes shining. She had confided to Andrew how much she wanted to go to college and now he had done this for her. She would be forever grateful.

And perhaps, she thought, *it would be rather nice to be married to Mr. Andrew Snedden.*

Three months later, Tracy was enjoying college and doing well. She was deliriously happy. She spent every spare moment with Andrew, and it seemed inevitable that, one day, they would marry.

Even her mother had stopped her constant devaluations of her. Her daughter was achieving, after all. Mr. Berns welcomed the unexpected peace in his home.

The family looked forward to a fabulous wedding. Eleven months later, this took place.

CHAPTER 4

Tracy stood against the station wall trying to shield herself from the wind. Why hadn't she taken something warmer with her? Why had she not taken something that would shut out the night air, which was almost painful in its blasts? She became acutely conscious of places where her bones had been broken and mended. It was as if the wind and cold were determined to unhinge the healing process.

She looked at her watch. It was time for the train. She waited, tense, anxious, and expectant. Five minutes went by.

Could her watch perhaps be slow? Could she have missed it?

No, he had been quite clear that it was 11:15 p.m. and she would have heard the train, even from a distance, but she had heard nothing, except the wind roaring through the trees and the breaking of twigs under her running feet, and, perhaps, yes, the wild beating of her heart earlier.

She was beginning to feel a little dizzy and strange, almost as if she would faint. Where was the train? Had she missed it? Had she mistaken the time? Had the security guard accidentally mentioned the wrong time?

A faint siren was heard in the distance, together with a rhythmic chugging, which was becoming louder and louder.

The train was approaching. She felt weak with relief. She put her hand in her pocket, feeling for her money. The ticket would have to be bought on the train, as was permissible at this hour of the night.

The chugging and rumbling came ever nearer as the train drew into the station. Where she stood was hardly a platform. The train would stop for only five minutes.

She climbed into the compartment opposite her and sat, vaguely aware that there were two other occupants who were looking at her a little strangely. She was not surprised. To see a girl inadequately dressed for this weather, climb onto a train at this hour of night with no luggage, was indeed strange.

As the train pulled out of the mini station, she looked around her, unable to avoid the startlingly blue eyes of her two fellow passengers, a man in a fisherman's cap and a pleasant looking woman. They must have been in their late seventies, if not eighties or nineties.

"Are you all right?" the woman asked. "I mean, who are you running from?"

"I'm all right, thanks," said Tracy. "It's all right, also; they won't catch me."

"I'm sure they won't," said the man. "Not now, anyway. Aren't you cold?"

Without waiting for an answer, the woman got out a bulky travelling bag from under the seat and opened it, eventually pulling out a large purple jersey.

"Here," she said. "Take this."

"Thank you," said Tracy, hesitantly. "But isn't it...?"

The man looked delighted. "My wife knits and knits, all day and half the night. To be able to give one of her jerseys away to someone who would appreciate it would give her infinite pleasure."

Tracy took off her jacket, put on the jersey and put the jacket back on. She could immediately feel its comforting warmth, which made a tremendous difference. It was well knitted and surprisingly, she thought, very much in style.

She sank back into the seat, for the first time feeling a little relaxed. The woman once more dived under the seat and brought out a picnic hamper.

"You'll do a favour here, also," said the man. "My wife thinks she has to feed an army and it's only me, and I am far from an army." He laughed. "Please help us eat this."

She had not realised she was hungry, but she found herself gulping down the coffee, the cookies, fish, salads and rolls that the woman produced.

She found herself relaxing more and more. The train conductor had come and sold her a ticket. The journey to Johannesburg was to be many hours. The rhythm of the train was soothing and it was not long before she fell asleep. She awoke to find the sun peeping through the shutters of the compartment window. She looked around. She was alone, but there was a travelling bag beside her and a soft rug over her knees. There must be another passenger somewhere. However, where did the rug come from?

She saw that there was a note pinned to the luggage and she found herself reading it, only after a few seconds realising that it was addressed to her. It said simply:

Dear young lady

We know by the way that you came on the train that you must have been in some kind of trouble. We noticed you had no luggage. We hope you really have somewhere to go. We have sorted through the jerseys and found some that might suit you. We have also found you some other clothes. Please accept them as a gift from us. We have so many, and, at home, we have so many more. Please would you also accept the rug that my wife put over you? There is also some food in the bag and some biscuits. We saw that you had money, but we have put some more in the front pocket of the bag. Please accept it. We have seen a lot of trouble at various times in our own lives and people have helped us out. Please accept this as a little of the repayment. Perhaps one day you could do it for someone else.

With best wishes for a happy future.

David and Dina Silver

It was already 2 p.m. when the train pulled into Johannesburg Station. She had spent the last three hours planning what she would say to her parents. Had it been almost two years that she had been away? It was hardly believable.

She had not been able to help feeling a certain excitement as the train had approached the outskirts of the city and she had seen its familiar outlines.

She picked up her bag, wished goodbye to her fellow passengers who had joined her several hours back, and stepped onto the familiar platform.

How would her parents react to her homecoming? They had kept regular written and telephone contact, first together and then individually. Maybe they would be angry that she had left the rehabilitation centre, but she could not stay there. She felt a sudden pang of guilt. They had probably been informed that she was missing, possibly dead. What were they thinking? Would they be angry? Would they really want to have her home? Had the police been put on her trail? Probably... Also, if she went home, wouldn't she be in danger from whoever was trying to kill her?

A wave of guilt suddenly overcame her as she pictured her parents' faces. They will send her back to the Cape! They would never understand that someone was trying to kill her. They had never, ever reacted to her letters about her fears.

Her mind went back to the night before and she saw in front of her again the kindly blue eyes of the couple who had helped her. She found herself picturing them again; the man with his white beard and fisherman's cap. The woman had had white hair too, or had she? Her hair had been covered by a turquoise scarf that had probably brought out more intensively, the blue of her eyes.

She remembered the couple had given her money. She had glanced at it but hadn't even counted it. She opened the

---

63

side pocket of the bag they had given her. There was, in fact, more money than she had expected, enough, in fact, if she was careful with it, to keep her for a whole month. She would find a boarding house, find a job and support herself.

Her depressive feelings returned. What would her parents really say? Would they be angry with her? She had nothing and nobody. She had even failed her daughter. What could she do? She had no training, except for the year at college before she got married. She still had, when she was tired, a slight limp. Until a few months ago, she had not been able to read right though a book without losing concentration, and it had only been six months since her writing had improved to the point of being fairly presentable and legible. Yet, she still had these terrible waves of depression, which she was sure would always be with her despite the doctor's reassurance that that, too, was due to the accident and would pass. However, her life was in danger, wasn't it? Moreover, no one believed her. Neither would her parents. She was just a useless person. Where would she work? What kind of boarding house would she go to? She would be lonely and bored. Maybe it wasn't worth it at all.

She looked at the money again, money enough to buy a lethal collection of tablets. This time she would really take them, in a place where she would not be found. There was a chemist at the station. She knew about that. She got up to go towards it and suddenly she saw in her mind again those kindly blue eyes. The money had been given her to live on, not to die on, not to be destructive with. Then there was Andy; somewhere in the world, there was Andy. Before she could change her mind, she went to the phone booth and dialled her father's number. His delight and relief at hearing from her dispelled all her doubts. He promised he would not send her back and reassured her that at this point he would tell no one except her mother she was safe. He offered to leave home immediately and be there at the station within ten minutes. She begged him not to, promising she would keep in touch.

Ashamed at doubting him, and bursting with relief, she sat down again, staring at the wall in front of her. There was a notice on it and she got up again to read it.

'Have you ever considered a nursing career?' it read. 'Trainee nurses wanted urgently − Apply Matron, Stanford Hospital'.

She had had enough of hospitals, hadn't she? But strangely enough she felt that there was some relevance.

She remembered the time she had spent in hospital in her early teens when she had burnt her foot with boiling water. She had become quite close to some of the nurses and at that time, her total ambition had been to become a nurse. This had lasted for almost two years before it had faded into the background. Then her marriage, and then her time being a mother and then her accident and with it her hours and days and months spent with nurses. Could she bring herself to identify with them? Could she see herself as a nurse? She would love to work with people; she was quite sure of that. However, hadn't she had enough of hospitals? Did she really want to spend her whole life in them?

One thing she remembered now was that trainee nurses lived in nurses' residences close to the hospital.

She knew Stanford Hospital. It was on the East Rand, several miles out of Johannesburg. There was a train that would take her right to it!

However, what would they do if they realised that a doctor had told her she should be in hospital for several more months, that she was not normal, and that she was imagining things. She was normal, and she was not imagining things. She shuddered. She wished it had all been her imagination. She wished that the terror had been without basis.

Had her father really believed her? Had he understood? What would stop him calling the police? He would think it was for the best. She had virtually died, and this was part of her treatment. According to the doctor she was not normal. She needed treatment. Of course he would send her to hospital again until she was better. If her father didn't, her mother would definitely do so. She could not bear to think about it. Why should anyone believe her?

She knew she had to get away from the station immediately. Maybe her father had phoned. She also needed to get away from whoever was trying to harm her.

But where would she stay? What would she do? She looked again at the notice in front of her. Two minutes later she had disappeared amongst the crowds, going in the direction of the local train lines.

CHAPTER 5

The main part of Stanford Hospital was a large imposing building of solid brick, built at the turn of the century. It had, however, very quickly outgrown itself, and scores of additions of various shapes and sizes built or erected at various times, had made it look something of a 'hodgepodge'. It would still take time before some enterprising architect would devise a low cost way to combine the buildings in a way that would bring out the best in all of them.

However, such an architect had not appeared. One could not deny, however, that the place had 'atmosphere' and that it had taken on the characteristics of any busy hospital.

There were nurses walking briskly along the corridors, orderlies pushing trolleys and the occasional in-patient, stumbling across the lawns to sit in the shade of one of the many trees.

Tracy, for some reason, immediately felt at home in this environment. Here was a place in which she could serve a purpose, help people, and at the same time, study and sort out her own life. After all, without a hospital, just where would she have been? This had been her world for the last two years.

After touring the hospital at least three times, in and out

of various buildings, she finally found the matron's office.

She was interviewed and eventually found suitable, and was given forms to complete. She was happy to have given the matron certain details of her life such as her marriage and divorce and the car accident, though she had admittedly made light of it. She had not mentioned the child.

Home address? Nearest relative? Oh well, who would check? She wrote out her parents' names and address. Purely formality, she was sure, and, perhaps, in an emergency...

The matron then called one of the trainee nurses to take her to the nurses' residence where she had been allotted Room 724, on the seventh floor, of course.

The trainee nurse had filled her in on the general rules of the place, ushered her in, and shut the door.

She breathed a sigh of relief that she was in a room of her own, albeit small, with her own bed, her own cupboards and bookcase. The curtains and bedspread, though of serviceable material, were a pleasant colour and there was a small rug on the floor.

Suddenly realising that she was incredibly tired, she lay down on the bed...

She awoke in darkness to someone knocking at her door. A student nurse who introduced herself as 'Hilda' came in.

"Hi," she said. "I am sorry I woke you, but I thought you would want to eat supper."

"Oh, thanks," said Tracy, rubbing her eyes. "I hadn't even meant to go to sleep. I wanted to do some shopping."

"There is a little store still open in the hospital," Hilda said. "It closes quite late. I could take you there after supper. Otherwise, you will have to wait till tomorrow. I will come back for you in five minutes."

As they walked through the corridors to the dining hall, Hilda told her about herself. She had begun nursing four months ago, straight after she had left school. She had wanted to be a nurse ever since she could remember.

"Did you always want to be a nurse?" she asked Tracy.

"I did at times," said Tracy, quite truthfully.

Hilda went on and on about how she had been hospitalised due to a particularly bad ear infection.

Tracy just let her talk, having to respond only minimally. It was good to be with someone who didn't really mind if you did not answer.

She was beginning a new life, different to her life at home, different to her life with Andrew, and different to her life in The Crawley Centre... a good, fulfilled, uncomplicated life, helping people, caring for people in a way they really needed. At the same time she could begin her search for Andy, though she had no idea where this could begin.

They reached the dining hall, collected a tray and served themselves from the large pots and huge salad bowls. They sat down at a table with several other student nurses to whom Hilda immediately introduced her.

"Oh, you are the mysterious new nurse who arrived with hardly any luggage and slept all afternoon," said a red-haired, freckle-faced, pleasant-looking girl. "We resisted the temptation to wake you. We reckoned we would have plenty of time to talk; loads of time. Where's your luggage? I mean, where do you come from?"

"I've been travelling," said Tracy vaguely. "Just with one bag."

"But where do you live?" asked the girl again, whose name tuned out to be Kerry.

Tracy was rescued by a small, dark girl who rushed up to the table with her tray and banged it down.

"I hate that sister!" she shouted. "She thinks she can just say what she likes to students. And I am sure she is wrong about that drip. I mean, I had looked at it five minutes before. There was nothing wrong with it, and she spoke to me as if I had set out to kill the patient. I hate her!"

"Is the patient all right?" asked Hilda, somewhat anxiously.

"Of course he is," said the girl. "But his arm is a bit of a funny colour. He'll be all right, I suppose. Do you think he'll be all right?" she asked, suddenly alarmed. "Thank goodness the sister took over!"

With that sudden change of attitude, she settled down to eat.

Tracy was off the hook. The rest of the meal was taken up with conversation about drips, injections, sisters, matrons and doctors. The matrons, in fact, sounded like sergeant majors. She had met one, hadn't she? And she hadn't been so bad. She had been quite friendly, in fact. The girls had warned her that first impressions did not always last, especially at Stanford Hospital.

*　　*　　*

Thirteen months passed, thirteen relatively uneventful months. Uneventful that is, except for extreme pressure of work. She had sent several messages to her parents saying that she was well and happy, and studying but she was careful never to give details of what she was studying nor return address. She had also made many unsuccessful attempts to find Andy.

The chronic staff shortage had reached crisis proportions and all nursing and medical staff were working one and a half times, or even twice their usual schedules.

For Tracy, one day followed another in fairly quick succession. She rose before sunrise and was busy in the wards most of the day, only to collapse into bed at night, exhausted.

Then there was the night duty that seemed to sap her strength completely, where, though exhausted, she would only sleep fitfully during the day, to go on duty once more at night.

At times, she was so tired she felt she had become some kind of machine.

She had no time to worry or to be anxious, or even to think. Except for her constant efforts to find Andy she hardly had time to think about her past, her present, nor her future until...

"Tracy, it really is you?"

Thinking it was one of the male nurses, she turned around to come face to face with Duncan, one of Andrew's friends. He had been engaged to a somewhat over-effusive girl called Peggy.

"Tracy, it can't be you! You were supposed to be...."

She blushed, crimson. She had been trying to find Duncan for months, hoping he would have news of Andrew.

"We have been thinking so much about you. It seemed so terrible that such a thing had to happen to you. Tracy," he said. "Peggy would love to see you... But what are you doing here? Why didn't you contact us when you came out of hospital? We have always been your friends."

Tracy stood, still crimson, not knowing what to say or even how to begin to say it. She was due to be in the ward in five minutes and instinctively she looked at her watch.

"You are in a hurry, aren't you," said Duncan. "What time do you come off duty?"

"Seven tonight," she said, as if hypnotised. Didn't he have any idea of how hard she had tried to contact him?

"I'll pick you up then, outside the gate," said Duncan. "I'll tell Peggy to organise a really good supper for you. You must be really sick of hospital food. I remember your favourite... chicken a-la-king. We'll organise it right away... and plenty of mushrooms."

Before Tracy could collect herself to say yes or no, he had disappeared down the corridor.

Though her meeting with Duncan totally dominated her thoughts as she walked into the ward, an emergency with an elderly patient who had a cardiac arrest drove that and everything else out of her mind.

She only had time to think about it again around 3 p.m. when there was a lull in the busy ward. What would she say to Peggy and Duncan? She hadn't seen them for several weeks before the accident. She hoped, oh how she hoped that they could help her find Andy. She again became extremely busy in the ward and it was only at 7:20 p.m. that she finally arrived at the gate, still in her uniform.

Duncan was waiting for her in the car. His face registered relief as he saw her and he got out to greet her.

"Peggy was delighted to hear that you were here," he said. "She would have come with me, but the baby fell asleep and we didn't want to wake him."

"Ba-b-baby?" she began. Then she remembered. She had been away long enough for Peggy and Duncan to get married and have a child. Maybe they could help her. Maybe they could understand.

Duncan drove her to their tiny apartment, which was not far away from the hospital. He spoke about trivialities, as if sensing that she did not want to get into any 'heavy' conversation.

Peggy, holding a ten-month-old baby girl who looked just

like a miniature form of Duncan, opened the door.

Tracy found herself really excited to see her. She had been a good friend, hadn't she? They had been Andrew and her best friends whilst she was at college, hadn't they? She was introduced to Jenny and was asked to hold her whilst Peggy was busy at the stove.

She smelled the delicious aroma of chicken-a-la-king and suddenly felt at home. After all, they had been her friends as well as Andrew's. They were just regular, normal, well-meaning people. She asked them if they could help her contact Andy and Andrew and they looked at her with sympathy, saying that they knew nothing. There was, however, a slight hesitation in Duncan as he said this and she wondered if there was more to it. She tried to push this out of her mind, finding that it disturbed her very much.

She went back to the nurses' residence, happy that she had found her friends again, with a supper invitation for one week's time.

The following week she was eagerly awaiting Duncan's car and when

they arrived at the apartment Peggy once more greeted her cheerfully.

"I want to discuss something with you, Tracy," said Duncan, while they were eating. "I contacted your father just to say we had met you again, and I did not realise that, though you had kept contact, he had not been able to get in touch with you, and he needs to do that."

Tracy drew in her breath. Had something happened?

"Your father lives in an apartment now," said Duncan. "Your mother moved to her sister in another city."

"But... But when is she coming back?" asked Tracy.

"She is living there," said Duncan. "I don't think she is coming back here."

"But... But my father... I mean, are they divorced?" She was flabbergasted!

Duncan looked at her sympathetically. "As I said, your father wanted me to tell you," he said. "Your father left your mother shortly after you came here. I am not sure if they are actually divorced."

"Please tell me where he lives," said Tracy, still too shocked to even begin to truly comprehend what was happening. "I must go and see them."

"Your father didn't want to upset you," he said. "I have to give you both of the addresses and your parents' phone numbers just in case you need them. Your father is 14, Carogall Apartments," he said, reading. "On the first floor, Lancet Street. Here is your father's phone number, and your mother's." He handed her the paper he was reading from.

"No!" said Tracy, still trying to digest the news of the separation. "No, I can't believe it. I have a lot to think about. I have to get myself together. Is my mother all right?"

"I suppose so," said Duncan. "I wouldn't really know."

Tracy suddenly felt overwhelmed with guilt. Had she broken up her family by going away?

Peggy saw how anxious she looked and she tried to change the subject. Tracy followed her with relief, and they were soon talking amicably about 'old times'.

However, Tracy could not again feel the excitement that had been with her the previous week. Everything felt flat and unreal. She was tired also, and she found herself withdrawing into herself. Peggy and Duncan did their best to get her to cheer up.

"I am sorry," she said. "I have been working hard. We have been very short staffed."

She herself knew this was not the reason for her mood. She felt guilty and worried about her parents. She would phone them, contact them, definitely, and do that immediately.

Just as they were about to take her home, Duncan made a statement about Andrew that she would have followed up had she not been so concerned about her parents'. He said that he appreciated that Andrew had desperately tried to pay off his debts but that the money had come from a numbered bank account in Switzerland, which was impossible to trace. Debts? She had not known he had any serious debts. Andrew was rich, extremely rich.

Duncan and Peggy arranged to see Tracy in two weeks' time– again for supper. In the meanwhile, Tracy had resolved that she would set about contacting her father. It was strange to think of him as a separate entity from her mother. He had seemed to be so much under her domination that she had hardly seen him as more than an inadequate extension of her. Apart from the phone call from the station, she had never really dared communicate with him. Such an action would have caused a storm of her mother's wrath.

She suddenly had a longing to see him again.

CHAPTER 6

For a few seconds, father and daughter looked at each other, neither knowing what to say. Both found tears beginning to form.

"Tracy," said her father at last. "Tracy, you have come back. You look so well, just like the old Tracy. I thought... I thought I would never see that old Tracy again."

It took almost a full minute before Tracy could answer. "I am me," she said. "I am Tracy. I feel so different, so much better. There is nothing wrong with me anymore. It is just that someone was trying to kill me. The doctor thought I was paranoid. But it happened. It really happened."

There was silence for a few minutes, and then her father spoke. "You know that Mum and I are not together," he said.

"Yes," she said. "Duncan told me. But he didn't say why or anything."

He sighed. "It was just that I could not take it. I didn't realize how much I couldn't take it until you decided not to come back. In fact, I think I had been staying in the marriage because of you, because a child needed a father."

He ushered his daughter into his somewhat austere apartment and they were soon drinking coffee from colourful mugs. He had found a packet of biscuits in his cupboard and had put these on a paper plate.

She nibbled at them, her appetite having left her completely.

They spoke at length, Mr. Berns telling her how he had left the house and exactly what had happened.

"What did Mum say?" asked Tracy.

Her father paused. "She cried; she cried a great deal," he said. "And then she began to plead with me, and weep and beg. And do you know what was terrible?" he asked. "It was terrible to see how someone who had always been so strong and dominating could become so weak and vulnerable."

Tracy felt a pang of sympathy for her mother. She had always sensed a certain vulnerability in her but had never really admitted it, even to herself. She had not been all that surprised at her reaction.

"Have you heard from her?" asked Tracy.

"I have, very often," said her father. "I have a whole pile of pleading letters, and I get phone calls with her crying at the other end. But I can't go back to her. There were some things she said, and I couldn't forgive her."

Tracy suddenly felt sick. She hadn't, even in her wildest dreams, thought that her parents would split up.

"When did the divorce come through?" she asked.

Her father was silent. Eventually, he said, "It isn't through. I haven't been to a lawyer. I couldn't bring myself to do that. She hasn't, either." He, too, looked vulnerable. Before Tracy could protest, he said, "Tell me about the hospital you are working at. I was really thrilled to hear your voice this morning. Tell me about everything."

She proceeded to do so, surprised as to how much she was able to tell him, sharing things that she had hardly become aware of herself.

"I cannot tell you what this means to me," said her father after she had finished speaking. "I had been trying to find you with my computer."

"Your computer? How? You have one here?" she asked.

"Yes, have a look in the spare room. I need it for my work. It saves me spending so many extra hours at the office."

"Hey, Dad, I never realized you had a computer," said Tracy excitedly. "I didn't know you would have one. Can I try it? Do you have games?"

"A few," said her father, "but not the big ones like Descent and Zork. I have my Solitaire and Tetris, which I have been playing on the computer for years in my spare time."

"I can play those," said Tracy. "I don't often get near a computer, so it will be really great. But, Dad, where you really trying to find me? How were you going to find me with the computer? Why, Dad?"

"Well, I had no idea where you had gone, and, even though you sent regular messages to us, there was no way to work out where these things were coming from. I mean, there was no way that we could contact you. I just left some messages, which I hoped you would pick up."

"I am sorry, Dad," she said.

It was later that Tracy asked if she could see some of the messages he had sent to her. "They won't be there now," he said. "They don't hold them for that length of time. I did it more in the beginning, but, after a year or so, I had kind of given up."

"But where did you place the messages?" she asked.

"I did a lot of research to come up with this," said her father. "I went to all the 'find people' sites and left messages and typed in your name until I found 'Towermail', which is a very user-friendly people-search site, and I decided to use that one."

"Assuming they are also looking at Towermail," she reasoned.

"Yes, that would be it. The person would have to be looking for you, too."

"Well, I wasn't, really. I kind of knew where you were."

"Or the person could also be looking for someone else," he added. "I thought you might be on that site, because you were looking for... well... Andy, because she might be looking for you."

"But she is..."

"She is almost nine now," said her father. "Children seem to find their way on a computer very early nowadays."

Tracy's face had blanched. "I have never thought of this. I never, ever imagined that. I wrote letters to lawyers and all kinds of people, but I never thought of using the computer. Hardly anyone has a computer in the nurses' home, and those who do only have the old 486 or maybe the first Pentium, which is all they can afford. I never thought of that. How do you do it?"

It took her father hardly any time at all to get into Towermail and Tracy, after a few minutes, typed in her message clearly, asking if someone knew of the whereabouts of a child named Andy who had been, or still was living in South Africa and who had a birthmark on her shoulder, which she described in detail, and who had curly blonde hair and large light blue eyes. She would be eight years old and her birthday was March 22.

"Oh, do you have to pay for this?" she asked, as a request for a credit card number came up.

"Don't worry, I will organize it. I will ask them to run it twice a month for a few months. One never knows when someone will dial up. I will also put money in one of their accounts for you, so that they can just take it off. It is better to go to a 'paid site', because it stops all kinds of casual surfers just writing messages. One has to be serious about what one is doing; therefore, the fee. Also, Towermail has people looking out on the big search websites, and gives us any information they can find."

"Will everyone be able to see her reply?" she asked.

"Not really, unless you make it general. You will have to put in my password. Later, you can get your own. I will give it to you, and then you can dial up to this from anywhere."

"Yours is the only computer I have access to," she said. "Can you dial up every day and see if there is a reply?"

"I won't be able to resist dialing up at least twice a day," he said, laughing. "This is my granddaughter you know. You have no idea how much I miss her."

"Then why didn't you put in a notice before?" she asked.

"I did not know how to contact you," he said. "I wanted her to see you, and then us."

They chatted for another hour and then she prepared to return to the hospital. "Can we check Towermail again before I go, just to see if there is any response?"

He dialed up for her but, as he had expected, there was no response.

"I suppose it is just another feeler I am putting out," she said, disappointed.

"I will keep looking at it for you," said her father.

*   *   *

A stint in plastic surgery was on the cards. She had always been interested in this field of nursing knowing that she had had certain minor procedures of reconstructive surgery. In the rehabilitation centre, she had seen patients with completely rebuilt jaws, noses and ears and had, in her last couple of months at the hospital, admired the handiwork of the doctors. She was still feeling very new and inexperienced in this section, but she learnt and worked wherever she could. There were several burn patients, as well as accident patients.

One morning, she came into the ward to find a new patient there, a rather pleasant youngish man with blue eyes peeping over a very swollen, misshapen nose of various hues of purple, blue and crimson, varying to pink. Despite his smile, he looked as if he was in a lot of pain, and she found her heart go out to him.

"What happened to you?" she asked, as she straightened out his pillows.

"One of my patients bit me," he replied, as if on cue.

"Your... Your patients?" she asked slowly. "How could one of your patients..?"

"I am a vet," he said.

"Oh... Oh, of course you are a vet; you would have to be. How could I even have thought that a human patient...?"

He laughed and suddenly stopped, obviously in a lot of pain.

"But how did your... er... patient get to bite you on the nose?" asked Tracy. "I mean, what kind of patient was it?"

"His name was Ruff, and he was a white bull terrier."

"With pink eyes?" she asked.

"With pink eyes... He had been in a fight and had been quite bitten himself. He was very edgy and frightened, and suddenly went for my nose."

As she went to take out the thermometer she had put in his mouth a few minutes earlier, she looked at his hands. There were scars on them, scars that must have been at least a year or more old.

"These are also from your patients?" she asked.

"Yes," he said, "but not from a dog. These are from penguins."

"Penguins?" she asked in surprise. "Do penguins come to you as patients?"

"I actually go to them." he said.

"But not here, obviously," she said. "We are so far from the sea."

"Right," he said. "I have to be in Cape Town; near Cape Town, that is. The penguins are mostly on Dassen Island and Robben Island."

"There is another place," she said slowly, trying to strain her memory to those friendly birds, indeed, the only little people at one stage that she could call her friends. "There is another place, but not on an island."

" Boulders," he said. "Those penguins are quite tame compared to the ones I am talking about. They are the same kind of penguins, but much more civilized and used to humans, I would say."

"What kind of illnesses would penguins have?" she asked as she looked at the thermometer. She remarked that he still had a temperature, and shook the thermometer.

"There are a lot of things," he said. "I will tell you. Your nursing experience will help you to understand. Well, first there are the parasites that can lodge anywhere within and outside the body... Ticks, fleas, lice and things. Then there are various worms that occur in the gastro-intestinal tract, and some in the kidneys and lungs."

"But what illnesses?" she repeated.

"Well," said Lewin. "There is aspergillosis, a fungus that affects the lungs, particularly if penguins are stressed or overcrowded, like in conditions where they are being treated after, say, an oil spill. Funguses are very difficult to treat and take a long time."

Tracy nodded as she busied herself around his bed.

"Then there is a condition known as bumblefoot. It be caused by the Staphylococcus bacteria and is associated with damp floors."

He went on describing the maladies that penguins could suffer from, realizing that Tracy was hardly listening, but he found that he did not want her to leave so he continued.

"Then there is haematozoa, a kind of avian malaria, and there is also babesiosis, which is endemic to African Penguins, and then there is Newcastle Disease, a virus with very high mortality, and very contagious. A vaccine can be prepared, but we don't know how effective it is."

She was looking at him and he found he was becoming disturbed by the beauty of her large light blue eyes.

"Then, of course, there is avian cholera, which has, in the past, killed some of the penguins at Dassen Island," he continued. "And then, of course, we have all the infections like viral or coccal pneumonia, and we treat that with amoxycillin." This nurse was really getting to him. Why did he have to meet such an attractive young lady when he was all bitten and defaced by that dog, Ruff? However, without Ruff, he would not have been here at all.

"Nurse Berns, I want you to keep a special watch on the Blackman child, Charles, our burn patient in the side ward over there. In fact, I want you to focus completely on him. Everything else must become secondary. I can't spare a trained sister to be with him and, apart from that, you are the nurse I trust most. Even though you are only finishing your second year," she added, with a rather significant look at the veterinary surgeon.

Tracy blushed at the compliment coming from Sister Mathews, the senior sister in the ward. After all, she had been nursing for under two years and others in the ward had been there for much longer. However, she was, it was true, several years older than they were.

She was disappointed that she had to stop nursing the vet, but she really had been given no option.

She followed the sister into the private ward where the child was lying and, at that point, everything else went out of her mind.

How could such a young child bear such an incredible amount of pain?

"He likes you," said the sister. "I have noticed that. He becomes much calmer when you are in the room. If we want to pull him through, we have to keep on strengthening his will to fight, his will to live."

The child seemed to sense she was there and he stopped his constant moaning, only letting out a quiet sigh, every few seconds.

"He's already calmer," said the sister. "I want you in this room all the time you are on duty. He seems to respond to you more than to anyone else, and the will to live is of primary importance here!"

"I am on seven-seven – 7 a.m. to 7 p.m. – for the next few days, anyway," said Tracy.

She went to the child and stroked his hair. His head was hot, very hot. She wet a sponge and folded it over his forehead.

"You're a good nurse," said the sister. "You've got a good heart."

She went out of the room.

—

Tracy sat next to the boy. Maybe he was the same age as Andy. She checked the chart, found that he was a few months older, and stifled a sob. She had made so many phone calls, and, on her off days, made so many visits in the hope of finding some word on Andy and Andrew, but without even the slightest success. They had vanished without a trace. Perhaps Towermail would help. Wasn't Andy really too young?

The boy was a little cooler already, and he looked calmer. He was obviously in a lot of pain, however. She frowned. Surely his pain control was adequate. She looked at his medicine chart. He had had a pethidine injection scarcely two hours ago. He surely should not be in so much pain.

His family would soon be here. One or other member always came at afternoon visiting hours and in the evening. His mother and father came and sat with him often late into the night. It must be so difficult for them to have a child this ill.

She wondered how her colleagues were doing on the rest of the ward without her. Why had the sister in charge wanted her to be solely in this room? They had other patients who were as ill, or more ill, she was sure. They were also fairly short staffed. Anyway, who was she to argue? She wished she had brought some of her study notes. She could have got a lot of work done... She would make sure she brought them the next day.

She suddenly straightened as she heard voices outside the room. She must have dozed off. How could one do that on duty? What kind of nurse was she becoming? The child looked more peaceful, although he was still obviously in a lot of pain.

Had his last injections not worked at all? Had he had his last injection? She checked again. It was written up. He had definitely had it.

She let the visitors into the room. It was Charles' two older sisters who had come straight from school to be with him. Well, perhaps she could go and have tea in the ward staff room.

"Tracy, where have you been?" asked Hilda her friend, who was nursing with her in the ward. "We thought you had just gone off somewhere. I have been looking after that animal doctor now. He really is nice."

"How is he?" asked Tracy. "How is his nose? Is he getting better? I really would like to see him again."

She came into the ward with Hilda, and the vet smiled at the two nurses. "You really have disappeared," he said to Tracy.

"I am looking after a child who got burnt," said Tracy. "They want me to be there all the time."

"You will be good for him," said the vet. "He needs a lot of understanding and love, due to the trauma of being burnt. You will be able to give it to him." Then, under his breath, he added, "But I wish you could have continued to give it to me."

"Is Hilda looking after you?" she asked, a little sharply.

"Oh yes," he said. "Don't worry. And Sister Gravesend is also doing so; keeps me from feeling too sorry for myself. But do pop in occasionally. I would like to see you." Again, he berated himself inwardly. Why did this nurse have such an effect on him, and, worse still, the age difference would be far too much if she was only in second year. He would just have to forget about those wonderful blue eyes.

She explained about Charles and they understood, though Hilda was a little puzzled. Was he that ill?

Tracy went back to the room to find Charles' two sisters, both were reading a magazine, occasionally stroking Charles' hand. She needed to ask them a question, but not too directly. Eventually, in the midst of conversation... "Does your family have a computer?"

"Oh yes," said one of the sisters, "but it is not being used so much anymore, because Charles is not home."

"That is amazing," said Tracy, her heart thumping. "Can he work with things like email?"

"Of course he can," said the girl, laughing. "He seems to know much more about the whole thing than we do. Some children seem to do that. I often have to ask him questions, and he always answers them. I have no idea how he picks up the information."

So there was a chance. There really was a chance.

They left after an hour.

Charles was becoming very restless and was moaning in pain. It was time for his next injection.

Alice, a sister from the ward came in. The sister looked surprised to see her. "What are you doing here, Nurse?" she asked.

"Sister Mathews asked me to stay with Charles all the time I am on duty," she replied.

"Well," said Sister Alice, "I am here now, to give the injection. You can go and see if you can still get some tea."

"I already went for tea whilst the visitors were here," said Tracy.

"Well, go for a walk then," said the sister. "You need a break. I will stay with him for a while after the injection. Come back in... say... twenty minutes."

When she came back, she found that Charles had fallen asleep. The injection had obviously worked.

She was happy when she left Charles. He seemed to be so much better. She alerted the sister on duty that she was going and then left.

It was early when she arrived the next morning, and she went to the vet to see how he had been getting on. He seemed delighted to see her but she could not stay long.

As she got into the children's ward, she noticed again that Charles was very restless and though he calmed down somewhat with her presence, he was still obviously in pain.

93

She looked at his chart. No, his injection had been given regularly. Strange that the pethidine wasn't working. It had worked very well that late afternoon. Perhaps they had forgotten to give it to him. She spoke to the ward sister. They could not increase the dosage as it would be dangerous and for the end of the four-hourly period he was in an increasing amount of pain till the next injection. Nothing could be done medically.

Memories began to flood her mind. She too, remembered the warm feeling of the pethidine as the pain began to vanish and the stress she began to feel as the hours would pass and slowly but steadily the pain would re-emerge and would engulf her with horror. The memory followed her as she prepared to sleep and followed her into her dreams. As she had done almost every night, she would hear Andy calling her, crying to her. "Mummy, Mummy, where are you? Mummy, please come back to me. I can't find you."

"I thought I would discuss it with you first, Dad. I really think I should go see her. I mean, especially as you say that she is so upset." Tracy turned to her father.

"My baby," he said, gently, using the name he had used when she was a child. "My baby, I don't want you mixed up in this. I don't want her to hurt you again."

"She's my mother," said Tracy.

Mr. Berns seemed to withdraw, and suddenly become distant. "That's right," he said, shortly. "She is your mother."

"Dad, don't be like that," said Tracy. "I mean, I sort of feel I should go and see her, no matter what. She must wonder why I haven't been to see her yet."

"She doesn't know you have seen me," he said, slowly.

"You said she was in touch with you quite often," said Tracy, looking confused.

"Oh yes," he said, "but I never mentioned that you had been to see me."

Tracy held herself back from asking why and just remained silent.

"I didn't want to have her phoning you. I didn't want you to cut contact again. I am so happy to see you. I am afraid you will run away."

"Where would I run to?" asked Tracy. "How long can I carry on running?"

Her father was silent.

"All right," he said at last. "I will let her know you are here and see what the reaction is. Maybe it is right that you should go and see her. She has changed, I must admit."

Tracy suddenly lost courage. "What do you think she will say about my being away?" she asked.

"So much has changed since then," said her father. "So much... I don't think she will go on and on about it."

"And Dad," she said wistfully. "Dad, did you go into Towermail? Is there an answer?"

"I am sorry, my darling. There isn't yet."

"Can I look now? I think I know how to do it myself."

He left her to do this staying with her only long enough to see that she had entered successfully.

She gave a sigh as she saw there was nothing and saw that her father had left a message also. He had also put a considerable about of money into the account. That meant he was very hopeful.

She came back into the lounge a little disheartened.

Her father had obviously thought more about her contact with her mother. "I will let your mother know I have seen you and that you are coming to see her," he said again. "I suggest you phone and make arrangements with her sister. She always was a sensible woman. I am really pleased she is able to look after your mother."

"Dad," asked Tracy. "Dad, are you happy without her?"

"Yes I am," said her father. "Things were becoming quite impossible. Now I can be myself without being nagged and criticized at every turn. But I certainly admit that I do become lonely at times... Quite lonely, in fact."

*   *   *

Tracy was surprised to find herself trembling almost uncontrollably as she opened the gate to the house.

She paused. She had to get herself together. She couldn't allow her mother to see her so disturbed. She had been quite unmoved during the bus trip. She had thought out all kinds of things that she would say to her mother... rational, common sense things. She had planned, in detail, how the meeting would go... A few tears, perhaps. If so, why was there a lump in her throat? Why had she forgotten everything she had planned to say, and why was she shaking?

For a few seconds, she thought of running away. But how could she? She had phoned and made the arrangements. They knew she was coming. They were prepared for her and she was prepared for them.

Perhaps it would have been better, though, if she had spoken to her mother on the phone. Her mother had not been there and she had spoken to her aunt. Her aunt had been pleasant and had said that her mother would be very happy to see her, she was sure.

However, that was what her aunt had always been like... pleasant, polite and somewhat denying of any problems. Tracy could never recall having seen her upset or in a temper. She was her mother's older sister, at least seven years older than her mother. She had always been strong, confident and competent.

She started to walk up the cobbled path, thankful that the shaking had become less marked. She could even enjoy the miniature roses in delicate shades, and the pansies turning their faces towards her.

Her aunt certainly was a good gardener. She was quite sure the garden had not been tended by her mother.

She steeled herself to walk to the door, feeling a shock run through her as it suddenly opened. This was followed by an immediate sense of relief that it was her aunt who opened the door and at the same time a resurgence of her desire to run away. Her aunt came towards her.

"So glad to see you, Tracy, dear. Your mother was so happy to hear that you were coming. She has had a hard time away from her family."

Tracy's feelings of guilt increased and again a shock went through her as her mother arrived at the door, but these feelings were quickly replaced by a wave of pity.

Her mother, who had been somewhat on the overweight side, had lost several kilos and in actual fact looked thin and her face looked drawn and pale. All the spirit seemed to have gone out of her as she smiled at her daughter with a smile that betrayed her insecurity.

Could a person change so much? But then, she had lost so much.

Spontaneously, she ran over to her, hugging and kissing her. Her mother seemed to relax and then to stiffen in her arms as she began to sob. Tracy led her to a settee and sat beside her, tears falling from her own eyes. Her aunt, practical as always, handed them a box of tissues and retreated to the other side of the room. She had always found emotional outbursts somewhat distasteful. Too much intensity embarrassed her. It wasn't right, wasn't 'decent'.

She left the room to put on the kettle to make some tea. She came back some ten minutes later and was relieved to see Tracy and her mother sitting upright with only their eyes somewhat red to show what they had been through.

Tracy had her mother's hand in hers and was listening to her.

"I can't live without him," she was saying. "I just can't live without him. He told me I was strong and dominating and controlling, and perhaps I came over that way, but none of you realized that, inside, I am weak, insecure and unsure of anything I do. You didn't realize that, either... Did you, Tracy?"

"No, Mum," she said. "I didn't."

Tracy had been silent, engrossed in what her mother was saying. She reached over and poured her another cup of tea.

"Go on, Mum," she said. "Please go on."

They spoke for a long time, sharing things they had never been able to do in the past. It was as though she had met and known her mother for the first time.

They soon got onto the subject of Andy and Mrs. Berns said she had been doing some of her own investigations into Andrew's whereabouts with little success.

"I think he must have gone back to the UK," she said at last.

"But, Mum, he didn't come from there," she said.

"He apparently did, way back," her mother said. "He once told me about it. I think he had a grandfather from there or something."

Tracy was thoughtful.

"When are you due for your leave, Tracy?" asked her mother. "I mean, we could really do all sorts of things together."

Tracy suddenly smiled. She hadn't even thought about that...probably because there was nowhere she could really go on leave. But she could now. She could spend time with both her mother and her father. She calculated that she was due for over a month's leave, if not more. She could surely take a week or two of leave from it.

She approached the matron the next day and they discussed various possibilities, one of which was that a nurse who had had leave approved had suddenly cancelled it for valid reasons. Tracy could take some of her leave in her place. The child, Charles, had become much improved and would soon be discharged, and she no longer needed to look after him so intensively.

Tracy returned to the ward overjoyed. She had permission, if she wished, to start her leave as soon as she got off work.

She had stopped at the tearoom to grab a sandwich and to quickly telephone her father at his office. He was delighted with the arrangement to fetch her at 8 p.m. at the nurses' home. He would buy a pull-out couch and have it brought over that very afternoon. It would be more than a pleasure to have his daughter staying with him.

For some reason, it seemed as if a load had been taken off her shoulders. She hadn't felt this way in years.

The day passed quickly and very soon she was with her father in his small apartment, unpacking her case into part of the cupboard and admiring the new armchair-come-fold-down bed, which he insisted he was going to sleep on. She was to have the bedroom.

He had also brought in all kinds of foodstuffs, which were still in their supermarket bags on the floor of the small kitchen. She unpacked these enthusiastically, feeling really pleased at the way her father was so thrilled to be having her stay with him.

She realized that she needed a complete break. She hadn't had one for a long time.

It felt so good sleeping in the tiny bedroom with the comforting presence of her father in the room next to hers. She had forgotten what it was like to relax.

Now she could spend the time reading some of her father's novels, transporting herself into another world. She needed this leave desperately and she would enjoy it. Of course she would contact her mother and spend some time with her, or at least visit her a few times. She did not want to upset the relationship, so perhaps she should not, in fact, actually stay there.

She would be able to browse the shops, to walk into libraries... things she never had time for before.

Force of habit made her wake up at 6 a.m. the next morning, and she went to the kitchen and began making a cup of coffee and reaching for some biscuits. Her father was still asleep, but woke up as soon as she passed him.

"Oh good," he said, laughing. "Coffee in bed, at last. Two spoons of sugar, you remember? Heaped spoons."

Tracy smiled. Her mother had always insisted that he only needed one level spoon of sugar in his coffee. This was part of his 'rebellion', as it were.

She made him some coffee and cut some of the creamy chocolate cake he had bought the day before. They sat together and ate it, discussing what they were going to do that day.

"Sleep, Tracy, go back to bed; you are on holiday," said her father. "But stay up a while with me. I only leave for work in an hour and a half."

"Did I wake you too early, Dad?" asked Tracy apologetically.

Her father smiled. "Well," he said. "It is somewhat earlier than usual, but it is a pleasure, more than a pleasure." He pretended to look disconsolately at his empty cup.

Tracy took it from him and within a minute was back with another cup of coffee.

They chatted about all sorts of things and Tracy fried eggs for both of them. She burnt the toast slightly, but was reassured her when father said that he rather liked burnt toast.

All too soon he was looking at his watch. "I have to be gone in ten minutes," he said.

He rushed around for a few minutes collecting his things and was soon out of the door.

Tracy poured herself another cup of coffee and went back to bed. It was so good to be able to relax and not worry about anything. It was so good.

The telephone rang and she answered it to hear her father's voice. "Tracy," he said. "Please could you buy a few things for the apartment? I meant to tell you. I left money on the dresser with a small list, but we got talking and I forgot about it completely. Please could you attend to it? And I did want to get you some of those peppermint crunchy chocolates you so enjoyed."

"Thank you, I will do that, of course," she said. "Oh," she added, "how do I get back into the apartment?"

Her father sounded apologetic. "I'm sorry," he said. "I meant to tell you. There is a spare key in the drawer next to the bed." He waited till she found it and checked that it fitted the door before he put down the phone.

She sat on the bed, thinking. She should contact Duncan and Peggy. She wanted to spend time with them, and also , they had said something strange; something she wanted to follow up; something about Andrew sending them money that he owed. Had Andrew done something with other people's money? Surely not! He had had plenty of his own. She would question Duncan further.

Now she could spend time with Peggy, talk about old times, spend time playing with the baby, and, most of all, she could chat about what had happened after the accident. Had they seen or spoken to Andrew? When she had been there for dinner, the time was all too short and she always had to go home early so that she could be prepared for the intensive shift she would have to work on the next day.

It was Thursday. Tracy had arranged to visit her mother. As she travelled there she thought about how different her mother's feelings had become towards her. She now felt a certain warmth and a confidence in her relationship with her. As she thought about this, she felt a pang of guilt. Was it her mother's weakness and vulnerability that had made her easier to get on with? Was she happier for her pain?

She put the thought out of her mind, having to admit to herself first that on a certain level, at least, this was true. However, that was not all of it... For the first time, on the last visit, she had seen her mother as a fellow human being, a person who had gone through her own conflicts and insecurities.

She was looking forward to discussing things with her. Perhaps, too, she might be able to tell her more about Andrew and Andy. After all, both Andrew and her mother had visited her every day and had often been together in the hospital. Perhaps she knew more than she realized and could perhaps shed some new light on the situation.

It was definitely worth speaking to her about it more fully.

She was looking forward to talking with her. Looking forward? Looking forward to seeing her mother? She laughed as she realized where her thinking had taken her. She had never in her life thought that she would look forward to a discussion with her mother.

She was soon at the gate of her aunt's home. How different were her emotions this time! She walked briskly down the path towards the house.

Her mother – did she look a little better? – opened the door.

"Come in, Tracy," she said. "I have made you your favorite cookies, and for lunch I have made lasagna with mince and cheese."

Tracy felt her mouth watering. She could smell the food from the kitchen. She was touched that her mother had made it especially for her.

They were soon sitting in the lounge, chatting. It was as though her mother had come to terms with accepting her daughter as an adult and a friend and seemed to find a lot of strength in this.

Tracy looked at her mother carefully. The bitter, angry lines around her mouth had changed and she had a certain softness about her. In fact, thought Tracy in surprise, her mother was really quite pretty. It did not take long before they were speaking about her father.

"Tracy," she said after they had been talking for a while. "Tracy, do you think there is any hope for us? Your father won't even see me again. I miss him so much. I can see what I was doing to him. I think it was because I have always felt so insecure that I kept thinking I had to improve him and dominate him. I realize that now. He was such a good man, a gentle man, but he was a strong man… and something inside me somehow had to try to kill that strength. And then I resented any show of what I saw as weakness. I knew I made him desperate at times. He hated being nagged, and I did that on and on and on. If only I had another chance; if only!"

"Mother," said Tracy, answering her mother's unspoken question, "I will do everything I can to try and bring you together. But it might take time. But I will work on it, of course I will. Who wants to see their parents divorced?"

At the word 'divorced', her mother seemed to collapse inwardly.

"We aren't divorced," she whispered.

"I know," said Tracy. "Dad told me that."

"What did he say? Please tell me, what did he say?"

Tracy hesitated. She did not want to be disloyal to her father or mother, but she had to try to do something and she wanted to give her mother some hope. Would it be false hope?

She thought for a while. No, it wouldn't be false. She had on a few occasions been aware that her father had not lost all feeling for her mother.

Her mother respected Tracy's silence; a contrast to the mother she had known previously whose rasping voice would have interrupted her thoughts and demanded to know what she was thinking.

Had her mother really changed so much, or would it be that, within a few months of the family being together again, she would revert to the unpleasant, controlling, nagging woman? How could she say this to her own mother?

However, her mother said it for her. "I have really changed, Tracy," she said. "I will not revert back to being the 'monster' I was. I have done a lot of soul searching and heart searching, and I have changed. I also hate the character I was. I would not have been able to live with her either."

Her mother started to serve the lunch.

"Where is your sister?" asked Tracy, suddenly aware that she hadn't seen her aunt.

"Oh, she went out for the day. She had to visit an elderly lady who now lives quite far away. She needed to take two buses. We will keep the lunch for her."

Her father looked at her quizzically and somewhat anxiously as she returned and they went straight into Towermail, disappointed, but not surprised to find no response. "Dad," she said, "I have decided I need to go to the police station to see the records of the accident. Please don't worry, Dad," she said as she saw his anxious expression. "It is just something I have got to do. I want to do it tomorrow."

Tracy was nervous at what she might find and it took a long time before she fell asleep. Even then, she tossed and turned in her bed, seeming to wake, towards morning, almost exactly on the hour, every hour.

She kept dreaming – vivid, colourful dreams about the about the hospital...mostly about Andy. She fell into a troubled sleep. She awoke at 10 a.m. with the sun streaming in through the window. Her father had gone to work long ago.

She went through to the kitchen and found some neatly cut-up salmon sandwiches for her breakfast and she smiled. Her father was so good!

She looked at her watch... 10:15 a.m. Was it too late to make an appointment at the police station? She phoned, to find to her satisfaction that they could arrange for her to view the file at 2 p.m. She just had to bring her identity document.

The police station was large and cold, but she was grateful to find waiting for her an inspector who knew everything about her case. He looked at her identity document for several minutes and then looked at her closely. "A walking miracle," he said. "Truly a walking miracle. I don't know if you know what a terrible accident this was. Are you sure you want to view the material?"

"Actually, I am terrified," she began. "I don't know why, because everything is over... finished, and I am better now."

"Amazingly so," said the inspector. "We thought you were finished. No one held any hope for you at all. Even the doctors didn't seem to hold out any hope. Are you sure you want to see the car and the pictures?" he asked again.

"Yes, I am sure," she said. "I have to see them. I have to know more about what happened."

"I have forgotten all the details," said the inspector, "but you have quite a hefty file with the court."

"Why?" she asked, her heart sinking as he led her into a room, asking her to wait.

Did they think it was a suicide attempt? Had they gone into that? Why would she have attempted suicide? She remembered someone talking about that... didn't she, remembered in some vague, confused way. The doctor and someone had been talking together about it... That she did remember, or did she?

Her daydreaming was interrupted by a brown, somewhat tattered file being placed squarely in front of her. A young woman in uniform had come in without a word, placed the file on the desk and again without a word had walked out of the room. Well, it was a somewhat bulky file. Her name was written on the cover together with the date of the accident, the police officer in charge and the hospital to which she had been taken.

Politeness stopped her from looking further. After all, she had not been told that she could look at it. However, then why had it been brought and left in front of her?

She looked around the somewhat dingy room. The heavy wooden door was closed and there did not seem to be anyone around. Would she have heard footsteps even if there had been any?

The silence was eerie, whilst, so close to her, was the busy reception area of the police station.

Tracy acted quickly, curiosity suddenly overtaking her, and she found herself slowly opening the file.

The first page was a form that had probably been filled in by the paramedics. Yes, they had used the Jaws of Life to cut her from the car, and they had used a fire engine. Had the car been on fire? She was not aware of having suffered any burns. She flicked over a few pages and came to the pictures of the car and drew in her breath in amazement. It must have turned over and over as it rolled down the cliff. It was battered and shattered that some parts were unrecognizable.

How could someone possibly have come out of there alive? Had she done it to herself? Had she felt so disillusioned with life, so unhappy that she had decided to end it? However, she would not have left her child.

She shuddered as she flicked through the pages, pausing as she saw a blown up picture of the side of the car, an arrow pointing to pieces of red paint intermingling with the shattered white of her car.

On the opposite side of the page the word suicide had been crossed out. What did that mean? What did it all mean? What were these red marks? Blood? No, there was blood around the rest of the car; this was dark brown, or, if red, a very different red. This was bright, post-box red.

Red... Red... A flash of red... Eyes... More red...

She shook herself out of her reverie as she read through more of the file, feeling sick as she read the details.

It had become clear. There was another car involved... a hit and run. At the end of the file was a note that a stolen red powerful car had been recovered several days later with white paint on its left front mudguard and paint scratched off the body near the left front wheel. No one knew the identity of the driver. No fingerprints had been recovered.

Feeling too shaken to carry on she closed the file. A slip of paper, which, over the two years, must have become unattached, if it had ever been stuck down at all, fluttered to the ground. She picked it up and found on it a name and phone number of a lawyer in Pretoria. Did it have to do with her case?

She quickly jotted down the name and number, and slipped the paper back into the file. Perhaps this lawyer might know something about the whereabouts of her daughter. Once again she opened the file, this time with a fierce questioning. Were there other names, other phone numbers? Was there a contact number for Andrew? Would she be able to find him? She had to find him. There was no other way, no other way to answer the cry of that little girl. However, she would not be so little now, would she? She was getting bigger every week, every month, every year, getting bigger and bigger, and moving further and further away from herself... her mother.

She saw another note written on the file. A Mrs. Tabby had been phoning constantly saying she wanted to speak to her. The police officer had insisted that it was not possible at this time. Eventually she had stopped phoning, but Tracy now jotted down her number.

There were no more phone numbers more than she had already. Rising, she closed the file and prepared to leave.

"Oh, Miss, I meant to join you. Are you all right? I got tied up with a case over here, a very difficult one, which suddenly came up. Are you all right? Do you need any help? Are you finished with the file? You can see it again if you want to. I can arrange it for you."

Putting on her bravest smile, she thanked him, emerging out of the police station into the bright light of the afternoon sun.

As soon as she returned home, she phoned the number of Mrs. Tabby who asked, almost breathlessly in her excitement at hearing from her, if it was possible for her to come and see her, the most convenient time being... right away.

"I don't think you know me," said the woman, pushing away a wisp of grayish-white hair from her face. "In fact, I am sure you have never met me. I just had to come and see you. I wanted to see for myself that you are really alive." The woman stared at her as if wanting to read on her face that she was healthy and physically in good shape. "I can't believe it," she said, standing back for a few minutes. "I just can't believe it." She stood staring at her admiringly.

"Please sit down," said Tracy, a little unsure of how to react.

The woman sat, and her face became blood red.

"I thought you were going to die," she said, obviously overwhelmed by emotion. "I really thought you were going to die. I kept phoning the hospital to check that you had not died."

"That was very caring of you," said Tracy. "That was really nice of you. But why? You didn't really know me; at least, I don't remember that you did."

The woman's color had changed from red to a ghastly white. "I-I saw it all," she stammered. "I saw it all... The red car, everything. I should have gone to the police, but I don't like to be involved with the police. Anyway, you were going to die, but you didn't, so I have come to you. I am sorry."

They chatted for almost an hour, at the end of which Tracy knew for certain that every question of suicide had been ruled out, and it remained an almost successful attempted murder.

As if on a relentless quest she phoned the lawyer. He was delighted to hear that she was well but denied all knowledge of Andrew and Andy's whereabouts. She insisted that he had to see her to which he somewhat reluctantly agreed.

"But you must know where my daughter is, you must know." She stared at the lawyer incredulously. "I mean, surely I have certain rights. Surely I have the right to make contact with her. I am not a criminal. I haven't treated her badly in any way." She studied him carefully. Was there a trace of embarrassment?

The corners of his mouth seemed to quiver.

"Miss... uh... well, your doctor did say that there was no chance of recovery, at least not as far as... eh... your brain faculties were concerned. If you did live, you would just be a..."

"A vegetable," she said.

"Well... yes," he said. "That is what they said," he said defensively. "We even have written reports to this effect."

She suddenly burst into tears, causing the man to twitch severely.

"I want my baby," she said. "All I want is my baby. I want to see her. I must have the address. Where have they gone?"

"Out of the country," he said.

"But where... Where?" she pleaded.

"I don't know. I really don't know. I just know they left the country. They didn't leave an address."

"But didn't you ask them where they were going?" she asked, not believing what she was hearing.

He again insisted that he knew nothing. "You were not in a condition to.... You were never going to be in a situation to..."

When asked for more information about the actual accident, he suggested that she look in the archives of the local press. "They keep all their newspapers," he said. "They bind them up into huge volumes. I am sure you will find something." Reassuring her that he would be there if she needed any further help, he quickly ushered her out of the office, obviously highly embarrassed about her survival.

To go to the newspaper offices would be a good idea, however, and she contacted them right away.

The man at Enquiries obviously had a bad cold, which he was trying desperately to control with an almost-empty box of tissues. "Yes, Miss, we have all the newspapers from way back... much further back than you are asking for, in fact. If you go down that corridor right to the end of it and turn right, you will find Mr. Ntuli, and he will help you."

He gave a loud sniff and then a sneeze and made a grab for the tissues, Tracy finding that she had involuntary jumped backwards.

"Shouldn't you be at home in bed?" she asked, somewhat concerned.

"Yes, maybe I should, but I have had too much sick leave this year, and I don't want them to take money off my salary. Thanks for your concern." He blew his nose loudly, and then turned to her. "That's better," he said. "That should be okay for another few minutes at least." He once again pointed down the corridor. "Mr. Ntuli. You will find him very helpful."

Indeed, helpful he was, except that she, too, with lightning speed, felt she had instantly caught the cold, until she realized it was the dust on the newspapers that had been filed into large books.

"The Sunday paper should also be useful to you, Miss," said Mr. Ntuli, a fairly elderly gentleman with his dark curls already tinged with grey. He had already given her the two massive heavy volumes of the relevant daily papers and brought her the *Sunday Times* next to them.

She sneezed.

"I'm sorry, Madam, about the dust," he said. "We dust these things, but the edges of the papers are not straight like a book, so the task becomes almost impossible."

However, her mind had become fixed on the newspaper published the day after the accident. There was a photograph of her car, an earlier picture of herself and a photo of Andrew and Andy. She shuddered as she saw the caption, 'Was it an accident?'

The papers had been more imaginative than the police file, obviously. The red markings had been mentioned, and some really ominous statements made about murder, suicide and hit and run driving. The paper stated that she had been critically injured and was not expected to live.

She gave a gasp. Even though she knew, obviously, that she had survived this, it still gave her cold shivers to see it written.

She looked at the next day's newspapers and the next but nothing at all was written. Could people forget so quickly? Well, maybe that was what newspapers were about.

She was preparing to leave when she remembered the *Sunday Times*, which she opened carefully to the Sunday after the accident. They had more or less repeated the incident, this time stating that she was still in a coma in critical condition in the hospital. For a few minutes she just stared at the page. Well there wouldn't be much further on if there had been nothing in the daily papers.

She started to sneeze as the dust caught her nose and she reached in her bag for her tissues. Her eyes were watering and she felt decidedly unpleasant. She had better get out of there fast.

Absentmindedly she turned the pages and caught sight of an advertisement for a sale in one of the stores. Why did the prices seem so much lower? Had they really increased in the space of a few years... and so much? There was no way she could buy anything at that price today, but maybe that was because of the sale.

She turned more of the large pages and then looked at one right at the end of the volume, only to be riveted by a small insert somewhat near the bottom of the page to the effect that Andrew Snedden had left the country without trace, having left a trail of debt behind him. It was stated that he had lost people's entire fortunes and that many were now on the poverty line due to his mismanagement of funds. He had left no forwarding address even with the caretaker. His ex-wife had been injured and was lying helpless in a hospital possibly with irreversible brain damage.

He had taken his almost five-year-old daughter with him.

She felt her heart starting to pound. That was what had happened! That was what Duncan had not quite told her. Perhaps this was why someone had tried to kill her, but she could not believe this was true. In fact, had someone tried to kill her? She could not be sure. She felt confused and angry and worried. How was Andy? Did they manage financially? Was he able to care for and look after her?

She realized that tears were pouring from her eyes, and gave a large sniff as she saw Mr. Ntuli looking at her sympathetically. "I had better go," she said, wiping her eyes. "The dust is too much for me. Maybe I will be back. Thank you for everything. I really appreciate it."

As she passed the man at reception, he was still glued to his tissue, and looked at her sympathetically.

"I really didn't mean to give you my cold," he said. "Maybe we spoke too long. I am sorry, Miss."

She went out of the main door, reassuring him that she held nothing against him, and that it was impossible for a cold to be transferred so quickly. "The dust," she said, reassuringly. "There's an amazing amount of dust inside those newspapers." She started to leave, and then turned back to give him some of her remaining tissues.

As she came out into the sun, she realized that she was badly shaken. This was something she had not really known nor suspected. Except for Duncan's vague hints, this was something that had never even entered her mind.

She would need to talk to her parents about it. Perhaps they would know something.

As she was thinking she remembered a Mrs. Tyrone, an elderly woman that Andrew had mentioned who was a distant relative of his mother. She managed to find her number and her address.

"Oh, I haven't seen Andrew for many years," said Mrs. Tyrone. "I mean, I had never met you, had I? Though I was sent a photograph of your wedding." She looked around vaguely as if she expected to see it floating by.

Tracy realized that it would take a great deal of time for her to find. Her writing desk, stuffed with papers of all descriptions would not close and most definitely was not leaving any space for writing on.

She also had a chest of drawers that seemed to be stuffed to the brim with papers.

The woman's next statement was therefore no surprise. "It is definitely here, most definitely. I never throw things away, especially important things like letters and papers and envelopes. The photo is definitely there. I also got a letter from my sister saying you had a little girl. What was her name, very much like Andrew's name, I remember.... Yes … Yes, it was Andrea, I think you called her Andy, wasn't it?"

She smiled, pleased that her memory had served her so well.

"You wouldn't know where I could find Andrew, would you?" asked Tracy.

"You mean he is missing?" asked the woman as Tracy felt her heart sink. Mrs. Tyrone had obviously known nothing about the accident.

"Well, you see, I had a terrible accident," said Tracy, preparing to tell her.

"Oh yes, yes, I remember now," said the woman. "That was a very bad accident."

"Andrew went away after that," said Tracy. "He took Andy."

"And left you, my girl," she said sympathetically. "I am sorry. He must have gone back to Lisbon."

"Lisbon?" she almost shouted. "Why Lisbon?"

"Now don't get cross with me. I really don't know where he would have gone. How would I know?"

"But you said," she began.

"I didn't say anything at all," she affirmed, and no persuasion would get her to reveal one more thing.

She is becoming somewhat forgetful, thought Tracy. *Lisbon, really...* Andrew was not Portuguese. Why on earth would he have gone to Portugal?

She put this out of her mind.

One day, she wanted to go to Pretoria to visit the hospital that had saved her life, but, at this time, she knew she was not ready for it.

CHAPTER 7

"Nurse Berns, could you please go to the storeroom and see if you can find an extra baumanometer, one on a stand… the older type? I know we had one, and it is going to be so much easier to use it with Mr. Moss."

The ward sister looked despairingly at Mr. Moss's bed. He was really being quite obstreperous and noncompliant.

"None of you will ever be able to take his blood pressure this way," she added.

Tracy found her way to the storeroom, which was at the end of a small corridor. It felt strange to be back at work and she had returned to an overfull schedule on her first day.

Why did people always leave storerooms in such chaos? All right, it was neat and tidy, but there seemed to be no real order as to how everything had been put away.

She leant against a steel bed frame and looked at things as systematically as she could. There were all kinds of things in the storeroom, fascinating things: drip stands, steel cots, wooden and steel lockers, but where was the baumanometer?

She looked more carefully around her. The sister was quite definite that it should be in that room. Oh, why did she always have trouble finding things?

She started as the door behind her clicked shut. It must have been the wind. It made the room quite dim, almost dark. She went towards the light switch. It made a clicking sound but no light came on. Perhaps there was another switch. She felt around for one... Nothing. Well, she could see with the door open; quite well, in fact, with the light coming through from the passage.

She turned the handle of the door. It turned easily, but the door would not open. Somehow, it had clicked shut hard – locked? Why had she not checked the latch? Why had she allowed it to close behind her?

As she groped around in the dark she tripped over several of the orthopedic appliances, which caused several more of the heavy ones to fall over on top of her followed by at least ten pairs of crutches, which seemed as determined to entrap her. Suddenly, she was trapped inside a very odd, but complicated, construction, and could not free herself for several minutes. She found that, for some reason, this caused her intense anxiety and a feeling of utter panic. When she finally managed to extricate herself, she stood helplessly, hardly daring to move.

Still trembling, she sat on one of the steel bed frames, which was quite uncomfortable without its mattress, which had continued to be used by the hospital on a far more modern bed. Her uniform caught onto the steel springs. Thank goodness they didn't make beds like that any more. These must have been quite uncomfortable.

Well, she had better do something!

She went to the door and knocked at it. No one responded. She knocked harder. Surely someone would hear her. However, the room was very isolated. Perhaps if she screamed she would be heard, but people would think she was crazy. Which nurse screamed when they were locked in a room? She would wait until the sister would decide that she was taking too long. She would surely realize what had happened and come to rescue her. How ridiculous she had been not to make sure that the door could not lock.

She went to the door and knocked loudly again. There was no response. Well, there was the tiny window high up, almost at the ceiling. Perhaps she could climb on something and reach that, but she would only do that if she was desperate. It would require quite a major acrobatic effort.

She again sat on the bed. Well, she would just have to wait.

For a moment, she leant back onto the hard bed springs, sitting up quickly again as she realized that more of her uniform was being caught on the springs. She looked around again and, this time, the old and broken hospital stores looked weird and sinister.

She shivered. The room felt cold and unfriendly.

The feelings of fear that had been so much of her world before she went to the nursing college were beginning to find their place firmly inside her. Well, what was there to do? She could only be alone with her thoughts.

She started to think about her marriage to Andrew and her missing daughter, and she suddenly felt her eyes filling with tears. She felt in her pocket for some tissues and within a few minutes she was crying. Now, she didn't want to be rescued, at least until she had stopped crying. How embarrassing if anyone should come now and see her crying.

Then slowly her thoughts changed as she remembered something her friend, Hilda had said, less than an hour ago...something that she had hardly taken notice of at the time because there had been a crisis in the ward and it had somehow slipped her mind. She had been disappointed to be told by Hilda that Dr. Lewin Green, the vet, had been transferred to another hospital for more expert plastic surgery on his nose.

Whilst she was away he had had an operation on his nose and Hilda had nursed him as he was coming round. "Tracy, I would say that this patient was in love with you. He kept talking about you and about your eyes, and saying how he wished you and he could be together."

Tracy had muttered something about anesthetic doing funny things to people, and had then been involved in a surprise resuscitation that had taxed them all to capacity. Everything came back clearly now, and, again, she forced it out of her mind. "Anesthetic makes people think and say funny things," she muttered to herself.

Feeling, however, strangely more optimistic, she once again walked towards the door and, for at least the twentieth time, turned the door handle. This time, she did it a little differently, pulling it out a little before she turned it. It turned, and the door opened. Had she been dreaming? It had been locked. Now it was open. Had she made a mistake? Was she going crazy? She looked up. There was the machine she had been looking for. With the additional light she could now see it quite well. Taking care that nothing else could fall on her, she somehow dislodged it from where it had been so carefully stored. She went outside and pulled the door closed again and then tried to open it. It would not budge. This time it did not matter. She was on the outside and she had the instrument she needed.

Feeling a little sheepish, she wheeled it along to the ward, hoping her eyes didn't look too red.

She looked at her watch. She had been gone almost half an hour. What would the sister say? She was pleased to find that the sister wasn't even in the ward. She did, however, make a note that the lock on the door was faulty.

Eventually she wheeled the baumanometer into the duty room and went on with her routine work. She was very shaken and found it difficult to concentrate. The hours dragged by and it was eventually time for her to go off duty.

She finished what she had to do and , busy with her thoughts she popped into the vet's ward only to confirm he had been discharged. Hilda had told her that, hadn't she? She could not understand why she felt so upset about that. Perhaps she was feeling generally vulnerable. After all, she had been through a fearful experience. Why had she reacted so strongly to being behind a locked door and being trapped under the orthopedic appliances? Why was her reaction stronger after her 'rescue'?

That night, the dreams began. She was once again trapped inside the room, unable to get out. Her panic was even stronger than it had been during the actual experience. She was feeling a sense of claustrophobia and of intense pain and fear...almost as if she had been compressed into a ball inside a continuous crushing metal case. She realized she was shaking and crying even as she awoke. Yes, it was the accident! It definitely was. Her dreams were taking her back to the accident. Deep inside she knew it. She had been trapped in the car and must have been conscious for at least a few seconds in her twisted solid metal cage. She had been trapped in the car unable to move, unable to get out and unable to call for help.

She had the dream the next day and the next, each time increasing the terror, until she was unable to sleep and finding it difficult to be fully awake. Why were these things coming back to her now?

On her regular visits home, both her father and mother realized that something was wrong. Her face was pale and drawn and she was definitely starting to lose weight. Eventually she told her father about the dreams she was having.

"My darling Tracy," he said. "Please go and see someone about this. You have been through so much stress with the accident and everything else. Maybe you need to speak to someone. Maybe you need medical help. Maybe you need to see a doctor."

"A psychiatrist?" she asked sharply. "You also think I am crazy." She began to cry.

Her father looked very distressed. "You are not crazy," he said. "You are not crazy at all, and you never have been crazy. It is just that you are not yourself and the terrible traumatic stress of the accident is getting to you."

"No, Dad, I am fine," she said, suddenly resenting his suggestion. However, she had to admit, she did not feel like herself at all. She realized also that, although her work was always of a high standard, she was finding it increasingly difficult to find the energy to keep up with it.

She began to make sure she was eating properly and taking it easier when she could. She was glad that her father would often fetch her for a meal after work. Although she would have eaten at the nurses' home, a home-cooked meal was always welcome.

One evening, she was walking to the main gate of the hospital, feeling somehow despondent about things

Her father's car was there to fetch her. She gave a sigh of relief and was soon in the security of his small apartment.

As usual, Tracy made her way to the computer, but this time was different!

As soon as she got into Towermail, she was astonished to find a message directed to her and signed, simply, 'Sky'.

Dear Tracy,

I have been reading your messages for nearly a month now from when I first started to learn the computer. My name is 'Sky' and I am ten years old. My mother died when I was very young and I hardly remember her. I don't have any mother to tell things to, things that frighten me, make me happy, make me sad. I need to ask someone all kinds of questions and that person must be a mother.

Tracy, I know this sounds a very strange thing to ask you, but I long so much for a mother and I see you long so much for your daughter. Could I write to you and talk to you like I would to a mother? I mean, you are always going to be on Towermail looking for Andy, so when you log in, please could you write to me. There is no one here I can really talk to and though I can talk to my father about some things, he is often away and I am left with various friends or with someone paid to look after me. Could you sort of adopt me, just through email, and just for a while?

Love

Your maybe adopted daughter,

Sky.

Responding immediately to the child's loneliness, Tracy wrote back.

Dear Sky,

Of course you can write to me and I will try to be as much as I can of a mother to you. You must miss your own mother terribly. Please write back.

She went on to write about her nursing, and about things in general, asking Sky a lot of questions about herself.

There was an immediate reply of a delighted child who, as all motherless children do, had been searching for years for some mother substitute. Thus began a correspondence between Tracy and Sky that sealed a friendship between the two, and that was, eventually, to have far-reaching results.

She stared at the computer for a long time and then went back to the Nurses' Residence. Could Andy be missing a mother like that, or had Andrew perhaps married again and Andy had a stepmother? Would that stepmother be a real mother? That night she slept relatively peacefully, her first peaceful sleep for many weeks.

As the days went on, her work kept her more than occupied. She was in an extremely busy ward, nursing patients who were either very ill or who, besides their illness, craved reassurance and attention.

One day, by mid-afternoon, she was dropping with tiredness. For the fifth time that day, at least, she answered Mrs. Paddy's call. She was an elderly woman with progressive lung disease who found her security in her oxygen cylinder. If for any reason it was taken away or became nearly empty, she would immediately have an anxiety attack, proclaiming that she was going to die. She was a difficult woman, but a likeable one…one however, who took up a great deal of time and energy.

Again she looked quite exhausted as her father fetched her, but she was soon at the computer, looking quite enthusiastic as she looked for something from Sky. She was not disappointed. There was a message waiting for her.

Dear Tracy,

I want to tell you about school. I am in class with both boys and girls, which I think is not always a good thing because the boys can often fight and we girls only do that with words. Did you go to an all girls' school or did you have boys in your class? Please tell me…also I think I am really going to like History this year…

Sky's letter went on for several pages giving school news, sports news, news of her friends of her likes and dislikes.

Tracy responded as always, making her letters full of news of herself and of the hospital and of her parents.

Sky was thrilled as usual

131

and responded with many and detailed questions. However, even with Sky and the excitement of communicating with her, the old fears had returned, attaching themselves to her every waking and, indeed, every sleeping moment. There was really no practical reason for her to be afraid, yet why did a sickly sense of fear keep washing over her? She felt at risk, even though there were two sisters and three nurses working with her in the very busy trauma unit, and the nurses residence where she stayed was filled to capacity.

She was not alone... Definitely not alone, and she was working hard as they all were. Several of the patients were extremely ill, reminding her of her own situation...whatever she could remember it.

One afternoon, as she left the ward, Tracy was suddenly overcome by an overwhelming desire to sleep.

"Tracy, you don't look well... and you are looking so jumpy and nervous these days," said Hilda, who had been walking with her. "Perhaps you should speak to someone. Perhaps you should see a doctor."

"There isn't anyone I can talk to," she said. "I must go to sleep; otherwise, how can I go on duty tomorrow? I don't know who I could speak to."

She went to her room, locked the door behind her, and fell into bed. She was exhausted... She felt herself drifting off, but, for some reason she was not falling asleep; in fact, she was becoming more wide awake by the minute. That was a nuisance. That meant that she would be exhausted the following day. She would just lie there and hope that sleep would overtake her.

Half an hour later, she was wide awake. She switched on her bedside light and took out a book from her bookshelf. She read a few paragraphs and then put the book away.

Why couldn't she sleep or, at least, why couldn't she concentrate on her reading? Maybe she should get up and tidy her room. She hadn't done that for a very long time. She just had not had the time.

It was so long since she had had the time or the energy to really tidy her room that she had to stop things from sliding out of her cupboard every time she opened it. Well... if she couldn't sleep, now was as good a time as any to do some tidying up. Strange how she had collected so many things over the past months. After all, she had arrived with only an overnight bag; so long... Was it so long ago?

She yawned; she was tired, but not sleepy, if one could make such a distinction.

She almost mechanically emptied out one shelf after another, repacking them neatly.

As she put it all away, she found the sweater that the kind people on the train had given her. She would never forget them. As she touched the soft wool she felt a comforting sense of warmth. She wondered how they were doing. If only she could have somehow contacted them. They had appeared from nowhere to become a warmth and comfort at one of her lowest points in life. She suddenly again felt overwhelmingly tired, got into her bed and, this time, fell fast asleep.

She awoke with a start. She was late and she stared at her alarm clock suspiciously. She must have forgotten to set it, or more likely, she had put it off in her sleep.

She quickly got dressed and went to the door, dashing as fast as possible towards her ward.

As Tracy left the ward later to go to the tearoom she was given a message to go to the matron's office. Any such message from the matron had to be obeyed right away and Tracy, very anxious, made her way to her study.

The matron looked at her carefully.

"Don't worry, Tracy. You haven't done anything wrong. It is just that your ward sister and several others... Other members of staff, are saying you are definitely not yourself, that you are depressed, anxious and jumpy. Tracy, I think you need to see someone. Though I must admit you are a good... an excellent, nurse. No one questions this. But, for the sake of everyone and for my peace of mind, you must see a doctor. I have already made arrangements. You will see him tomorrow."

Tracy just nodded. Well, her father and Hilda would be pleased. In fact, she herself felt a little relieved it was taken out of her hands.

The matron called her on the next day and sat her in the empty outside office next to hers. Tracy blushed as a new psychiatric registrar came in. Was this what they all thought...that she was in urgent need of psychiatric help?

However, they were soon left alone in the office.

"The matron called me," the doctor said. "She said I should speak to you. You have apparently been looking almost burnt out, and she feels something is worrying you. Would you like to tell me about it?"

He smiled, and she could not help having a certain amount of confidence in his smile. Why did his blue eyes look so familiar?

"Is this really confidential?" she asked, knowing immediately that it was. "I had a very bad accident several years ago," said Tracy. "Of course, after my accident, I was in Union Hospital in Pretoria for many months." She stopped, realising that her telling of the story was somewhat disjointed.

He nodded when she mentioned Union Hospital.

"I used to go to the hospital there every day. As a registrar, as you know, I am busy doing psychiatric specialisation, so I spend six months in each hospital. It was quite a long drive over there every day, but it isn't worth moving every half year, and I am not sure where we will end up. I was so busy at the hospital. But what about you? What's the matter? Are you all right?"

Tracy looked at her watch. She was beginning, more and more, to feel like she wanted to tell him everything, but would he send her back to the rehabilitation centre? No, there was no reason.

"It's all right," he said, laughing. "I have seen all the overdoses, done at least six emergencies, and I haven't got anything I really have to do for at least an hour, maybe an hour and a half... unless something drastic happens, Heaven forbid." He said the last part under his breath.

She found herself telling him her whole story from beginning to end. He frowned when she started telling him about the strange things that had been happening to her from the time of the accident and even in the rehabilitation home. To him the whole thing made a horribly realistic terrifying picture. He did not even entertain the question of paranoia.

She told him what had happened in the last two years, her meeting with her parents and even her search for Andy. She told him about the dreams that had been haunting and terrifying her. "Am I all right?" she asked eventually.

"More than all right," he said, laughing. "Though you do have some post traumatic stress disorder symptoms that we must treat."

He handed her his card and, for the first time, she saw his name: Dr. Raphael Silver.

A memory seemed to stir and flickered inside her, and it then went blank.

"Your name, you are so familiar. You look like someone," she said.

"Me?" he asked. "I look like myself."

"No," she said, suddenly struck by the resemblance. "Who are your parents? Where do they live?"

"Well," he said, "let's say just outside Cape Town. On the train line, actually."

"Your parents," she said. "They caught the same train. They could... They could have been the people who helped me with the money and the clothes."

She described the incident, which she had already mentioned, in more detail. She could not remember their first names, however, but she was sure it had been something like Silver.

He thought for a few moments.

"I do remember something like that," he said, "only those are my grandparents you are talking about, I am sure. They catch that same train quite often. I will ask them. That is just the kind of thing they would do, and my grandmother is always knitting. Soon, when our child is born, we are going to have an incredible amount of baby clothes."

Was she imagining things? It surely had to be. There was such a resemblance, the unusual blue of the eyes, the good-natured, understanding smile, and the same train! Now, at last, she could thank them.

The doctor's bleeper went off. He was wanted urgently in the psychiatric unit.

"I'll report to the matron," he said. "Don't worry, I won't say much, just that you have some post traumatic stress disorder symptoms because of an earlier accident. We can deal with that together." Then he was gone.

Dear Mum,

It is very strange writing to someone and calling them 'Mum', yet it is something I have wanted to do ever since I could remember. I hardly remember having a mum though, obviously I did have one. I just know I would always dream of what she would be like, of how she would have a smile just for me, that I would be precious to her. She would care for me if I was hurt or upset. She would notice if I was sick She would look at my school report and she would speak to the teacher about me. She would know who my friends at school were and what I was doing. She would notice if there was a hole in my tights and either sew it up or get me new ones. And, of course, we could discuss all kinds of things.

My dad does some of these things but he is not really home a lot and he is really very busy. I mean, I love him but he hasn't got that much time for me.

Once he had a girlfriend and I thought he was going to get married and I thought I would have a mother, but she didn't really like me at all. She bought me things and tried to be nice in a way, but at times when my father was not listening, she could be quite nasty. So I thought I could be a bit nasty back and that somehow would always be told to my father and I realised she never, ever really would be my mother... even if she did marry my father, which, thank goodness, she didn't. I am not sure of the reason. They never told me.

Please could you love me?

I don't want to tell you where I live. I will one day but not now. I mean, I will obviously tell you a lot about where I live but not actually where it is. I don't know why, but I just can't now because I want to tell you so many things that I can't if you *know where to find me. Is that all right?*

Love

Sky

Though she was somewhat puzzled, Tracy responded in a reassuring way, saying that Sky need not tell her where she lived and that she would love to hear about all the things was doing, and, of course, she would love her and that love would grow as they shared things together.

The matron looked relieved when she bumped into Tracy on the way to the ward and nodded to her in a friendly way. Dr. Silver had apparently helped them considerably. He had apparently reassured them about Tracy's psychological soundness and competence, mentioning the car accident and saying that she just needed to talk things through and to have a bit of a break.

Tracy breathed a sigh of relief when she heard this, but she also knew, as Dr. Silver had suggested, that she needed a break.

She was due for leave again as soon as she had finished her exams and had been relieved when the doctor had said the break could wait till then. Writing her exams meant a lot to her. She knew she would do well as she always did. Then she would take leave.

This time, she would make sure she got to the Union

Hospital to visit the staff who might remember her and see what she herself could remember. It was something she just had to do. Dr. Silver had been encouraging about it.

"Dad, will you come with me to the Union Hospital?" asked Tracy. "I have always wanted to, or, rather, needed to go back there. I suppose I have some awful memories of the place hidden away."

"I also have some very traumatic memories of the hospital," said her father. "You are right; maybe we should go together. I will drive you there and we can look at the place, and I can show you where your ward was and everything, and maybe take you around a bit."

"And then, Dad," said Tracy, "then we can go for lunch somewhere and perhaps... No... I have not been there for a very long time."

"The zoo, Tracy, I know you have not been there since your accident, and I know that you have always loved it," said her father, laughing. "Don't worry. You don't lose your love for the zoo like that. I also love to go to it. And, remember, there is a little restaurant there. We can go there and eat lunch."

"Great," said Tracy. "That will make the visit to the hospital so much easier if we can go to the zoo afterwards."

She remembered how her mother had always said that she and her father were like ridiculous children the way they always visited the zoos both in Johannesburg and in Pretoria. She had always made very scathing comments about it.

She pulled herself short. Her mother had changed now. She definitely had changed. The old abusive derogatory remarks were a thing of the past.

There were places she really wanted to go with her mother, and now they had been shopping together for hours, enjoying each other's company. One of the things she realised was that her mother never gave her advice on what she should buy and what she should wear and even when specifically asked she was somewhat hesitant. It appeared she had really thought through the things she had been doing.

She and her father travelled almost in silence, both busy with their own thoughts.

As they approached the Union Hospital, Tracy was expecting to feel apprehensive and anxious but she was surprised to see that it was her father breaking out into a sweat and breathing with a degree of difficulty.

"Dad, what's wrong?" she asked.

"My darling," he replied. "You have no idea what terrible memories this brings back for me. You have no idea what it meant to travel on this road and seeing you lying there with no hope at all, or so we were told. I remember going along this road, praying, just praying that we could somehow have you back." He suddenly laughed, breaking the tension. "And here you are. Here you are as alive and whole as you ever were… All my dreams are fulfilled."

"Dad," she asked, "do you remember when I was brought here?"

"Well, Tracy," he said. "We had Andy to look after, but your mother kept her that afternoon and, as soon as I heard which hospital you had been brought to, I came here to the trauma casualty. Andrew was here and was looking utterly devastated, saying that the doctors had told him very definitely that there was absolutely no hope at all. I had to almost suppress anything I felt to try to comfort him. But here you, my own daughter, was dying, and we could not get to you."

"Why not, Dad?" she asked. "Weren't you allowed to see me?"

"No, not at all. You were in the operating theatre. You had been taken there as soon as you had arrived. There was no waiting for you to go in at all. There was absolutely nothing we could do. You had been taken in straight away. Now and then, a doctor would come out and nod to us very seriously, and then move on. We did not even ask. We thought it was a matter of time before they would come through and say that you were gone."

"But they didn't," she said.

"No, they didn't, but they did eventually come out and say that they had done all they could, but there was very little hope of you being alive even the next morning. If, by any chance, you did survive, you would be a... A..."

"Vegetable," she said, putting in the word for him.

"You don't look like any vegetable I know," he said, laughing and crying simultaneously.

"An onion," she said, seriously, "with many layers nobody knows about."

"Yes, and capable of making people cry," he said.

She looked at him, realising that the tears were rolling down his cheeks.

"Sorry," he said, sniffing. "It is just coming here again, just the awful memories."

She squeezed his shoulder. "Dad, thank you for just being you. You have no idea what an inspiration you have been."

"Now I wanted to come here to see if I remembered anything. Now I want to see if they remember anything."

Nothing looked familiar as she came into the foyer of the busy trauma casualty. There was a queue of people wanting to see the doctor. People were also waiting outside because they were comparatively only lightly injured, with broken arms, hands, feet, legs and various stab wounds and minor gunshot wounds. The serious cases were inside, she knew that. She went over to the desk and produced her card. "I would like to speak to the casualty doctor who admitted me after my accident," she said. "There are things I have to know, to sort out, things that I need to know for medical reasons."

The woman looked at her card and then looked at her doubtfully and then sent in a request for a microfiche of her file. "This was a long time ago," she said. "If we were one hundred percent a government hospital, I could not do this for you, but, seeing this is partially private, I will put this down as a private consult. It is at least five times the price."

"Thank you," Tracy said, satisfied.

She sat in the foyer with the other patients. It was nearly two hours later that two doctors and a nurse came out of the trauma unit and walked over to her.

"You are Tracy Sheldon?" they asked.

The one tall fair doctor smiled. In fact, he almost jumped with excitement. "I can't believe this," he said. "You were dead. We had to start your heart at last twice, and you clinically died in the ward, also. There wasn't any hope for you at the time and, if by any faint chance you survived, well, you would never have been right."

The nurse and other doctor were looking through the notes excitedly. "You are a miracle," the nurse said. "A walking miracle. Please come and talk to us all. And, Mrs. Sneddon, is this your father? Please come, too. In fact, would it be all right for you to be presented at our ward round as a successful case? Would you be able to come back to us next week or the week after, or whenever we manage to arrange it? Next Wednesday, we have a meeting with the trauma professors and, in fact, the whole trauma unit. We could put it to them then. You know, when you came here, there was almost zero hope. Perhaps, if possible, even less than zero. You know, so often we have to deal with ghastly, horrific things. You are going to be our inspiration."

Tracy smiled.

"You know," the doctor said. "You have no idea what a miracle it is that you can smile and that your smile is equal on both sides of your face. People have no idea what a blessing that is, and it was definitely not so when you left here."

"I don't remember a lot," said Tracy, "but I remember, for a long time, I had a weakness on one side, and I couldn't actually smile properly."

They spoke excitedly for several minutes, but then had to return to their waiting patients.

As he left, the first doctor said. "I am Dr. Sidney. I will take a breakfast break in half an hour for twenty minutes. Please wait for me, and I will take you to your ward. I just have to see their faces when they see you. Please go to the canteen in the meanwhile, and come back here in exactly thirty minutes."

"And your breakfast?" asked Mr. Berns.

"This is much more interesting than breakfast," said the doctor.

They went to the canteen that caused more trauma to her father as he remembered the devastating times they had had there. He remembered weeks of anxiously picking at his food or else gobbling it down as if he had not eaten for days, which was often basically true. He never seemed to have the time or the motivation to eat.

They went back to casualty as they had arranged with the doctor and he arrived, shortly after, almost out of breath.

"Okay I can leave for twenty minutes," he said. "There is nothing absolutely drastic that I am needed for."

He gratefully accepted the sandwich they had bought for him eating it on the way to the ward. He also quickly drank his orange juice.

Mr. Berns was becoming more and more quiet as he went along the passageways that had, for so long, been so familiar, the horrifying memories engulfing his mind; for him, more than for his daughter, who had very few memories of it.

For him, this had been a place of horror. Every corridor, every turning had been, as it were, soaked with his tears, with his wife's tears, Andrew's tears, and more openly, Andy's tears. His heart seemed to convulse within him as he thought about his granddaughter. If only they could find her or even if she never contacted them again, if only they could be sure that she was happy.

He was feeling physically and emotionally exhausted when they arrived at the familiar, dreaded doors, yet, through these doors, Tracy had somehow been brought back to life.

He saw her chatting animatedly with the doctor and felt he could say nothing. There was now not even a trace of her accident.

As they got to the ward and went through the doors, Tracy gave a gasp.

"Yes, yes, I do remember it," she said. "I remember I was in this bed."

At that moment, the sister came out and stared at her for

several seconds. Then she caught sight of Mr. Berns and her face paled. "This can't be Tracy," she said slowly. "This surely can't be Tracy."

Tracy caught her hand and shook it and then gave her a spontaneous hug. "Sister Jennet, I am so pleased to see you again. You were the one who believed I would get better. You were the one who really encouraged me. And I want to tell you that I have already finished two years of nursing and I am busy with my third one."

Even the student doctor with her was very impressed with that information as Sister Jennet who could not believe that Tracy actually remembered her name, called excitedly to the rest of the staff. Some of these people had treated Tracy quite intensively and they looked at her with absolute amazement and joy.

The best moment was when the doctor, hearing the excitement, came over. Recognising her immediately he almost gave a leap in the air. "I knew it!" he said. "This is a miracle, nothing less or more than a miracle."

He looked into her eyes, and noted that she was alive and aware of everything.

Tracy laughed. "I am nursing now," she said. "I have started my third year. I have passed all my exams. See." She laughed. "I did not turn out to be a vegetable at all."

The doctor and some of the nurses blushed. "Who told you that?" asked the doctor. "Who would have told you that?"

"Well, people said it around my bed."

"You heard that?" asked the doctor. "You were in a very deep coma."

She started to tell them the exact words that some of the staff had said around the bed and they blushed.

The casualty officer looked at his watch. He had been enjoying this. "I have to go back," he said. "But we want to present her case, with her and her parents present, at a ward round in a couple of weeks' time. We can demonstrate this to them then."

The nurse looked a bit uncomfortable, but Tracy gave her a reassuring smile.

One of the nurses suddenly frowned. "We heard that you had committed suicide whilst you were at the rehabilitation centre. That is what we heard."

"I escaped," said Tracy. "Missing, believed dead."

"But there was something more," said the sister. "They said you were frightened that someone was trying to kill you."

The nurse was looking at her intently and Tracy just nodded.

"Did it happen there, as well?" the nurse continued.

"What do you mean?" asked Tracy, her heart beating fast.

"Well, there was a time here, I tried to report it, but people said it was my imagination, but one day there was a man here, and he seemed to be trying to switch off your life support machines."

"Yes," said Tracy. "Yes, I am sure it was. I looked at the police files about my accident, and it stated that someone had deliberately knocked me over the cliff."

The nurse was very pale. "So I was right," she said. "I always knew I was right. The man even came a second time and, when I saw him, I went to your ward before he got there and just sat with you. I wasn't even in uniform. I was off duty. I had just come back to the ward to fetch something I had forgotten. So he went away."

"That is very serious, Sister," said the doctor. "Did you report it?"

"I can show you the entry," said the sister. "I wrote it on the card."

The doctor just stared at her.

It was with some relief that they were going out of there to the Pretoria Zoo.

The Pretoria Zoo ranked amongst the best in world, and was home to thousands of Southern African and exotic animals..

Tracy and her father arrived just in time for a guided tour that would be leaving in forty minutes. That should just about leave time for a quick lunch. They booked their tickets and went to the closest restaurant. They had not really felt like walking around for hours and the tractor-bus would take them around everywhere with time to stop at each place.

They enjoyed the zoo thoroughly, the highlight for Tracy being the visit to the penguins. "These are different," she said, "different to those I met in Cape Town at Boulders when I was ill. These are larger, sort of more formal looking."

"Emperor Penguins," said her father. "They are royalty. Look how they hold themselves."

"They probably aren't as friendly," she said, "and they are so much bigger."

"Was it your cousins who took you to the penguins... my brother's children?"

"Yes, and those were the visits that kept me sane and inspired. I sometimes think that, if it wasn't for them, I would not have coped. Maybe I would have gone crazy over there. Going to Boulders was kind of life restoring."

*   *   *

All too soon Tracy's holiday was over and she was back at her hospital.

She went back to her ward and quickly slotted into the work she had been doing. She was feeling happier in this ward. It looked out on to the west side of the hospital, on to the least built-up area of the town. Nothing overlooked them except a row of tall trees. It was pleasant and peaceful.

On her third day, Tracy helped to set up a drip on a badly dehydrated patient, made sure the old woman was comfortable, and carried on with checking temperatures, pulse rates and blood pressures. She was about to go for tea when one of the patients called her.

"Nurse, please could you help me? The pain is so bad."

Tracy turned around and went over to the bed of the woman calling her. Immediately all her thoughts and anxieties were pushed to somewhere else in her mind as she tried to help the patient. She was, indeed, in a great deal of pain and was being given three-hourly injections to control it. The woman was also in obvious distress, confiding that she was feeling extremely lonely as she had no visitors.

"Family?" questioned Tracy.

"No family," the woman said. "Many years ago, I had a husband and daughter, but I was ill, in a severe depression, and my husband divorced me, took my daughter and left the country. I have never heard from them again."

Tracy found herself shaking uncontrollably as she straightened out the woman's blankets, puffed out the pillows and left the ward. The woman was not young and it must have been years ago that her daughter left. Why, the daughter herself probably had grown up children. She had a sense of desperation and for the first time she doubted her ability to find Andy. She was disturbed for the rest of the day and went home with a confused, hollow feeling.

When he fetched her after work her father saw she was looking a little dejected and knew something was wrong. He decided to speak to her after the meal when they were more relaxed. He was about to say something when the phone rang. It was Tracy's mother wanting to speak to her. Their conversation lasted for some time and her father busied himself around the apartment.. She looked around for her him and then walked into the bedroom to find him. He did not hear her come in and when she saw what he was doing, she tiptoed quietly out.

He had in his hands a picture of her mother and was looking at it, an expression of thoughtfulness and confusion on his face that she could not quite comprehend.

Dear Mum,

Dad and I went for a holiday for the weekend. We went to an island to the north of us. You would have loved it, because there were so many birds. There were shearwaters, guillemots, kittiwakes and, would you believe it, puffins. I love puffins. I think in a way they are a bit like penguins.

We stayed at a guest house on the island and I do hope we can come here often.

Love you so much

Sky

Tracy's determination to find her daughter Andy strengthened. She was sure that Duncan knew far more about Andrew than her was telling her. In many ways he had indicated this to her. She needed to get the whole story, no matter what it entailed. She accepted the next invitation for supper with a determination to find out what she could.

They were eating chicken-a-la-king, and discussing more about Andrew's involvement in financial disasters before he left, when she asked a casual question "Could his creditors be so dangerous?"

Duncan looked at her for a long moment before he replied: "As I hinted before, it is more than his creditors. Andrew was working for an arch criminal; without realising it, of course. Andrew, as it were, betrayed him. He was involved in all kinds of crime such as drug dealing and armed robbery and even had a hijacking syndicate using cars that would be hidden in an underground garage outside Johannesburg. He was involved in outright, violent crime, to say the least"

Tracy's face had blanched as she realized what must surely be the truth. None of that sounded good. It was sounding more and more sinister as he continued to speak. How had it affected Andy?

The tense atmosphere was broken by the unexpected ring of the telephone. Peggy went to answer it.

"It's your father," she said to Tracy. "He sounds worried," she added as she watched Tracy pick up the phone.

Tracy knew it was a strange time for her father to phone her. He had always adhered somewhat rigidly to some kind of rule that said that no one should call anyone after 9 p.m. unless it was an emergency.

Was this an emergency?

As soon as she heard her father's voice, she knew that it was.

"It's your mother," he said. "She has had some sort of heart attack. Your aunt phoned. You must go to her straight away; she needs someone with her. The doctor is on his way. She said not to worry, it isn't too serious, but we can't have her being alone and her sister is not always there."

Tracy flinched at the mixed messages given, and still hesitated.

"They could not reach you," he repeated.

"Dad, I will go straight away, but you must come with me. This is a thing we have to do together."

Her father did not need much persuasion and he arranged to fetch her in ten minutes. "I am really worried," he said, "really worried."

"Did she say how serious it was?" asked Tracy.

"Well my sister-in-law said it was serious and not serious. I don't think she knew, because the doctor had not arrived there yet. I tried to speak to Mum, but she could not communicate at all." His panic was rising.

"Fetch me now," said Tracy. "We can use the cell phone in the car and see how she is then. Perhaps after she has seen the doctor, she might even be on the way to the hospital. We will confirm everything. I will phone whilst you are on the way here."

She phoned her aunt whose usual unruffled demeanor seemed to have left her. Yes, the doctor had been and an ambulance was coming to take her to Hillside Hospital. They should meet her there.

"Can I speak to Mum?" asked Tracy.

Her aunt hesitated, and then she heard her mother's voice, breathless, anxious and weak. "Don't worry, darling, I will be okay," she said.

"Mum, we are coming now, Dad and I."

Her mother thanked her, seeming to have no energy to continue the conversation.

By the time they reached Hillside Hospital, Mrs. Berns had already had an ECG, was on a drip, and was ready for admission.

Tracy kissed her mother, relieved to see that she was looking better than expected.

Her father went over to her and just took her hand in his for a few seconds. A faint smile played on her mother's lips.

It was very late when she returned to the nurses' home. She was anxious about her mother but was reassured when she saw her father had left her a message saying that he would be staying near her mother until she was ready to return to her sister's home. He felt that even though they were separated, he was needed at this time.

It took several weeks before Tracy's mother was completely well. Tracy visited often and slowly became aware that her parents were becoming closer, closer than she had ever known them to be. They were treating each another with a respect and love that she had never seen between them as she was growing up.

When she returned to her sister's home there was a definite change, in that her father became a regular visitor, almost, she hoped, as if they were courting again as things once more fell into a regular routine.

"I want to tell you something," her father said to Tracy as they sat together in his apartment, just before she was about to return for the night to the Nurses Residence. He seemed to be choosing his words carefully. "You know, when I first met your mother, she was one of the most beautiful women I had ever seen, and I could not put her out of my mind until I had made her my wife. I absolutely adored her and would do anything for her. Nothing was too much, just to see her smile. And then... And then slowly she started to take advantage of that and seemed to have lost all respect for me, and she would just order me around and dominate me. She did the same to you, and you know the rest. She became domineering and impossible. You know that is all gone. She really has changed, as you pointed out to me a few months ago. You know I have come to see that I still love her to the point that I can't, and don't, want to live without her. And you know what, she feels the same way about me, so we... We..."

Tracy got up and flung her arms around him. "I would be so happy if you got together again. When is she coming back?"

"Well, I haven't really told her yet. I thought we should move into a bigger apartment first."

"You can move into a bigger apartment afterwards,' said Tracy. "Tell her tonight and help her pack up her stuff."

"You always give good advice, my girl," said her father. He was looking delighted.

"Are you sure she will agree?" asked her father suddenly insecure.

"I am sure she will," said Tracy, "but why don't you phone her and check it out?

He paused only a few minutes and then went to his room. He came back some time later with his eyes shining. At that point he looked like a delighted love-struck teenage boy.

During that week, Tracy's mother came home, and Tracy

helped them to look for a larger apartment, which they moved into a few weeks later. Now there was peace in the home except for the agony of the persistent search for Andy, made more urgent by the real element of danger. They searched Towermail every night each time hope arising anew. Towermail had organised for the details to go on other sites but to no avail. No one gave up; however, there was a possibility that, as Andy grew older, she would want to find out about her mother. The older she got, the stronger that possibility was.

The correspondence with Sky increased and deepened. They shared a lot and learnt a great deal about each other however, Sky continued to refuse to give any indication of even the continent she was living in. Her address and all personal details were under the confidential protection of Towermail.

CHAPTER 8

Tracy's time of nursing training ended, and she did not sign the contract offered to her to work as a sister in the hospital. She wanted a break and needed to find her daughter. She would decide later what she would do. She needed to go overseas somewhere, but she was not even sure where to start. In many ways she found she could not settle to do anything constructive

A few days after she had left the hospital, she tidied up her room and left to do some window shopping, holding endless conversations with Andy in her mind.

She was awakened from her daydream world by a greeting from Peggy who was taking the baby...now a toddler for a ride in the stroller.

"Hi, Tracy," she called. "You look as busy as I do. I have a well-visit appointment for Jenny with the child specialist, and I was sure it was at one, and I see he has us booked for three, so we have to stay around until then. It's not worth going back to the apartment."

They were soon on their way to the nearby park, having each bought a bag of chips and a soda.

They sat on a bench beside the lake, trying to convince the rather puzzled looking ducks that chips were good to eat. They definitely seemed to have a preference for bread crumbs and strutted off haughtily towards a woman with a large plastic bag, who obviously fed them regularly on their chosen diet. Jenny was fascinated though a little afraid of them.

Tracy saw a man walk past her, his newspaper open to the sports page and she found herself reading the large letters on the reverse side of the page.

She felt a surge of interest as she read the headlines: 'South African Oil Tanker Sinks – Thousands of Penguins in Danger'. Walking through the park she went to a stand and she bought the newspaper. Didn't she remember something about penguins being oiled? As clear as daylight she saw her friendly Boulders penguin friends standing in front of her, the sea sending out beautiful sun filled spray behind them.

She sat on a bench beside Peggy and became absorbed in what she was reading.

The iron-ore ship that has been in trouble off the Western Cape coast for the past few days, the Treasure, *sank early this morning. It went down eight kilometres north-west of Melkbosstrand, almost exactly opposite the nuclear power station at Koeberg. The place of sinking is approximately twenty kilometres north of the African Penguin colony on Robben Island, and about forty kilometres south of the colony on Dassen Island. The ship had one thousand three hundred tons of fuel oil on board. It seems almost an inevitably that penguins will be oiled.*

That did not sound good   and she read further.

The ship had developed a fifty-six-foot-wide hole in the hull, but its cause was not immediately clear. All twenty-nine crew members, most of them Chinese, were airlifted to safety as the Treasure – en route from China to Brazil – went down before dawn whilst authorities were trying to tow it farther offshore to reduce the risk of pollution.

The twenty-square-mile slick was a danger to Robben Island. The island was now a museum and World Heritage Site and home to a large colony of penguins and other birds. Plans were being put in place to protect the Robben Island penguins and the Koeberg nuclear power station on the mainland.

Further down the page they mentioned something about needing volunteers.

"What are you reading so intensely?" asked Peggy, curiously.

"The penguins," said Tracy. "They are in danger of being oiled. I wish I could go and help them"

"Why are you so concerned" asked Peggy?

"I love penguins," she said. "When I was in the rehabilitation centre, my relatives used to take me to Boulders Penguin Colony. I hope they are going to be all right. At one time, they were my only friends."

"But when was that? How was it that these birds were your only friends? I mean, how long were you in the rehabilitation centre?"

Tracy explained how she

had been after her accident and Peggy looked at her in amazement. "I, of course, knew you were in an accident," she said. "I mean, I don't think I quite realised how serious it was afterwards. I knew you were almost killed and that people thought you would never make it, but I did not realise how long it took to actually get better. I mean, you look fine now. I mean... there are no scars, and.... well, how was it that you could hardly communicate with anyone, and why penguins?"

Tracy told her about the rehabilitation centre and about her cousins who did not really communicate much with her, and about her visits to Boulders. She was about to tell her about the way she was being hounded by some sinister force, but decided against it. She had learnt not to confide these things. She rather told her about the vet she had had as a patient in the plastic surgery ward and about his love and concern for penguins. She also told her how he had been bitten on the nose by one of his patients and had several scratches from penguins.

"Have you ever thought of getting married again?" asked Peggy, noting her enthusiasm when she spoke about him.

Tracy looked startled. "No, no, I can't do that," she said.

"Why not?" asked Peggy. "You are divorced."

"I know I am divorced, but... No," said Tracy. "Some place, somewhere, I have a daughter."

"But you can still get married," Peggy insisted.

"But I have to find her," said Tracy. "This is my life's purpose. I can't do anything until I find her..."

"Do you think this vet will be at the oil spill if they ask for volunteers?"

"Maybe; probably," said Tracy. "But I am quite sure I would not recognise him. He had a very swollen nose, which made his whole face misshapen. I think I would never recognise him again."

"What else was there about him?" asked Peggy.

"Well, he was a vet, and an extremely nice person."

"Was he married?"

Tracy blushed crimson. "He probably is now. He wasn't then."

"How did you know?" asked Peggy innocently.

"Well, I checked his records and saw he was not married. And then he was thirty-six. He must be thirty-eight now." Tracy's blush was deepening. "Listen, he was a wonderful person, but he was not the slightest bit interested in me; at least, not after he left the hospital."

"And when he was in hospital?"

"Well, we enjoyed chatting, and he was lonely and in a lot of pain and, whilst he was there, we spent time together. When I got moved to another ward, I would visit him in my tea breaks just to see how he was doing. There was nothing in it at all. I just liked talking to and listening to him, and I think, whilst he was vulnerable, he felt the same way. The ward sister wanted me to stop visiting him, but I said I just wanted to see how he was. He had had a second operation, and I wanted to know how it had gone. He was very drowsy as he spoke to a friend of mine, a fellow nurse, coming around from the anaesthetic, and he said some things that I am sure were meant for someone else. I thought he would be in hospital for many weeks, but, when I came back from leave, he was gone, transferred somewhere else. I thought he might have contacted me again just for friendship's sake, but he didn't. He had just been responding to a friendly nurse in a hospital. That's all. I didn't see him in that light. I just respected his love for animals."

"Did you think about him afterwards?" asked Peggy.

"Please don't ask me these questions. Why are you asking me these questions?"

"I really hope you meet him again," said Peggy earnestly, ignoring her comment. "I can see you are seriously considering going down there. Maybe you will meet him by the penguins in Cape Town."

"I will see how they are tomorrow," said Tracy as she read the article again. "The oil might not even get to them at all." She walked with Peggy and Jenny towards the doctor, and went back to her parents' apartment.

Perhaps the spill had passed Robben Island and the penguins were no longer in danger. She hoped so, but she was soon disappointed.

When she bought the newspaper on Sunday, she saw that the news was not good. By Monday, she would make up her mind. Perhaps she would find more of this on the Internet.

She could not sleep that night. Peggy had suggested that

she and Duncan find some way to set up a meeting between Tracy and the vet. Though she had occasionally toyed with the idea of meeting someone again she had put it out of her mind. No, she couldn't meet him. She had dedicated her life to looking for Andy. How could she get married? There was no way she could get married. How on earth could that ever be possible? It had been so long ago when she had nursed him. Her imagination was playing tricks on her. Eventually, she fell asleep.

The next day, after a thorough search on the Internet, she went onto the University of Cape Town Avian Demography Unit site.

The report was dated June 24, 2000, which was that day, and gave details about what was going on. They were following the oil spill very carefully and exactly. Volunteer workers collected hundreds of oil-coated penguins and prepared to scrub them clean on Saturday, a day after the tanker sank. As of Saturday afternoon, no oil had reached Cape Town's beaches, which were amongst the country's most popular tourist attractions... This meant the penguins from 'Boulders' were safe. The penguins lathered with oil were being gathered from Robben Island and mainland beaches to be scrubbed clean at a rehabilitation centre run by SANCCOB, the Southern African National Foundation for the Conservation of Coastal Birds. The foundation expected to collect up to one thousand oil-drenched penguins on Saturday alone. It warned that the spill could have a devastating effect on the aquatic bird population. The initial oil slick covered their main feeding ground and most penguins would be swimming through oil to get back to Robben Island. They mentioned that the officials who were trying to contain the oil from spreading said there were some encouraging signs. 'The flow is not constant and the quantities are not large'. Perhaps they would be all right; however, the next day was to make up her mind.

In Cape Town a stretch of coastline had become coated in thick black sludge. Air surveys revealed heavy oil collecting at the mouth of the Cape Town's harbour. Volunteers were using nets to round up birds and herd them into ventilated cardboard boxes for transport by boat to the mainland, where they were to be cleaned. The operation to evacuate the endangered birds was expected to become one of the largest of its kind in the world. She caught her breath at the further mention of volunteers. This was just what she needed at this point. She needed to be away from everything, to work out how to find Andy. She also might meet the vet who had been bitten by so many penguin patients, but she quickly put that out of her mind. This was, temporarily, to be her place. She knew this without a doubt.

After discussing the matter with her parents and Peggy and Duncan, none of whom were surprised about her decision, she booked herself on a bus to Cape Town and prepared for the long journey down.

Several people on the bus were coming down as

volunteers and during the many hours she got to know some of them. They were all excited to watch the beautiful scenery out of the windows until they came to the Karoo... huge, semi-arid country that covered about one third of the area in South Africa, mostly in the Cape Province.

She was booked into a boarding house where she found her room and almost immediately fell sound asleep.

The next morning she arrived fairly early at the cleaning station.

What an incredible collection of people, she thought to herself as she saw the scores of volunteers waiting to be given their various duties to save the penguins.

She found herself waiting with a somewhat overweight, pleasant girl who announced herself as Johanna. She had also been staying at the boarding house, and they recognised each other immediately.

Tracy felt a little strange in the large white gum boots, thick gloves and oilskins she was given, but comforted herself with the fact that everyone around her was dressed in a similar way. She and Johanna looked like each other with slightly embarrassed smiles.

They stood somewhat hesitantly surveying their surroundings until a young woman, identifying herself as Pam, gave over her three-day-long expertise, which seemed vast compared with Tracy's.

"You first have to learn to catch them, and then to keep

them," she said, showing her some rather nasty peck marks on her left wrist and thumb. "If you don't learn fast, you can get bitten to pieces."

Tracy examined a particularly nasty bite, which was angry and red around it. "That is getting infected," she pronounced, thankful to withdraw into her nursing profession in which she felt comfortable.

Pam was looking at her strangely.

"I am a nurse," explained Tracy.

Pam immediately responded by asking her what she could do about the bite, as it was becoming more painful by the minute.

"There is some kind of first aid station here, isn't there?" asked Tracy. "Go to them and ask them to put something on it."

"You know, these birds just go for you in the same spot over and over. That is the result of at least eight bites."

"And you are still here?" asked Tracy.

"Well, I love birds," said Pam, "and these are so vulnerable and frightened. I have learnt now to more or less handle them. You have to for pure survival; otherwise, they bite hard. I think I will give you some hints first as to how to catch and hold on to them. Then I will go and get this fixed up. You don't want to work here as a nurse instead, and help them over there, do you?"

"I have been nursing all the time," said Tracy. "Now I will work with these wriggly little chaps over here."

"You have no idea how wriggly," Pam said under her breath. "I will take you to your feeding team," she said, more audibly. "There will be three feeders and one carrier. You will see."

Tracy looked at her a bit blankly.

More than a hundred portable swimming pools were constructed as temporary pens to house the birds inside the disused railway warehouse in Salt River.

She was taken to a pen containing about one hundred and fifty penguins and watched the members of the team sitting on upturned milk crates with buckets of sardines alongside. She saw the feeder nearest to her catch one of the penguins and immobilise it by means of holding it quite firmly between the thighs and force feed it three sardines plus one special fish, which she afterwards learnt contained medication. She watched this procedure done several times by the feeders until she was invited to her own milk crate, and given a bucket of sardines and she proceeded to feed a penguin and at the same time protect her thumb, which the bird seemed determined to include in his diet. This was not going to work. Perhaps she should just volunteer as a nurse. After the first penguin had somehow had the three sardines and the medicated fish forced down his throat without the thumb being included, she found herself just watching the rest of them, who seemed to be so expert in what they were doing.

"They are starving," said one quite elderly gentleman who seemed to have mastered the art of feeding. "Just carry on. It will become easier."

He demonstrated how to hold the bird so that his razor sharp beak was away from his thumb, immobilising the feet to prevent the bird's claws from scratching him deeply. It seemed to work and she gingerly and immediately more forcefully took another bird from the pen and proceeded to feed him. For the next couple of hours this process was repeated and repeated and then there was a coffee break of ten minutes, and then another exhausting few hours.

At the end of the day, 8 p.m., to be exact, she arrived at the boarding house they had been accommodated in, feeling that all she wanted to do was to fall into bed. As she peeped into the lounge, however, she saw that there was a computer there that someone was using. Everything else flew out of her mind.

"Are we allowed to use this?" she asked. "I mean, who does it belong to?"

The young woman on it turned to her. "Well, it is one of the services at the boarding house," she said. "But, at certain hours, you are only allowed on it for twenty minutes at a time, and at later or less convenient hours, you are allowed longer. But you have to buy a password from the residence, and you can join. The password registers how much you are actually dialled up and using the phone, so, of course, you are charged for that. At hours like these, it is better to book, though, because a lot of people want it around about now."

"Where can I make arrangements for the password?" she asked. "Do I have to wait till tomorrow?"

"I am sure Bess is still in her office," she said, indicating one of the women in charge. "Speak to her, and take a look at the timetable to see how you can slot in."

Tracy did exactly that and was more than happy that she could save a space for herself at 9:20 p.m.

She went upstairs to rest until that time, feeling her whole body stiff from exhaustion. She had wanted to go and see the sea, hadn't she? Well that would wait for tomorrow. In the meanwhile, she would rest, after bandaging a thumb that had been attacked several times but by some miracle was still attached to her hand. Were her hands going to look like Dr. Lewin Green's hands? She allowed herself to think about whether Dr. Green would be here helping to stabilise the penguins. Would he be in Cape Town? She would probably not even recognise him. Her heart started to race and she quickly turned her mind away from thinking about him.

As she got onto Towermail, she saw that there were two emails from Sky but no mail for her about or from Andy. She had almost become used to this, but something made her continue checking. She had put the message on several other search sites, but there was, as usual, nothing. Perhaps there was another way. She might even have to phone up the lawyer again. She emailed Sky and her father, telling them about her day. As she saw her twenty minutes drawing to a close she got ready to leave after booking for the computer on the following evening.

"Your thumb doesn't look too good, either," said Pam, coming to meet her at the gate as she arrived the next day.

She was welcomed by her team into the pen and they looked knowingly and sympathetically at the bandage on her thumb. "Protection, too," she explained.

He would get a breakfast of bandage as well as thumb. Determinedly she took hold of a penguin and held him firmly, realising as she did so that she had somehow mastered a bit of the technique. Lowering her guard for a few seconds she was rewarded with a razor sharp bite on the most tender part of her thumb, right through the bandage.

"We can't feed, anyway, just yet," said the leader of the group. "We've run out of sardines." He smiled wearily.

"But aren't there sardines here?" she asked, pointing to a bucket that was obviously full of the fish.

"Frozen solid," he said, putting his hand into the bucket and feeling the icy sardines. "No, wait a minute, they aren't so bad. At least we can separate them now. The sun has warmed them up a bit." He took a very stiff, cold sardine, patted with his hands for a few moments to make it more subtle, grabbed a penguin with perfect technique and proceeded to attempt to get it down his throat. Naturally, the ease of inserting a hard-frozen, seven-inch sardine down a penguin's gullet has to be done a great deal more carefully than a nice fresh slimy defrosted one.

Tracy stood up uneasily. "Could I try to get you some defrosted ones?"

She could not even begin to think how she was going to feed a pecking, clawing penguin with a solid, cold, fish.

"You can try," said Harold doubtfully. "As far as I know, all the sardines arrived frozen solid. Everyone has them. There is a huge demand for sardines, which is generated by a steadily increasing number of volunteers; the defrosters are overwhelmed. But you can definitely try."

However, her pleas for warmer fish went unheeded and she returned, trying to join them in feeding the even more reluctant, but starving, penguins. This was the position until about three hours through the day, when the natural heat of the day did the job. After this, her feeding job seemed much easier and except for a few pecks on her thumb and wrist she left exhausted but relatively unscathed.

The next day, she was fully prepared mentally for another demanding day of feeding, but not too unwillingly was hijacked away by a director to the washing bays to work on a new team being set up to pre-oil the birds for washing. The woman in charge explained that this was the equivalent of a washing machine pre-wash, and that, by gently spraying each bird about to enter the wash bays with a light vegetable oil, which acted as a solvent, it made the actual washing process much easier. "Appreciate this whilst you can," said the woman to Tracy. "If this goes on at this pace, our supplies are going to run low."

Relieved, and rubbing her painful wrists and thumb, she joined them, convinced that this would be easier away from the frozen sardines and the razor sharp beaks. The process started off beautifully with them working in pairs, she with a girl called Heather. They oiled away, with oil that smelled slightly like citrus, but the problem of the oil soon manifested itself, as the oilskins and gloves soon got a liberal coating of the vegetable oil and made control of the now very slippery bird ever more challenging. She was left, however, with a strong sense of achievement and an exhaustion, which was now becoming part of her.

She was beginning to feel the team spirit of the rescue mission and was soon greeting people she had met on the days before. During the coffee break, she went around the washing bays absorbing the process of what happened to the penguins who were about to be cleaned.

Each section consisted of two wash bays, being converted showers and washrooms previously used by the railways employees, a rinsing section, being the ex-toilet area, and the drying rooms, being the old changing rooms. In each wash bay were ten overturned plastic forty-five-gallon drums that contained five-gallon plastic washing basins, which would be filled with warm soapy water by the 'water boys'. Each bay would be manned by between four and seven pairs of washers, one holder and one washer to a team.

A team would collect a bird from the holding pen outside the door, where, at any given time, about fifteen pre-treated birds waited for about twenty minutes for the vegetable oil solvent that they were working on, to do its work prior to washing. The bird would be lowered into the warm soapy water, where a combination of its kicking and struggling, plus some vigorous rubbing from the washer soon removed about seventy percent of the oil.

The bird would then be swung into a second basin and the procedure repeated, the dirty basin being changes by the water carriers, until the bird was clean from the neck down. The water would often have to be changed four or five times.

The next basin was dedicated to cleaning the neck and face, the most sensitive area, which needed to be done with a great deal of care using a toothbrush, and having a rinsing bottle of fresh water handy for when a bit of soapy water got in the eye. The cleaning process was continuously repeated and repeated until the suds coming off the feathers were clean and all traces of oil gone.

Tracy spoke to Sam, a young man who had obviously been working as a washer for some time. He continued to explain the process.

Once the washer was satisfied, usually about five minutes after the holders arms are about to break, the bird is carried through to the rinsers, where every vestige of soap is sprayed off using a hose. At times, the birds were returned as not quite clean.

Washing and rinsing time could vary from ten to forty minutes depending how heavily oiled the bird was. To Tracy's surprise, she was told that some people did forty to fifty birds a day.

She enjoyed meeting volunteers from all over the world and all parts of the country and from all ages and walks of life. She quickly saw that the team spirit was something very special and the dedication to helping the penguins quite phenomenal. Everyone had a pride in the job allocated to or selected by them.

Everyone was throwing in whatever time they could spare. Many had decided to extend their stay from the original intended three or four days till two or more weeks. However, for every five hundred penguins sent out clean, another one thousand new, oily arrivals would appear. The work was hard and challenging but rewarding in so many ways. Tracy was very moved to see that people who lived on the street were brought in to help, and were fed, along with everyone else, whilst they were happily hard at work.

The next day, she was allocated to the drying room to handle birds for one of the attending vets, an elderly man wearing bright green oilskins, black rubber gloves and white gumboots. The room was situated at the end of the washing section and, once the birds had been washed and thoroughly rinsed, they were bought through. The room was equipped with infra-red dryers where she was to take the bird and hold its trachea open for the vet to insert a thin plastic tube into the stomach and inject one hundred and twenty millilitres of glucose electrolyte solution for re-hydration, followed by an injection into the keel muscle of five millilitres of a multivitamin. Then the process would be completed by the fitment of a plastic flipper ring. The bird was then deposited into the drying pen until the following morning when the penguins they had managed to clean on the previous day would be boxed up and transported to SANCCOB in Table View, where they would sit out two to three week period until they recovered their feather mesh and natural oil-air waterproofing, which would allow them to return to the sea, without getting wet to the skin and chilled. Once a bird has been cleaned, it needed to be cared for in a rehabilitation centre for about a month.

Being informed that his helper was a qualified nurse, the vet explained to her the treatment the birds would receive. Birds arriving at SANCCOB were initially stabilised, if this had not been done immediately after capture, with rehydrate solution and charcoal. All incoming birds were also treated with Terramycin, to prevent eye infection, and given an iron injection to counter potential anaemia brought on by ingestion of oil. Each bird was given a plastic tag with an identity number and a card on which its place of capture, medical history and other details could be recorded. No birds could be released until they were completely free of oil and their natural waterproofing had returned. Another stringent condition that had to be met included weight... No birds under two and a half kilograms were released. There were blood tests to check that counts of both red and white blood cells were normal, and blood smears to ensure that birds were free from any sign of infection.

The next day, she was to work with a different vet. This one was younger and she could see intense green eyes beneath the oilskin hat he was wearing and for some strange reason she found herself blushing. When she had introduced herself as Tracy there had been a slight smile and a definite change of face colouring in the vet as well.

He did not introduce himself, but just nodded and continued with getting his equipment ready. She took a penguin and held it for him to inject, aware that her face had become a fiery red. There was a flash as the bird's razor sharp beak caught his hand.

"My patient bit me," he said to her, stretching out his hand. "Would you be able to fix it for me?"

She opened her eyes wide in sudden recognition. "Did you ever have a patient called 'Ruff', a white bull terrier with pink eyes?"

"Oh, I didn't introduce myself, did I?" he continued. "And did you ever have a patient called Lewin?"

"Yes, but..." She stared at him. "But you looked so different. Your nose was all red and blue and swollen, and now you look so... So..." She blushed, embarrassed as she saw the way he was looking at her.

"Now you look... wonderful," she said, stammering a little.

"So do you," he said.

"I mean..." she said. "I mean... I meant that medically."

She bandaged his hand, wondering what to say and

wishing her colour would return to normal. In fact, it took at least an hour before the hard work they were doing together returned things to normal. She was also trying to avoid looking at him. Off her guard again she allowed herself another look as she prepared to ask him a question about one of the birds.

He looked up, meeting her eyes and Tracy found herself forgetting what she was going to say, almost as if she had been captured by that look.

She scolded herself inwardly. She was a woman with a child and a husband...no...an ex-husband. He had divorced her. She had not seen him for five years. Yet why did she feel a sense of loyalty towards him? Why had she never looked at anyone else? She was free, free to make her own choices, free to pursue another relationship. But why had she not thought of this before? Where had she been? Possibly there had been no one she had met that made her need to assess her situation in this way. She found herself beginning to blush and she turned away noting that he too, turned several shades redder.

Well, this was her imagination she was sure. He was probably by now a happily married man. She found herself looking for a ring on his finger but found none. But then most married men did not wear rings as women did and anyway, it would probably interfere with his veterinary work. He was getting grey around his temples and she knew his age to be several years older than herself, and married, most definitely married. She would put any new, ridiculous ideas out of her mind. What if he wasn't married? Well, if he wasn't married, why wasn't he married? He was probably one of these people who never would make a commitment. That was why he wasn't married.

She tried to blast the ideas out of her mind, but these were replaced by daydreams about going to coffee with Lewin and about getting to know him.

Forcing herself on another thought track she chided herself, *Tracy, your life is dedicated to finding your daughter. There is absolutely no way you can get involved with anyone.*

All this time, she had been trying to gently struggle with a particularly frightened and therefore aggressive penguin who did not feel that he needed any treatment. She finally 'got him to agree' and she replaced him in the pen gratefully, again catching the doctor's eye as he said, "I have been watching you with that little chap. You certainly persuaded him."

She again found herself stuck for words and promptly went off again into a whole mind trip.

"We can break for coffee," said Lewin, putting another penguin into the pen. "You also look as if you could do with a break."

They walked together towards the coffee shop. "I will buy you a cup," said Lewin as the woman at the shop asked for their order. "After all, you have been a tremendous help to me all morning. Working with you, a trained nurse, makes all the difference."

"I have only just finished the training," she said.

"You came straight here, then?" he asked.

"Yes," she said. "I love penguins. I love them a lot. They helped me, and I wanted to help them." As she said that, she realised that this might sound a little odd.

He smiled, and she felt her heart turn over. What was wrong with her? Even Andrew had not had this effect on her.

"Maybe we should have dinner together tonight," he said. "I just have to hear this story. Would you be free if I fetched you at around, say, 7 p.m.?"

"Yes, yes, of course," she said. "That would be great."

Again, he looked at her, this time with something in his eyes that she could not fathom, and that made her feel a little strange. She had better watch herself, but why? Maybe he was married, maybe...

She had some of her questions answered before he fetched her that evening and she had not even asked the questions.

Almost everyone in the guest house had come to help with the penguins and the gossip in the lounge went through almost every main figure at the cleaning station.

Her attention was riveted when a young man began to talk about Dr. Lewin Green. He was apparently thirty-eight years old – older than herself by seven years – she already knew that. Well, that was a good start, she reckoned. However, was he married? Had he been married? He, apparently, was not.

The young man continued, especially when they realised that Tracy was going out with him that evening. His family had known Dr. Green for many years on a fairly close level.

"We have known him ever since he moved close to us, ever since he started at the Onderstepoort Veterinary School, situated close to Pretoria. He had recently qualified as a vet and was now working in Johannesburg in a busy practice. When the crisis happened with the penguins, he had been asked to come down and work on the team, which he had regularly agreed to. For the last few days, he has been working on Dassen Island, sometimes on Robben Island."

Tracy was bursting to ask more questions but she held back, trying to see if she would hear more. He gave no more details and she decided she would speak to him later.

She found her heart beating wildly as she looked through the clothes she had brought, wondering what to wear, and she realised that her palms had become wet with perspiration. She certainly had not brought anything formal to wear. She would have to improvise with what she had, maybe a black skirt.

As she got into the car it was as if she had stepped into a place where she belonged. How could she feel like this? They hardly knew each other.

They very soon found that they had an incredible amount in common on all levels.

It was a magical evening but its magic turned sour just before they were about to eat the dessert of strawberries and cream. She decided that before they could go any further she had to be absolutely straight with him and tell him all the details about herself.

They had spent a wonderful evening discussing all kinds of things and found many important points, which they agreed on in many ways, and many ways in which they were similar and many ways in which they concurred in the important things in life. At the same time, they had found interesting differences of opinion, which would and could only enrich their relationship.

He was definitely very interested in her and she in him, but she had to share her background with him. She was sure he did not know that she had been married and divorced and had a child, nor did he know that she had been brought back from the dead from a critically serious accident.

It was so good to see him again, and again she realised that this was someone she could maybe spend her life with, but it was obviously too soon to think of anything like that, and he had to be told all the things that she had been through. Yet, he was so different from Andrew. If only she had found Andy already. After all, she had pledged her life to find her.

She found herself telling Lewin all about this, about her marriage to Andrew, about the accident and about her near-death experience where Andy had called her back, as it were, to this world.

"You see, Lewin," she said. "This is my life's purpose. I have to find her."

"I understand," said Lewin slowly. "I really understand."

She looked at him searchingly. Yes he did, he really did,

and it seemed at one point he had even brushed away a tear.

She started to tell him everything in detail and he listened attentively and her anxiety grew as she found his face changing colours. "If only I had known," he said, obviously distressed. "If only I had known before all this."

She felt as if he had given her a slap in the face. He obviously was not prepared to accept her past and she stood up, excusing herself, to the washroom, leaving him sitting there with a shocked expression on his face obviously very upset.

However, she did not go to the washroom. She went straight through the door and ran down the street towards the guest house. As she did so she realised she was being very unwise. South Africa was not a place where a woman could walk, or rather run about at night and she realised she was putting herself in danger, but the more she thought about it the more she did not care. She did not care if she was alive or dead. She had lost her first husband. She had lost her child and now she had lost Lewin. Why had she not told him she was divorced before she had ever got involved with him? Then again, they hadn't really known each other for long, except in the hospital, and he had not followed that up, even then. Well, he could obviously not accept her knowing she had been married and had a child. She supposed it could be a shock to any man. Or had it been that she had dedicated her life to finding Andy? She was so confused, so distressed.

The street was dark as she ran and it was very late. She realised she had a long way to go.

She started as she heard a car draw up beside her.

"Tracy, what are you doing outside here?" a woman's voice called. "What are you doing in the streets at this time of night?"

"I am sorry," she said, relieved to be getting into the car with Monica and her husband, Derrick. Monica had been putting several hours into the business of cleaning penguins and had got to know Tracy and, in fact, Lewin.

Soon, Tracy was telling her what had happened.

"I understand it completely." She was sobbing. "I understand very well that I should have said to him 'by the way, do you know that I have been divorced and married and, somewhere in the world, I have a child', and then she would not be so full of heartache and recrimination."

They sympathised and dropped her off at the guest house.

"Monica, I think we ought to tell Dr. Green what happened to Tracy," said Derrick. "I mean, he thinks she went to the washroom, and will eventually realise she has gone. He will be extremely worried."

They found Lewin at the restaurant desperately making enquiries about Tracy having just received news that she had been seen running alone along the road at least twenty minutes previously. He was very grateful to Monica and Derrick for having taken her home.

"Why was she so upset?" he asked. "Did she give you any idea as to why she was so upset?"

Monica explained it to him, and he gave a groan. "It isn't that," he said. "She misread it completely. I promise you it isn't that."

Tracy returned to the boarding house her whole self deeply moved and upset by her date with Lewin.

Why had she ever agreed? She knew she must dedicate her life to finding Andy. She needed to go overseas. She needed to find her child. She had delayed it too long. She thought about Sky, about the child craving for a mother who had provoked anew all her longing to find Andy. She had missed her computer time but no one had booked it for that particular time as she returned home and she wrote a long letter to Sky. She was happy that Sky could not see her tears.

*   *   *

Meanwhile, the penguin rescue was taking on a new dimension.

It was a few days later that Lewin rounded up some of the volunteers to tell them exciting news. A brilliant plan was underway and it looked as if it would soon be implemented. He went on to explain to them: This was all being done under the young maths genius, who had become the Minister of Environmental Affairs.

"The planners I was with have come up with a risky, hair-brained solution," Lewin said. "They want to remove all the healthy un-oiled penguins, box them and take them by boat off Robben Island. Then they would transport them nine hundred kilometres to Port Elizabeth and put them in the sea to swim back home to buy time whilst the oil dispersed. They have to be caught and transported, and find their way home."

"Tell us more; please tell us more," said Michael, one of

the volunteers. "How will they return? How do you know they will find their way? How do you know it will all happen? Have there been oil spills before?"

"I was part of a large team on Robben Island yesterday," Lewin continued, smiling at all the questions. "The oil has come ashore onto the main landing area, so all birds arriving and departing are getting oiled. We are getting absolutely swamped with oiled birds here, so we have to do something else. You might all, or some of you, be aware that, at this stage, we have to prepare ourselves to deal with a disaster up to double the scale of the Apollo Sea spill of 1994, in which ten thousand birds were oiled. We are working on some difficult decisions. We have to do our best for all the birds.

There are three groups of birds we are dealing with: the oiled birds, which we are beginning to know very well, the un-oiled birds on Robben Island, and the chicks on Robben Island. We are doing pretty well here, but we still have to face long, tedious and exhausting hours of cleaning, and, as I hear, some of you had to work by candlelight because of our over-strained electricity system. At present, we have about two hundred and fifty clean penguins from Robben Island who are flipper banded and ready for transport to Port Elizabeth tomorrow. They will take about ten to fourteen days to return, by which time their island's coastline should be cleaned up. If they are prevented from going to sea, they will dehydrate and starve; if they are allowed to go to sea on Robben Island, they will get oiled. We might have to do the same thing with the Dassen Island penguins."

The listeners gave a gasp. "You mean they are first being moved to Port Elizabeth. How do you know they will come back? That is hundreds and hundreds of miles away."

"They have started de-oiling the stretch of rocky shoreline where most Robben Island penguins land and go out to sea. An absorbent material is being used, and is doing quite a good job. We have had to fence in the un-oiled penguins on Robben and Dassen Islands to stop them going to sea and becoming oiled. The large chicks are being taken into captivity for hand rearing."

"But how can you do that?" asked Pam. "How do you know they will get back? Has it been done before?"

"We hope that, whilst they swim home, we can clean up for them here," continued Lewin. "To our knowledge, this is the very first time that such a translocation exercise has been tried for any seabird."

"But how can you be so sure they won't get lost?" asked Pam again. "If you took me away eight hundred kilometres and asked me to find my way back, I would not even know which direction I should go. They don't have a map, if they could even read one. They will get lost or eaten by sharks."

"Well, they have a very strong homing instinct," said Lewin. "But that happens with many animals. They find their way to distant places. We can discuss it if you like."

"Yes, but this is different," said Harold, another member

of the team.

"Why?" asked Pam.

"I don't know," said Harold. "We have got to know these birds here. How can they do something like that? We have got to know them and love them. But they are just ordinary penguins. And penguins don't migrate, do they? They don't have the skills. There would have to be some kind of miracle for them to find their way beck all that way."

"Well, maybe it is the same with the homing instinct," said Sam. "Let's ask Dr. Lewin."

"I heard all kinds of amazing things about birds flying long distances," said Dina.

"The barnacle goose, for instance, breeds in the Arctic Circle and travels south every winter in a long journey to England, and then, in the spring, it goes back home. The swallow and the cuckoo fly between North Africa and Britain every year, and the remarkable thing about the cuckoo is that the young cuckoos stay in Britain after the parents have left, and then take their first journey to Africa alone, with apparently no means of finding their way, yet they do find their way."

"I think we should speak to Dr. Lewin about all this. Maybe he knows all the explanations," said Benzie looking very thoughtful.

"It is a pity we can't follow their progress," he added. "I want to know where these penguins are."

"That's it," said Lewin, who had joined them again. "We

have a sponsor who will track, via satellite, the movements of three penguins to be released in Algoa Bay. The three instruments will be attached to the penguins."

"Won't that be heavy for them?" asked Pam.

"I gather not," said Lewin.

"So, Benzie, you will be able to track their every move," said Pam, leaving.

"That is amazing technology," said Benzie as soon as they were alone. He seemed to want to say more, but then changed his mind and went to work.

CHAPTER 9

Dassen Island was an incredibly beautiful nature reserve and, normally, a veritable paradise for the penguins, which had free reign over its five hundred and forty-five acres. The island normally had a population of about fifty-five thousand adult penguins, and only six humans. Visitors were not welcome.

However, there was now a human hive of activity. Ventilated boxes used to transport the birds were being ferried by boat to the island, where volunteers were helping assemble them.

The island has only a tiny harbour, so the birds would have to be shuttled to a big boat via small vessels, before they are taken to the mainland and trucked to the town of Port Elizabeth some five hundred and sixty miles east, where they would be released.

The volunteers crowded around to read the report:

On the island, at least ten thousand clean penguins are confined to barracks, fenced off towards the centre of the island so that they cannot go into the oiled waters and feeding grounds. Some have not have fed for five days, but they can apparently cope with this. A decision has to be made either to release them and let them go to sea, or evacuate them, to transport them to Port Elizabeth. This decision will be made on the basis of a helicopter inspection of the shoreline and surrounding ocean. If they were surrounded by oil they could not be released into the ocean.

Dr. Lewin came in and greeted the volunteers. Again he seemed very excited about what was happening.

"I know I have filled you in on some of this, but this is something really big. People are saying that this might be largest evacuation of animals since Noah's Ark," he said with a smile.

"They are calling for more helpers and are asking the South African Defence Force to send vehicles, planes and ships to help volunteers and international experts working to capture birds on the two islands."

"But can all these birds survive and arrive?" asked Benzie, still somewhat cynical.

Tracy had bought the newspaper on the way to the centre and read everyone the news:

The evacuation of the penguins on Dassen Island started today. Fortunately, the weather continues to be perfect. About three thousand five hundred birds were boxed and left the island by boat and helicopter. They are travelling to Port Elizabeth on a three-tier sheep truck. The first of these left Yzerfontein around lunch time today, and the second arrived at Yzerfontein at 4.30 p.m. whilst we were leaving. It was due to be loaded up immediately with the birds

that had arrived since the first truck had left, and will travel to
Port Elizabeth overnight.

It was all so exciting and so daring. If only she could have shared it with Lewin, but she had to somehow still her aching heart by working as hard as possible and every night falling exhausted into bed.

My dearest Mum,
I am staying with my friend Colleen and her family because Dad
is away again. this time, he says, for several weeks. He
apparently has very important work to do, which is top secret so
he can't even tell me where he goes, so now I don't even ask any
more. Mum, I like Colleen and her family. They are good friends
of mine. I like especially their loft of pigeons.
You know, in many ways, pigeons are like penguins. They find
their way home wherever they are. They get back to the loft even
if you let them go miles and miles away and the bird was not
really looking through the car window.
We took one with us for a long drive and he was back home
before we were.
I love you, Sky.

Whilst Lewin and Benzie were poring over some notes that Benzie had made with all the volunteers begging to be filled in on the information. Lewin's cell phone rang and he smiled as his mother, a hospital matron, told him that she was not missing the greatest penguin rescue in the world and would be joining them in a day or so. He told her she would be very welcome but the patients would be somewhat different to what she was used to.

As had been planned, three penguins were tagged with transmitters and Benzie had found the relevant information to share with them.

"I found out all about the transmitters," said Benzie. "I even wrote it all down so that I could read it to you all."

He pulled out a notebook and started to give them all the technical details.

"Peter, Pamela and Percy are carrying Platform Transmitter Terminals or PPTs. These instruments measure ten centimetres by four point eight centimetres by two centimetres, and have a mass of seventy-five grams. The mean mass of African Penguins is two thousand, eight hundred and thirty-six grams. The mass of the instruments is less than that of a good meal, so it isn't too heavy for them."

"PTTs are attached to the penguins using Velcro and epoxy resin. Velcro is glued to feathers on a penguin's back and to the bottom of the PTT. The two pieces of Velcro are then joined together. Because they are in the sea, the glue lifts after about forty days, when the Velcro will fall from the penguin's back. If the penguin can be found before this, the instrument can be recovered by removing the top piece of Velcro. That would be when he or she is back home on the island. Each PTT is fitted with an antenna, which transmits signals to satellites passing overhead." Benzie had obviously done his homework, taken notes, and gone into the matter quite deeply.

"Satellites need to pick up at least two messages from the same instrument on an overpass to provide a valid location. The satellites store information, and then, later, downloads it to the Argos data collection system in France, and, eventually, to the Avian Demography Unit in Cape Town, South Africa, so that the SAP map can be updated."

Thus began one of the most exciting and incredible journeys as the world held its breath for the daily reports of the progress of the penguins. Three penguins, Peter, Pamela and Percy had been chosen:

Although Peter, Pam and Percy are the only penguins tagged with satellite transmitters, they were heading home, together with twelve thousand five hundred penguins from Dassen Island and five thousand penguins from Robben Island. All of them were released at Cape Recife near Port Elizabeth after they had been evacuated from their home islands. They had arrived in the Eastern Cape after having been taken from the islands in boxes and crates by helicopter to the mainland in Cape Town. They had then been transported by volunteer truckers and others three to a crate.

"And now we wait and... pray," said Lewin.

"And now we wait," said Benzie.

"Dr. Lewin, could I please speak to you?"

Lewin looked at the rather troubled young man with his mop of curly black hair and large anxious green eyes, who always seemed to be standing close by; the person who always did very valuable research for the team and was always ready to help with everything.

"Yes, of course," said Lewin. "Of course you can. I just need to explain a few things to the volunteers, and then we can speak straight afterwards."

When Lewin had finished speaking he saw that the young man was looking towards the sea. Benzie suddenly realised that Lewin had finished speaking and he turned to him with an apology. He was also aware that most of his courage had run out, but he had to say something.

"Dr. Lewin," he said at last. "Dr. Lewin, I used to be very different, but that was a long time ago. I actually used to be happy."

Lewin nodded. "How long ago?" he asked.

"Well, I left home in New York three or four years ago. Something very bad happened, something that no one in the world could be asked to accept. Dr. Lewin, maybe one day I will tell you about it, but not now. I can't talk about it now. But it made me decide that there was no sense in the world, nothing was really organised or meaningful. Dr. Lewin, I asked to speak to you because I was going to tell you about it and ask your advice, but I can't, not yet. It hurts too much."

Lewin had been listening quietly, and he answered, "Whenever you feel you can talk to me, come to me. You are more than welcome."

Despite himself, Benzie smiled. "Dr. Lewin, I can tell you this much, I think of Peter, Pamela and Percy, who will be on their way home, together with thousands of penguins, swimming in waters they have never been in, and finding their way through hundreds of kilometres. Yet no one really knows how they do it, how they know where they are going, or what a homing instinct really is. I did not know it was all such a mystery, even today. Dr. Lewin, I want to tell you that I have made a decision. If all three birds actually get back to their islands and the transmitters pick this up, I will find my way back to who I was, if there is any way to do it. Dr. Lewin, I promise you that. I need to promise someone besides myself, someone I really respect."

"Thank you," said Lewin.

"I cannot keep running away forever. Maybe I will even make my way home. But that is impossible."

He was almost crying as he said goodbye and made his way to a solitary walk along the darkening ocean.

As Lewin watched Benzie go away he hoped he would get the courage to talk to him. He knew he needed to talk and for some reason he found a vet to be the person he could talk to. Then he whispered to himself, "Yes, everything is organised and has meaning. I just wish I knew what to do about Tracy."

He had been speaking to his mother at length, telling her

that he had at last found the girl he wanted to marry, but she avoided him at every point, would not take his phone calls and had make sure she was working in a place as far away as possible from him. How could he have blown it again!

Tracy was slightly overawed to be told that a retired matron from Groote Schuur Hospital, one of the Cape's main hospitals was to be coming to work with her.

Even though she realised this was hardly a hospital situation, she was a little uneasy at the news but at the same time pleased to have a senior colleague who could so effectively do the work.

She was suddenly flung into a situation of hyper efficiency run by an ex-matron who was busy attending to a level of bird care that did not need to be done by a veterinary surgeon but needed much more skill and experience than most volunteers could provide.

She was relieved to be away from Lewin though at the same time extremely disappointed. However, Jeanette, her name seemed to be Green also, kept her occupied at such a fast pace that she and her two other helpers, one a medical student and one an optometry student had no time to go on any kind of negative mind trips. They had to concentrate on what they were doing otherwise an agonising bite from a beak would remind them more than sharply of their immediate purpose.

There had, of necessity, to be a certain level of tension, but it was a hard-working and dedicated sort of tension, with no unpleasantness at all. The only horror lay within her heart. She had gone over and over, in her mind, the events of that fateful evening, but had not been able to find any solution at all. He had definitely reacted to her past, and in shock. She had not answered the three messages sent by him; in fact, she had not read them. She was sure he would have apologised for his reaction, but it was too late. It had been spontaneous and definite. She would never get married. Her aim and ambition was to find her daughter. That was the only reason she was alive. That was what she had, as it were, returned from the dead for. Nothing and nobody else mattered.

An attempted bite brought her back sharply to the present. Yes, this was important now, she had come to help these little chaps and she deserved to be reminded of her job, but she was glad that she was distracted from her thoughts to this extent. She had not realised how much the whole incident had hurt and disturbed her.

The entire day was taken up with this new section and the four team members were with each other all the time. Both tea and lunch were had together with hardly a break in the work and she realised they were performing at a high level of efficiency and accomplishing a lot.

At 6 p.m., they were asked if they were prepared to carry on for another two or three hours, and, after being promised a pizza and coke that another team would be bringing them, they readily agreed. No one minded the fact that they had to eat amidst the smells of half-rotting fish and distressed birds, as well as many other rather horrifying smells. They had long ago got used to it.

Exhausted, they were preparing to leave at some time close to 10:30 p.m. when they heard the familiar sound of a truck outside. At least a thousand new oiled birds were arriving, desperately in need of help. They settled back into work.

It was 1 a.m. when she returned home and, after answering her email, fell, exhausted, into bed, being a little upset when she saw that there had been no more messages at the boarding house for her to ignore, as there had been on the first two nights. Obviously, his concern had not lasted even forty-eight hours.

The next day, had been the same, and the next, and the next. On the fourth day, the matron had told the students to leave at 6 p.m., knowing that they had some student function they had wanted to go to for the evening, leaving Tracy and the matron to work alone, again very efficiently. At eight, they had a coffee break where they were given coffee by the night team …people who were occupied during the day and offered their services until late at night. Tracy noticed that the matron did not look the slightest bit tired and was really only stopping to give her a rest. She had become to respect her and to like her a lot. She must have been an exceptional matron where she 'ruled' her hospital by love, respect, and dedication to hard work that others could only follow.

The break was extended by the fact that they had finished treating the birds in the pen, and were waiting for another group to finish their procedure and to bring them some more birds, which was taking more time than expected. Tracy found herself talking, quite naturally, to the matron, telling her, eventually, about her accident, her divorce and her search for her child. The matron listened sympathetically, at times asking relevant and encouraging questions.

She eventually asked her if she had thought of getting married again, and Tracy suddenly looked incredibly vulnerable.

"I don't think I should ever do that," said Tracy quietly. "My duty and purpose is to look for and find my daughter. That is why I am alive."

"I also have one child," said the Matron wistfully. "A son of thirty-eight. I am really hoping he will marry one day and give me grandchildren. He was engaged once. He originally did accountancy, but two years in an accountants' office made him realise it was not for him, and he decided to do what he had, he discovered, really always wanted to do, and that was to become a vet. He had worked hard for the rest of the year, had applied to be accepted at Onderstepoort, and had decided to put himself through, doing people's books as a sideline when he needed money. He had been engaged to a girl who had been shocked at his intended change of career and told him she had no intention of being married to an eternal student who was not satisfied with his career, and she had, quite brutally, broken off the engagement and married his best friend, who had become very settled in the accountancy profession and had his father's millions behind him. From that day to this, my son has only has casual friendships with the girls in his class at Onderstepoort, which consisted of the odd conversation, and he is now something of a confirmed bachelor. I wish he would meet someone." She looked at Tracy expectantly, and she blushed.

"Anyway, he fulfilled his dream and became a vet."

Tracy was blushing crimson. Matron Green... of course. Lewin Green.

"He was always such a special boy," she was saying. "He would never hurt anyone no matter how much he was be hurt in the process. When he was in junior school, he would seek out any child who was badly hurt or lonely, and make friends with them, so he had a collection of lonely people, and these children would learn to do the same thing, and you had a whole group of children seeking out other children to join them, rejecting no one. Eventually, the teachers would call Lewin over and tell him about a new boy or girl in the school or the class, and he would make sure that he or one of the group would contact him and make friends with him. On Parents' Day, when Professor – my late husband and – I would attend the school meetings, the teachers would tell us what an amazing child our son was... but we knew. He was always collecting things that needed help. At home, we had dogs, birds and cats."

"Together?" asked Tracy.

"Believe it or not, together, as well as a rabbit, a tortoise and silkworms that his friends were forgetting to feed. Even though I say it myself, he was just the nicest child anyone could wish for, and he has stayed exactly the same, only wanting to do good."

Tracy had become very quiet. She wondered how much Matron Green knew, after all, her son had only taken her out once. There was nothing really between them, never had been. They just did not suit each other.

She tried not to take any of this personally. The matron was just pouring out her heart about her son, as she had done about Andy. But the next few words were obviously directed at her.

"And then, one day, he told me he had fallen in love again. He was in hospital recovering from a bite by one of his patients who had decided he did not like the shape of his nose. There was a nurse there who he really wanted to get to know better. However, it was pointed out to him fairly forcibly by a senior sister that she was only a second-year nursing student, and he had made a calculation and decided he could not ask a seventeen- or eighteen-year-old girl to go out with him. He would be cradle snatching."

Tracy caught her breath. Another explanation was beginning to form. The woman smiled. "Tracy, I really wanted to tell you that," she said. "I understood your reaction completely when he told me. He was extremely upset, for one thing that he had hurt you, and for another thing... Well... you can work that out with each other."

It was Tracy's turn to blush and smile, feeling that a heavy load had been taken off her shoulders, and replacing it had created a certain warmth and glow deep inside her.

"Thank you," she said. "Thank you, I really appreciate that."

"You see," the matron continued. "He did not have to wait; he could have..."

Again, Tracy said thank you, noting as she left that the matron had whipped out her cell phone and pressed a number. Tracy had scarcely gone for a few minutes when Lewin met her.

"Can we go out tonight?" he asked, his face flushed with emotion.

"Yes, yes, of course. I am sorry, I thought..."

"I am also sorry," he said. "I should have realised that my reaction might have seemed strange."

It was as though the temporary misunderstanding had brought them infinitely closer, had bonded them into some kind of unity. Both felt incredibly, deliriously happy.

For the next few weeks SANCCOB staff and many volunteers worked long hard hours, sometimes by candlelight when the somewhat temperamental power supply dictated, to ensure that as many birds as possible could be returned to the wild.

At the same time, they followed every news broadcast or hint of news about the penguins swimming home.

Peter, the first penguin that was tagged with a SAP Africa-sponsored satellite transmitter and released in the ocean at Cape Recife near Port Elizabeth on June 30, 2000, is now at Cape St. Francis. Pamela, released on July 3, 2000, is still at Cape Recife. She is probably feeding, as she went without food for some time before her release.

There was an 'exhaustion break' at the centre and some of the volunteers and workers crowded around Lewin.

"Please tell us how this all works. How are these birds finding their way? Are there scientific explanations for all these things?"

"No, there actually aren't, though there have been a lot of studies that only describe and don't, and can't, explain," said Lewin. "Many people – scientists, educationalists and others – describe the miracle of migration. Every year, several million birds make migratory journeys along a network of routes that encompasses the whole world. Sometimes, they travel tens of thousands of kilometres, crossing continents and oceans, going over the largest deserts and seas, the highest mountains and expanses of ice. And, a few months later, they fly back again."

"But where do they get

this kind of energy from?" asked Benzie.

"The energy used, especially on non-stop flights, comes almost exclusively from fat, which some long-distance migrants store up in such quantities that, if they are small birds, their pre-migratory body weight is twice as great as normal. The timing of migration is also amazing. Many bird species, particularly those breeding in the Arctic, arrive at their breeding grounds every year at the same time, to within a few days."

"But how does it all work?" asked Raye.

"These birds have comprehensive, detailed, innate spatio-temporal programmes for successful migration. Such programmes evidently enable even young, inexperienced birds to migrate alone, with no adult guide, to the species- or population-specific winter quarters that they have never seen before. They somehow get to the exact spot that generations of their family have gone to, without being shown the way. Obviously," said Lewin, "this navigational achievement, performed without complex boards of instruments, compass and map, and under constantly changing conditions, including sun position, wind direction, cloud cover and the diurnal cycle, is nothing short of amazing. Even a slight diversion off course whilst crossing the ocean would mean certain death in the open sea for migrating land birds. They have some kind of genetic clock, as well as physiological compasses essential for their navigation and orientation. During flight over wide, windswept stretches of ocean, a tendency to drift off course cannot be avoided. Such drift must be continually compensated for, as in a feedback system in control technology, in order to avoid losing energy by flying a longer route. The birds are equipped with a precise 'autopilot', which, apparently, is constantly measuring its geographical position and comparing the data with its individually 'programmed' destination. In this way, an economical, energy saving and direct flight is guaranteed. Just where this vital system is to be found and how this operating information is coded is known by no one today."

"How many miles do these birds actually fly?" asked Thembi, curious.

"The Arctic tern flies a phenomenal round trip that can be as long as twenty thousand miles per year, from the Arctic to the Antarctic and back. Other sea birds also make astounding journeys... The long-tailed jaeger flies five thousand to nine thousand miles in each direction. Long-distance migrants commonly perform non-stop flights of several hours, and some species fly for up to fifty to hundred hours when crossing oceans."

"How high can they fly?" asked Solly.

"Higher than Mt. Everest," said Lewin. "Bar-headed geese have been recorded flying across the Himalayas at twenty-nine thousand feet. Other species seen above twenty thousand feet include the whooper swan, the bar-tailed godwit, and the mallard duck. One of my favourite examples is of a manx shearwater that was taken from its nest burrow in the British

Isles, placed in a box, and flown to Boston, Massachusetts, a distance of some three thousand miles. It was back in its nest burrow twelve and a half days later. If the return was a straight-line flight, it would have necessitated an average of two hundred and sixty miles per day, most likely a minimum figure."

The volunteers gasped in amazement.

"That's true, isn't it?" asked Thandi. "How could it be true? When you talk about all these birds, I understand, but when you talk about one bird, it is all so real."

The others agreed.

"Look at the swallows," Lewin said. "They are usually quiet birds, but, just before they migrate, they will twitter and chatter, and begin to eat very seriously, almost doubling their weight in a few weeks. That is good for their flight of eight to nine thousand kilometres. They will be here one day, and gone the next, leaving overnight. They seem to use the stars and the Earth's magnetic fields to find their way, but, almost all, of this remains a mystery and a miracle."

"That is totally amazing," said Benzie. "You mean that science really can't explain it?"

"Not that and many other things," said Lewin. "Let me tell you some other things worth thinking about. There is a kind of genetic imprinting that is also mind boggling. A scientist took an egg from a nest in Holland and swapped it with an egg from Eastern Europe. Instinctively, the Western-conceived bird placed in the east flew west to find its own family route. It is a whole system more complex and more efficient than our aeroplanes."

Everyone was very excited by this information and they went back to their temporary homes, very thoughtfully.

Tracy went out with Lewin the next night, and the next, until she felt him to be an integral part of her life.

Meanwhile, they followed every newscast with bated breath.

Peter, the first penguin to be fitted with a SAP Africa-sponsored transmitter is near Plettenberg Bay – he has covered about a hundred and fifty kilometres since he was released on June 30 and has completed about twenty-eight percent of the long swim home. If he maintains his average speed over the past five days, he will get back to Robben Island on July 21. Pamela – released on July 3 – is now swimming just off Cape St. Francis after she had a late start because she lingered to feed before she started the long trek home. The third penguin, Percy, did not stop for feeding after he was released yesterday morning, and is making a beeline for Cape Town. He is at Sea View, just past Cape Recife.

The World and its people were glued to their radios, newspapers and TVs, listening, reading, waiting. Peter checked in again at 8 p.m. on Friday, July 7, when he was about twenty-five kilometres offshore to the south of George. He is still in the lead. We wish him well as he approaches Mossel Bay known for its seals and sharks, both predators of penguins. He is wise to be moving offshore.

At 11 p.m. on Friday, July 7, Pam was off the Tsitsikamma coast, some distance offshore. She was not much farther west than the previous day.

Percy, released last of the three, was about six kilometres off Elands River in Tsitsikamma National Park at 3 a.m. on Saturday, July 8.

All three are still heading home, but giving time for the oil between their home islands to clear.

Dear Sky,

They were having a very interesting discussion at the cleaning station today and lots of information came out that I must share with you, especially as your best friends have homing pigeons. It is almost unbelievable.

Have you ever heard of the Arctic Tern? He flies up to eleven thousand miles to the other end of the world, and then returns.

Oh and I forgot to tell you, I was also hearing that it's not only birds that migrate, they even mentioned butterflies. The painted butterfly also travels to Britain all the way from North Africa and many butterflies cross the English and French channel. And the American Monarch butterfly travels south for more than a thousand miles to roost in a Mexican forest.

And it isn't only birds and butterflies that travel like that, some fish travel great distances. Salmon make regular journeys from the sea to fresh waters. The Fresh Water Eel is born in the Western Atlantic and slowly swims north-eastwards, reaching Europe after two years, to live in a river. Then it goes back to the sea and travels the thousands of miles to the South Coast of

211

Bermuda where it was born.

So you see that these pigeons you were talking about have some kind of tracking device that we have no idea about. I know they are making the most amazing things such as cell phones and email, but these animals and birds seem to beat us all.

Dear Mum,

What you say is so exciting and interesting.

We are going for a holiday to another magic island where there are all kinds of birds and things. It is not too far from here, but it is, people say, like being in a whole different world. I am so excited. Just Dad and I are going.

I am taking a camera. It is not digital one, but I can find a scanner and scan some photos for you. Now that you are going out with Lewin, he will be very interested to see how the birds there look. Mum, you really sound like you like Lewin. I hope it works out for you.

Mum, I have to tell you all about the island. We will see so many birds and even some puffins. I found out about all the birds on the island so that I could name them for you....

Sky went on for several pages giving all kinds of details. She was really excited to be going there.

Tracy wrote back, wishing her a really wonderful trip and a request to tell her everything when she got back.

*   *   *

Lewin was busy looking at a somewhat forlorn penguin that did not seem to be able to stand on his feet. There had to be something wrong with him besides the trauma of being oiled. He started to examine him going through each part as with a fine-tooth comb. He looked at his flipper band. It was A5738.

Ah, there it was, a nasty wound under the left flipper, a wound that was becoming very infected. Probably the bird had caught himself on some wire or even a bush before his rescue.

He held the bird firmly, looking around for someone to help him. He saw Benzie and called him. As the young man came over, Lewin noticed that his usual enthusiasm seemed to have gone and the anxiety and depression that he had seen when he had tried to speak to him had once again appeared, but he quickly responded to Lewin's request for help.

He expertly and deftly held on to the bird for Lewin, trying to give the vet complete immobility in which to work, but, at the same time, being careful to keep the bird fairly comfortable and confident.

Lewin cleaned the wound carefully. It was deeper than he had thought and the bird must have been in agony, but knowing somehow that Lewin and Benzie were helping him he lay there, not even trying, after some minutes, to resist.

"There is actually something in here," said Lewin, as he probed deeper. "If I had known it was like this, I would have given this bird an anaesthetic, but he might have been too weak to take it, so perhaps this is best. But I hate to hurt anyone where it is not necessary."

He felt gently inside the wound until he emerged with the broken off head of a marker that the bird must have somehow fallen on and struggled to get free from.

As Lewin removed it the bird tensed but remained quiet. As he got it out the bird suddenly relaxed. The pain of having that foreign object inside him must have been agonising.

Lewin looked up at Benzie and saw him rather self-consciously brush away a tear, to which the vet gave a reassuring smile. "Could you get me some of that antibiotic powder from that cupboard over there? Terramycin powder," he specified. "I think we need to wash out all this infection, and then pour some in here. I just hope we can save this little chap's life. He must have fallen on the stake after being oiled and not had the strength or balance to get off it. Poor little chap. I will give him antibiotics by mouth, too."

He looked at the bird again. "What can I call you?" he asked, looking at the now more comfortable, but still very much in pain, bird.

"Maybe Benzie," suggested Benzie.

"Hey, Benzie is your name," said Lewin. "But maybe we call him 'Ben', okay?"

"Okay."

Both silent, they carefully cleaned the bird and Lewin gave him another injection. Ben, though still in pain, certainly looked more at peace.

"That was a tough one," said Lewin. "We could easily have lost him."

"That wouldn't really be because of the oil spill, would it?" asked Benzie. "I suppose birds do have accidents, and they do become ill."

"This is also because of the spill," said Lewin. "The bird was very weak."

He began to tell Benzie about the various things that could happen to oiled birds.

"But what can the oil actually do to the penguins," he asked?

Dr. Green became very serious.

"Well, the birds preen themselves and swallow oil, which causes ulcers in the mouth, the gullet and the stomach, leading to internal bleeding. Oil in the eyes can cause ulcers and blindness. Oil destroys red blood cells and the bird becomes anaemic. It also affects the immune system and can cause ulcers on the skin."

For a few days, especially after their short talks, Lewin had been puzzled about the young man working with him. Benzie was obviously intelligent, was pleasant to work with, and seemed dedicated to what he was doing. He judged him to be about twenty-three years old.

However, he had sensed about him a certain sadness. His large eyes held an anxiety and a sensitivity that belied his ready apparent confidence. Also his questions and statements had shown a certain disillusionment.

Lewin had the feeling that he was nursing a very deep hurt, and he had indicated as such, that somehow he had been traumatised from something that he could not find any way of recovery. He felt it was important to get him to talk. At least he had hinted at something wrong.

It was late when Lewin and Benzie were trying to finish off treating some penguins before they waited to go home and they were by that time working together alone.

"Benzie, tell me more about yourself," said Lewin, hoping that, perhaps, he might open up.

"Nothing more to really say," said Benzie cagily.

"Do you have family around here?"

A look of fear crossed his face. "No," he said, almost angrily.

Lewin decided not to say anything more. The young man obviously resented his intrusion, but it was Benzie who continued after a few minutes.

"Lewin, I haven't seen my family for three years. As I think I told you, I come from America. I have not heard from them or seen them for more than three years."

"They don't write?" asked Lewin.

"They don't; rather, they can't. I never gave them my address."

"So you don't want them to contact you?"

"No," he said simply.

"Are you sure?" asked Lewin.

"Well, they wouldn't want to, I am sure," said Benzie.

"Why not?" asked Lewin. "I am sure that cannot be true. They must want to be in touch with you. They are your family."

"No," said Benzie slowly. "I did something bad, extremely bad. In fact..." He sighed deeply. "In... fact... I killed someone."

Lewin gave him a quick glance. A murderer? Benzie? No, definitely not. There was much more to it.

"What happened?" asked Lewin. "Who did you kill?"

"My brother," said Benzie, suddenly bursting into tears. "My baby brother. I killed my baby brother! I just wanted to take him for a ride. I had just got my licence. I was so happy, and I wanted him to see that I could drive, and I wanted to take him to the shop and let him ride on those cars that you put money into, and I wanted to buy him some sweets. I took my father's car. I knew how to drive it, and I had taken quite a few lessons on it, and I did not really think he would mind if I borrowed it. Craig was really excited. I think I was his favourite brother." His crying became so intense that he could no longer speak.

Things were becoming all too clear to Lewin.

"You had a car accident?"

"Yes," sobbed Benzie. "Someone jumped the stop street and rode into us on Craig's side of the car. There was no hope. I had only fairly minor injuries. Craig... Well... He was..."

"He was killed on impact?" asked Lewin.

"Not quite," said Benzie.

"How long did he live for?" asked Lewin. He knew this was tearing Benzie's heart out, but he knew that it would be, on a certain level, healing for him to speak about it.

"I don't know," said Benzie. "I left him dying..."

"Tell me more," said Lewin.

"Well, there was the accident, and then all sorts of people came to us. I had a terrible pain in my arm and my leg, but, at that stage, I could not even feel it, because I had such a shock about Craig. He was lying very still, and there was blood pouring from his nose and mouth. I tried to get to him, but the metal was collapsed so that it encased him. They had to use the Jaws of Life to get him out. They put him into an ambulance and me into another one. I knew that it was my fault. I knew then that my life was over. Craig died physically, but I had died emotionally and spiritually. As soon as my leg and arm were even halfway better, I left home. I left Craig dying. I did not have to be there when he died completely. That very day, they were going to switch off the machines, and they had made it clear that it was only the life support machines that were keeping him alive. There was obviously no hope; everyone said so. There was absolutely no hope."

Lewin, who had spent the previous evening listening to Tracy's story, did not accept this completely, but he did not want to give any false hope. Too many miracles just did not happen. Perhaps he could make his own enquiries.

"That must have been terrible, really terrible. Which hospital was he in?"

"Grant Park Hospital," he said, with a shudder.

"How long ago was it?" Lewin asked.

"Three years and three months ago," he said.

He did not want to ask any more details to raise false hopes and he really believed there was very little hope of Craig being alive.

"Do you have other brothers?" asked Lewin.

"I have three older brothers and one older sister," said Benzie.

"And they are probably all married by now, and who is with your parents?"

"In that case, probably no one. Yes, they will probably all be married."

"So you have taken away another son from your parents."

"Craig, yes, I have," he said, looking miserable.

"No! Not Craig! I am talking about Benzie. You have taken away from your parents the pleasure and comfort of having Benzie."

"They cannot possible want me," said Benzie.

"Are you absolutely sure about that?" Lewin almost screamed. "Are you absolutely sure that they don't long for you to return, to come back and be their son?"

"They can't want me." Benzie sobbed. "I am sure they can't want me!" However, for the first time, his voice held a hint of a doubt. "I don't want to think about this," he said suddenly as his face cleared into a look of determination, and he carried on trying to treat the penguins. "I have work to do, and I can't be distracted. The penguins need caring for."

He was suddenly calmer. He was very thoughtful as he said goodbye and made his way to his walk along the ocean to be in communication with his own 'homing instinct'.

It is with great relief that we learnt that Peter had managed to pass Mossel Bay safely and that he stayed well out at sea. Mossel Bay is known for its Cape Fur seals and Great White sharks.

The next day, Benzie was busy working with the penguins when he noticed that one of them stayed close to him. He recognised him as Ben and confirmed it by a quick examination of his flipper band. He placed himself right opposite the bird and spoke to him.

"Ben, I want to have a serious discussion with you," he said solemnly, sitting on his haunches in an attempt to be more 'penguin size', ignoring the surprised glances he was receiving and the people who stopped in their tracks to listen to this 'conversation'.

"Ben," he said, looking at the penguin, which was playing his part and looking back at Benzie very solemnly. "Ben, you are an African penguin, also known as the jackass or black-footed penguin. See, Ben, you and all your companions have these wonderful webbed black feet. Ben, you are little more than eighteen inches high, and, although you stand to look at us, you are not very tall at all. And, Ben, as we all know, you are weighing about seven and a half pounds. Yet, my little bird, people are saying that you are able to be put into the sea, eight hundred kilometres away. You have not swum there. You have been taken in a truck in a closed box with two of your friends, or enemies, by the time you have made the journey there, and just let loose into the sea. And, Ben, you are able to find your way back to Dassen Island and find your old home. Ben, if they blindfolded me and took me in a car a few miles out of Cape Town and told me to find my way back, and I had no map, and I could not ask anyone, there is no way I would be able to do it. My brain, they say, is far more advanced than yours. Ben, where do you keep all this knowledge? Ben, how do you do it? Ben, I was listening to the professor over here, Prof. Underhill. He said that we can only marvel at the navigational feats of our penguins with their satellite transmitters. He is talking about your friends that are actually finding their way home, Peter, Pamela and Percy. He told us that, if a non-sea bird gets lost, it can fly a kilometre or so up in the air, and get its bearings. But you can't fly like that into the sky. The horizon is always a kilometre or two away for you penguins. He is the expert, and is as puzzled and amazed as all of us, perhaps more, because he knows so much more. Ben, I respect you and admire you."

At this point, the bird turned and waddled off only giving a quick glance backwards to see that he had not offended his friend.

Benzie stood up, slightly embarrassed as he realised he had an audience. "Amazing little chaps," he muttered. "Absolutely amazing little chaps."

The next day, Benzie came into the cleaning area looking very excited.

"They have this whole programme for adopting a penguin," said Benzie excitedly. "I just have to adopt Ben. I am sure they will let me."

The other volunteers crowded around him.

"What do they mean, adopting a penguin?" asked Sam. "They surely won't let you take him home with you."

"No, no," said Benzie. "They need the sea and all their friends. You can't do that. For five hundred rand, you can adopt a penguin and, for that, you receive a photograph of your penguin, a personalised adoption certificate, the SANCCOB newsletter, an annual status report on your penguin, and a report of any of the sightings of your penguin."

The next day, Benzie arrived a little late. He had been busy adopting a penguin, namely Ben, flipper band number A5738. He had also met Tracy there who was busy adopting two penguins and paying her one thousand rand. They were Peggy, flipper band A7689 and Priscilla, flipper band A8329. He had given his address to be informed of any of the sightings.

They were proudly showing their certificates to Lewin when he produced his, one of his first patients, Dassen, flipper band A2772.

PETER, PERCY AND NOW PAMELA ARE ALL HOME

Final progress report written on July 25 at 4:10 p.m., South African time.

Pam was seen last night on the beach at West Bay, Dassen Island, by staff of Western Cape Nature Conservation Board – identified from the uniquely numbered flipper band that she is wearing. She also transmitted signals to the satellite from the vicinity of West Bay. The second of the three birds to be equipped with transmitters, she is the last home but the first to be sighted.

Percy, the other bird from Dassen Island, also transmitted signals from Dassen Island last night and appears to be located on Boom Point, the north-western 'arm' of Dassen Island.

Peter, first to be released in Port Elizabeth, and first to arrive home at Robben Island, has left Robben Island and is now foraging in the vicinity of Dassen Island and Yzerfontein, which means that all three instrumented penguins are in close proximity to each other.

Somewhere along the coast, a young man read this, and decided to return home and reunite with his family.

He went to say goodbye to his adopted 'Ben' who somehow seemed to sense that this would be the last time he would see him. He stood opposite Benzie, just looking at him for a long time before he turned around and waddled off towards his companions.

Benzie went to the SANCCOB offices, making sure once again that he would be given details of sightings of Ben and word of what he was dong. Then he gave them his home address, this time his real home address.

He then went to say goodbye to his friends, promising to keep in touch.

Tracy felt a surge of excitement. Peter, Pamela and Percy were home! Peter first, and the thousands of penguins travelling with him! A group of sea birds had found their way home, following no map, yet returning to the island on which they had their home. She stopped in amazement, realising that her eyes had filled with tears.

However, the tears of joy turned very quickly to those of sadness. Peter, a bird, had travelled eight hundred kilometres to find his home. Why, oh why, could she not connect with her daughter? If a simple bird had a driving force towards home, surely a human being would have something of the same.

She phoned Lewin. She could not become so close to anyone. She had to find her daughter and this had to be her sole purpose in life.

"I am leaving you and going away," she said, the tears falling freely. "There is no way that this could ever work out. There are too many problems, too much against it. I have no right to look for another life. How can I just carry on living? You can't get involved with me. It is too complicated."

"I am involved already," said Lewin quietly.

"But it is just the beginning."

"I am involved very deeply. I think I have been involved ever since I met you. For you to go away would... break my heart. Do you not believe you could love me? Do you not believe we could have a future together?"

"Yes, of course I believe we could, and, yes, of course I could and do love you, but that is another reason I must go away, because it is something I can't take hold of. I have to find my daughter."

"And together; can't we find her together?"

Suddenly, the tears were just coursing down her cheeks, as if his words had unleashed a fountain. "We have got to find her," she whispered. "I hear her voice calling. I still hear her calling."

"Tracy," he said. "Tracy, I can't lose you. Please tell me, Tracy, please tell me just this. Tracy, will you marry me?"

She paused, knowing without a doubt what her answer would be. "Yes, Lewin, yes, of course I will."

Still filled with the almost overwhelming impression that Lewin had made on her she sat down at the computer, almost mechanically going into Towermail.

At the same time, she realised that she was happier than she had ever been. Without setting a date they had decided to get married within the year.

Dear Sky,

I have met the man I want to marry. I wanted to share that with you. In fact, you are the first to know. Guess who it is.

Love Tracy

Sky was already on Towermail, so she wrote back straight away.

'Dr. Lewin Green'.

'But how did you know?'

'Mum, I know you. I saw the way you were writing about him'.

'What do you think about it?'.

'I am, very happy for you. But you won't forget you have a daughter will you, I mean, besides Andy, your other daughter, Sky'.

CHAPTER 10

It was two months later. Thousands of penguins had been cleaned, and had gone back to their islands and beaches. Both Tracy and Lewin were in Johannesburg.

Lewin was working in his practice and Tracy was doing short nursing locums.

She was keeping constant contact with Sky but there was still no news of Andy...at all.

Lewin called her late that evening and when she met him he was looking exhausted.

"I have had a really heavy day," he said, slumping into a chair. "They brought in a dog, a large one, a retriever. She was pouring blood and gasping for air. There was a jagged hole between her ribs, which was allowing air into her chest cavity, taking up the space her lungs needed to inflate. The dog tried to compensate for the lack of oxygen by panting, causing more air to enter her chest and further compressing her lungs. Finally, her lungs collapsed. We had to keep other patients waiting and operate immediately. We had to draw the excess air out of the chest wound."

"With a chest tube, right?" asked Tracy. "That is what we would have done with the patient."

Lewin nodded. "Then she could be x-rayed," he said.

"I thought that was the end," said Lewin. "Some object had impaled the dog and gone in one side of her and out the other. Believe it or not, the x-rays showed that no major organs were damaged. But she still had a lot of free air in her chest cavity. But we managed. It was touch and go, but, already, she is starting to look better. Then, of course, I saw my usual clinic. But they all look much better."

"Lewin, but you don't. You look exhausted. How do you manage to relate to all your patients? I mean, they must have been in the waiting room for hours. What did they bark at you when you finally saw them?"

"Nobody likes to go to the doctor. I don't! You're sick, you're wary, you're a bit embarrassed, and animals are no different. There are weird smells, and animals are cued to things we don't even notice, even as far as a 'white-coat syndrome'. They don't know you, they don't trust you, and, every time they go in the car, they know they're not going somewhere for fun. One has to be very empathetic toward these animals. We have to remember they're not only sick, but also very afraid, and that can compound the problems they're having. Those are the most difficult ones. Any animal that tries to bite or act out, we take it in our stride. That's how they're expressing their fear. We do everything we can to reassure and calm them. Sometimes we have to slow on what we're trying to do to help them, because moving forward can be what pushes them over the edge as far as too much stress goes."

"But it must be difficult, because they can't talk," she said.

"But their owners can," he said. "If you listen to the history and ask the owner the right questions, ninety percent of the time you'll be able to come up with the right diagnosis with the owner's help. The keys are things like how much water the pet is drinking, has the appetite changed, what abnormal behaviours are being shown, etcetera. My secretary had asked everyone to come a little late, so it wasn't so bad. Though some of the owners were angry. Those are sometimes the most difficult."

The next day, Lewin was just as exhausted and he was beginning to wonder if private veterinary practice was really for him. He called Tracy, telling her about his day.

"I had a patient, today, a cat, in a terrible condition. He had, some time ago, it must have been, come across some plastic that had been wrapped around some fish and still had pieces of fish attached to it. Unfortunately, some of it became stuck between his teeth, causing an infection. Over some months, I am sure, the infection spread from his mouth to his sinuses, his face became swollen and painful, and he was eventually brought to me. I have no idea why the owners had not noticed before. I suspected an abscess at the root of one of the teeth. If the root did have an abscess, the tooth would have to be pulled. But it wasn't the first time the cat had required dentistry. He had already had two teeth removed on the same side as this tooth. I took an x-ray that showed that the cat's swollen sinus was, indeed, linked to an abscessed tooth. There was no doubt that the tooth had to be extracted. Anyway, I did that, and I am sure the cat will be much better now. It was a really nasty infection, and the surgery was delicate. I have to keep a check on him for quite some time. Then, of course, there was my usual clinic. There are times I really long for Cape Town and the penguins. They are still busy cleaning there and still asking for people to volunteer." He gave a sigh. "I really miss the little chaps a lot."

"Lewin, I was thinking, if you go back to Cape Town, maybe I should go overseas and start looking for Andy," said Tracy.

"I am not going to Cape Town," said Lewin. "Also, we have our future to think about." For some reason, he felt very deeply distressed, not really knowing why.

He decided to speak to Dr. Silver who, since they had got back, had become a good friend. They found that they both played chess and every so often managed to squeeze in a game.

"Hi, Lewin," he said as Lewin entered. "Good to see you."

They chatted for a while. Eventually, after a really good game, Dr. Silver asked, "How are things going with Tracy?"

"In a way, very well," said Lewin. "But sometimes I am afraid I might lose her, that she will just go away to another country to find her daughter, but she might not find her, and who knows when she would come back." Lewin looked dejected. Where was the glow that he had been showing since he met him?

"Why should she go overseas now?" asked the doctor.

"It somehow has become very urgent for her. I think ever since she has been corresponding with Sky."

"Sky?" questioned the doctor.

Lewin explained.

"You think she will really go?" asked the doctor thoughtfully.

"I think she might," said Lewin. "There is no way I can stop her from going."

"When would she be going?" asked the doctor.

"She wants to go straight away," said Lewin dolefully.

"You have not set a wedding date yet?"

"We want it to be some time this year," said Lewin, "but we haven't set a date for it. I really hope it works out…"

"You haven't thought of getting married sooner?" asked the doctor, with a faraway look in his eyes. "Like within the next couple of weeks?" He turned to him suddenly.

Lewin was caught completely of guard. "But the arrangements… Is it not too soon?" His face had turned a fiery red. "But the arrangements," he repeated. "And my work."

"You can get leave."

"Well, I can leave it to my partners to look after. They are used to me being away," said Lewin. "If I take my laptop and cell phone with me, I can still do a lot of work on my research from wherever I am."

"And she has not started another permanent nursing job

yet," said the doctor. "But she can well manage financially. I don't know if you realise, but you are marrying a very wealthy woman."

"Oh, I thought her parents... I thought they were comfortable, but not really wealthy. I mean, it is not that important for me at all. I love her for who she is."

"Her lawyer claimed a small fortune from the insurance, and also from her husband and, in return, made the divorce easier. He thought he was leaving someone who would never be functional in any way."

Lewin came home in a thoughtful mood and immediately phoned Tracy. "I would like to come over for coffee," he said. "Are your parents home?"

"Yes, they are, of course they are," said Tracy. "They don't go out very often. Have you had supper?"

"No, actually not," said Lewin, "but it is after 9 p.m."

"We will make you some," said Tracy, "and it won't take long."

"I will be there in about forty minutes," he said.

Her parents were surprised he was coming, especially this late to visit. Of course, he always came in and spent a few minutes with them when he was taking Tracy out, but this seemed to be a more official time he wanted to spend with them.

"Looks like we will be making a wedding soon," her father whispered to her mother when Tracy was out of earshot. "He loves our Tracy so much that I don't think he can be without her even for a few hours, and both are working so hard they hardly see each other."

Mother and Father took themselves a bet that that was what Lewin was coming for. After all, they had correctly guessed the engagement, now the marriage.

"Possibly, the sooner the better, if he has sense, which he has a lot of," said her father. "I know my Tracy, and she is already talking about going overseas to find Andy, though where she will actually go, I have no idea. He should marry her fast and go with her."

"How fast?" asked Tracy's mother.

"Well, right away, I suppose," he said.

Her mother had learnt not to argue, and, in fact, that seemed to make sense.

Mr. and Mrs. Berns greeted Lewin and then left the dining room for Lewin and Tracy to eat alone together.

Lewin had brought a few deep red roses, which he gave to her with a look in his eyes that made her heart turn over. No, she could never leave Lewin. She loved him so intensely, and she knew how he loved her, but she could not betray Andy. However, Lewin was already part of her and she had no idea how she could ever live without him.

As they sat at the table he looked deep into her eyes, those eyes that had captured his heart so long ago as he was lying in a hospital bed.

He had rehearsed several ways of asking her to marry him in two weeks time, but her eyes reflecting a love for him blew everything out of his mind so that he just used very simple words.

"Let's get married the week after next, or even next week. Then we can go and find Andy straight away. In fact, we can settle everything tonight. We can look on the Internet for a booking to England or some place and get married a week or so before."

Tracy had not said anything but she went to the computer and looked up South African Airways to London.

She left the booking dates for him to look at and he pointed at a date in just over three weeks time. He mentioned this and looked questioningly at Tracy. He filled in the booking details and then Lewin pulled out his credit card to pay for it and seal the deal. She had hardly spoken, but then said, "Shouldn't we call in my parents, and what about your mother? Shouldn't we tell them? I mean, if we are leaving in three weeks, when do we get married?"

"I told my mother already that I was going to do this," said Lewin, "and she was really happy. Let's call in your parents."

Slowly, Tracy tried to break the news to them that they had come to the conclusion that there was no reason to wait to get married and, therefore...

"Won our bet," said Mr. Berns with a twinkle in his eye. "You said this week, and I said next week."

They both gave Lewin and Tracy a bear hug and looked towards the computer. The message was that they had been taking too much time and would have to rebook. They did this, using exactly as they had been going to book before. Tracy blushed when she saw he had booked the tickets in the names of Dr. and Mrs. Lewin Green.

"Now we have to make that happen," said Lewin as he seemed to be playing with the Dr. and Mrs. Lewin Green as if it was something almost sacred.

"Whenever you want," said Mr. Berns. He was looking very excited.

His wife was flushed with the suddenness and excitement of it all.

"When can your mother come up here from Cape Town?" asked Mr. Berns.

"She has a few days' leave at the end of this week. She has to be on duty again on Monday."

"Then we can do it this weekend," said her father. He looked at Lewin, and then at his daughter. Both their faces were glowing, and he felt his heart lurch with happiness. "Settled then," he said. "Now we will leave you two alone for Lewin to eat something. Do you want to warm it again, Tracy? Everything has got cold."

"I can't eat," said Lewin.

"Tracy, help him eat it, but make sure he eats," said her father, disappearing behind the door.

The food became very much colder before they began to eat it, and between them, actually to finish it.

* * *

The wedding took place as planned with quite a few people present. Tracy and her parents had arranged everything tastefully and beautifully. What graced the wedding most was the undoubted affection and love and happiness that bride and groom shared with each other. They had even managed to plan a short honeymoon.

Immediately after the wedding they left for the South Coast of Natal for a tiny guest house in Shelley Beach. For the first two days they took things easy and on the third day they decided to take a drive further along the coast. Tracy had taken the wheel and Lewin was looking at her strangely. There seemed to be something very wrong.

"I am not saying you are not a good driver or anything," he said, "but is there any reason why you are going so slowly?"

"Well, I just want this guy behind to overtake. I get very shaken up when someone follows me so closely. I can't drive properly; I have to let him go."

"But he is not that close to you," said Lewin.

"But I see him in my rear-view mirror and that frightens me."

The driver behind her, obviously impatient, overtook her and sped off into the distance. She relaxed at once. "That's better," she said.

"But you were terrified only a few minutes ago," said

Lewin. "What was it?"

"I don't know," she said. "I just don't like a car following me; that's all."

"How long has that been?"

"Please let's talk about something else," she said. However, it was Tracy herself who resumed the subject. "My accident, those eyes, I will never, ever forget those eyes. I keep dreaming about them. I saw them in my rear-view mirror. I have never, ever seen such eyes!"

"Maybe you will recognise them one day," said Lewin.

She gave a shudder.

"How much do you remember of the accident?" he continued. He had often wondered about it.

"I don't know, I thought I didn't remember anything, but sometimes I get a faint glimmer of a memory. Once, they brought the Jaws of Life to get a woman out of a car after an accident, and I realised that it was a sound I somehow remember, yet I don't remember it at all. Yet, I remember the helicopter, but not much of it... just the feeling of being lifted straight into the air, and then only vague things of hospitals and things, and terrible pain, nausea and weakness, and, of course, these dreams. But I know they are just dreams. When they are happening, they are real."

Later that day, their travels seemed to become too much for Tracy.

"Lewin, I don't feel well at all, I really don't... My head feels so heavy. I feel that it is going to burst."

"Tracy, you are looking very flushed. I am sure you have fever. I wonder if there is a doctor around here."

"We did pass a chemist some time back," said Tracy. "Perhaps we can get something there. I really don't feel well. I mean, I am sure it is nothing drastic, just like flu or something, but I need medicine and I need to be in bed for a day or so."

He took over and swiftly drove to the chemist and then back to their guest house in Shelley Beach.

That night, she had a particularly vivid dream. She cried out in her sleep.

She woke up, obviously shaken, her whole body trembled and tears streamed down her blanched face.

"It was a dream?" he asked.

"Yes, it was a dream. I know it was a dream. But then it was more than a dream. It was a memory."

She tried to tell him everything she could.

The sun beat down on the road ahead of her and she turned up the fans in the car, hoping to dissipate the heat, but only more warm air blew in, making it, if anything, even hotter. It was a pleasant drive, one that she had enjoyed on a weekly basis, where she would be free to do her own thing, and free to pursue her own sports interests. She thought about Andy left alone with Andrew. This was their special time together. She knew it was important.

She concentrated on the road in front of her. It really was hot but she enjoyed going at a fair speed past the trees guarding the road, towards the steep winding road that would take her further on. She was glad that the rain had stopped. Driving on the road in that kind of rain had not always been pleasant. And then there was the car following her and the eyes, those dreadful eyes...and then as can be found in the magic of dreams, the scene changed.

She was in a desert, trying to cross the parched land. The sand was hot, and the sun beat down mercilessly. Oh why was it so hot, and why was she so thirsty? Surely there must be water somewhere. Surely there must be an oasis. Yes. yes, she could see it. There it was. She could see it now quite clearly. a few tall palm trees and a lake of sparkling, cool water. She would soon reach it, soon be there, soon be able to drink her fill from the cool refreshing water, but as she approached, the oasis seemed to be distancing itself, to be retreating further and further away, tantalising her and increasing her thirst at the opportunity of it being quenched so soon. The water was blue and cool. She needed something to cool herself off. Perhaps she would even be able to swim.

That is what she needed, a nice cool swim. But at the moment all she felt was hot and dry. Her lips felt as if they would crack into pieces if she did not find liquid to wet them. Oh for some water! Oh, for some cool water!

She could hear voices, distant voices, the voices of a man and a little girl. They were coming closer to her and they were talking.

"Andy," the man was saying. "Andy, my baby. Your

mother is still asleep. You can kiss her, Andy. Maybe one day she will wake up." His voice cracked as he gave a sob. "My Tracy," he said. "My beautiful Tracy. You will never be the same again. You have left us both, Tracy."

The child began to whimper. "Mummy, Mummy, please wake up, Mummy. Please, please wake up, Mummy. Daddy and I want you so much."

"We will have to go away," he was saying. "Far, far away. Andy, would you like to go away? We can start a new life, just you and Daddy. We can find a house far away."

"Want Mummy," said the child, raising her voice. "I want my mummy. I want my mummy! I want my mummy!"

Shivering, Tracy tried to explain. "Lewin, she said, "it was the most terrible dream. But I don't know if it is a dream or if I am remembering something. Lewin, I must find my baby. I must find my baby. I want my baby!"

"I know, my darling," said Lewin. "And we just don't know where to look. But we are going, soon, to London. We are leaving a week and a half after we get back."

"I heard them talking. They were talking just a few minutes ago, beside my bed."

"Who?" asked Lewin.

"Andrew and Andy. I heard them distinctly."

"You are delirious," said Lewin, concerned. "I must give you more of that medicine to bring your temperature down. You are very flushed, and I can see by your eyes that you are not well at all."

"I heard them distinctly," said Tracy.

"No, Tracy, you are delirious." He saw by her reaction to his words that she was about to become hysterical, so he quietly soothed her. "All right, Tracy, tell me all about it. Tell me every word they said. You have to get better, my darling. You have to be well enough for our trip next week; okay, the week after."

"Well," said Tracy, "I was in the desert again where I used to be so often when I went to hospital after the accident. And then I heard them talking."

"But what did they say? What did they sound like?"

"I will tell you exactly," she said, repeating the conversation, tears coursing down her cheeks as she gave over Andy's words.

Lewin could not help but be influenced by what she was saying. He too, was asking the questions: was it a dream, was it delirium, was it a stirring of a forgotten memory, or was it some kind of combination of all three? How could one be sure?

He filled a glass with water and gave her medication.

"Please, please let us go to look for her," she said.

As the medicine was beginning to take effect, Tracy lay back with a smile.

Lewin breathed a sigh of relief. He colour was better and her breathing more easy. The medication had definitely helped.

"I wish we could get in touch with Andy," said Tracy. "I

mean, even though I don't know where to look, I want my Andy. I hear her calling me. I still hear her calling me."

"I know, my darling," said Lewin. "We are going to London after next week. I am beginning to hear her calling me, too. We have to find her. A little girl needs her mother, perhaps more now that she is ten."

"Eleven," mumbled Tracy sleepily. "She is eleven now."

The time for their trip was coming closer and there remained only a few days left as they made last minute arrangements.

Dearest Mum,

I am beginning to get very frightened and I can see that, for some reason, my father is frightened for me. I think he has been receiving some sort of letters and things.

Maybe I must not think about it. It was just so good to share with you.

Try as she might, Tracy was not able to really find out why the child was afraid...until...

Tracy, please help me. There are good and bad things happening. There is going to be a school picnic and that is good, and I will be with my friends. But my father is going away for a few days and, for some reason, he has been very worried about me and about everything. He had a phone call and saw someone in town.

Tracy I am, really worried...

I saw a note in his study. He does not know I have seen it.

Please Tracy, I am, really scared. Please write back to me and I will pick up the email after I have eaten supper.

Tracy responded immediately, noting that her email had just been sent. She asked Sky for details they had for some unspoken reason not shared before. She wanted her surname and her address and her home telephone number and also her father's cell phone number. She was not going to leave the child alone in this.

There was no reply, not the next day and the next.

"Lewin I am worried about Sky. There is trouble there and I feel I can't desert this child."

"I know," said Lewin. "My adopted daughter, too, three adopted penguins, and two adopted daughters. Well, it certainly gives us a direction in which to start our search for Andy. If we can really find out where she lives, we can go there first and, from there, we go on to Portugal, to Lisbon, though, as you say, you really have never connected Andrew with Portugal."

"Have we got any lead at all as to where Sky lives?"

"No," said Lewin. "But it is time we found out where she actually is. This time, I don't think we can wait. She is definitely not in South Africa, so London is a good start to anywhere."

"How do I find out?" she asked.

"Maybe from Towermail," he said. "She must have some kind of email address, even if it is from another computer or an Internet café. It has to have some kind of email address."

"I will try to find out," said Tracy."

She sounded exhausted, and his heart went out to her. If only they could find these two girls. It had seemed as if it was going to be so easy.

"I will go onto my laptop, too," he said. "But I am so tired. I am sure I will get my energy back in an hour or so."

He must have dozed in front of the computer because he woke some forty minutes later finding Tracy in another chair sleeping but still connected to Towermail. He saw three more messages from Tracy, the last one sounding quite desperate, but there had been no response from Sky.

He went further down the page until he found the email address of the Towermail line and then a telephone number in America. Glancing at the time, he dialled the number.

"I am very sorry, but we can't give out that kind of information," said a rather irritated woman's voice on the other side. "I don't know why people have to put in panic messages. You are the third person who has called about it."

"My wife has called twice?" asked Lewin.

"Well, if Tracy Green is your wife, she has called once. Apparently, the message was to her. There was another query from a man in the UK, someone with a foreign accent," she added. "He was aggressive when I would not tell him what country the message had come from. The girl was using our own Towermail's email address. It is web based, and can be sent and picked up from anywhere in the world."

"But Towermail itself might have another address" said Lewin.

Irritation again seemed to flood her. "Excuse me," she said. "But the other man was also asking these questions. We just cannot give out the information. I am sorry."

"Thank you," said Lewin. "My name is Lewin Green, Dr. Lewin Green. Who am I speaking to?"

"I shouldn't tell you that, either," said the woman. "But it is Lettie. And good luck!"

"Thanks," he said. "I really appreciate it." He was about to replace the phone when he managed to catch her before she did. "I would like to give you my phone number."

She was about to become irritated again, but caught herself and took it down. "I really don't know what for," she said. "I won't be using it."

"Thank you," he said again, this time replacing the phone. Very quickly, he was online and sent Tracy a message from Towermail again.

'I love you', he wrote, 'from Lewin'.

Two minutes later, she stormed into his study.

"Lewin, what are you doing?" she asked indignantly.

"I was just getting across a very important message," he said, laughing.

"I love you, too," she said, "but rather don't say it on the email line."

"I wanted to speak to you," he said, "and I wasn't sure if you were awake." He proceeded to tell her everything that had transpired.

"The UK," she whispered.

"I don't know who the man could have been," said Lewin. "I have a funny feeling about the call, that it has something to do with the danger."

"We have to go to England and we are," she said. "Maybe that is where she is."

"But maybe it isn't," said Lewin soberly. "But then, as we agreed, maybe it is as good a start as any, and then we can check out Portugal. Let's try to check into it more. The woman on the Tower email line was Lettie."

"Short for?" questioned Tracy.

"Short for... Lettuce," he said.

"It can't... Oh, Lewin, how can you joke about a thing like that?"

"I love you," he said. "I keep thinking Towermail has the address, but they won't give it, and I somehow feel uneasy that someone else was asking for it. We can't waste time."

Tracy was staring at him. "Lewin, you mean we go tomorrow? Change our booking?"

"Well, I think we should check with the airline how soon we could change our tickets. We already have our booking, so, with an extra fee, I don't see it can be a problem. We have been dealing with the airline on the Internet, so let's just finalise things."

"Why not?" she asked, excitement beginning to grip her. "Why ever not?"

The booking was changed, and they would leave on the following evening.

"In the meanwhile," Lewin said, "I think we should go through all her emails together. Maybe we can pick up some kind of hint."

He suddenly saw how tired she was. "Do I have permission to go through all these letters myself?"

She nodded. "She is your adopted daughter, too," she said, as she handed him a diskette. "But she has never indicated the name of a town, city or country."

He called up the files into Microsoft Word and began to read. When he got to the latest emails his face flushed with excitement. Written in the one email were detailed descriptions of birds on the island she was visiting with her father. She had described several kinds of birds and to him it was as if she had drawn him a map. Britain, yes, probably, but far north. He wanted to share this with Tracy, but she was sound asleep.

CHAPTER 11

They had been travelling for several hours and were now probably somewhere over Central Africa. Everyone had finished their meal.

The lights had been dimmed and most of the passengers had settled down to sleep. Though dozing a little, neither Tracy nor Lewin were really sleeping. Both were busy with their own thoughts.

The movie was still on and occasionally they would glance at the screen wondering if any of the passengers would have on their earphones and be watching it. It did not look very interesting, and they remained in their semi-dazed state.

They became aware of a flurry towards the back of the plane and saw the flight attendants walking quickly along the isle towards it. Vaguely they wondered what was happening but both were too much in a daydream world to really get involved.

Not five minutes later a voice came over the speaker of the plane apologising for any inconvenience caused and asking if there was a doctor on board the plane.

Both Tracy and Lewin tensed and looked at each other. They heard another man get up from somewhere on the plane and presumed a doctor had answered the call.

However, a few minutes later the call came through again, this time the voice sounded more urgent.

Tracy and Lewin both got up and made their way to the back of the plane. "I am a veterinary surgeon, and my wife is a nurse... for humans," he added, as he saw the look of doubt on the flight attendant's face. "Perhaps we could help."

"Maybe," said the attendant. "Yes. Maybe you can. No one knows what is going on here, not even our paramedic. No one has answered the call for a doctor. I am sure you can help."

They moved aside to reveal a young boy of about ten who was lying back unconscious but rigid in his seat. His mother, close to hysteria, was sitting in the seat next to him and his father looking not less anxious but somewhat more controlled, was leaning over the seat trying to wake his son.

The parents moved over quickly to let Lewin and Tracy closer to the boy. Tracy was within seconds taking his pulse whilst Lewin checked his vital signs.

"He's alive," he said, looking at the mother. "His heart is beating regularly and he is breathing."

"We know that," said the paramedic a little indignantly.

"But the parents didn't," said Lewin as they saw the parents' faces become flooded with relief.

Tracy found it strange and somehow rewarding to be the nursing sister assisting Lewin. She forgot in a way that he was Dr. Lewin Green, veterinary surgeon, and slotted naturally into the doctor and nurse situation. Only when she saw him stroke the boy's hair and pat him did she realise that that was what he probably did with most of his patients.

He looked up and indicated that he needed the oxygen mask, which he attached to the boy, noting, at the same time, how convenient the oxygen masks in a plane actually were. The boy seemed to stir and the mother breathed a sigh of relief.

"What is wrong with him?" asked Tracy as she tried to calm the mother. "Has he been ill lately? Has he been to the doctor?"

The woman was shivering, and Tracy signalled to the attendant to bring her something hot and sweet to drink.

"He was once treated for epilepsy," she said. "That was three years ago. He had been put on medication and he stayed on it for two years, and we went to the doctor regularly. But he seemed so much better and he was going to start school, and we thought he had got over it, so we just stopped the medicine and nothing happened. I mean, we were going to ask the doctor about it, but he seemed so much better. I mean, he seemed to have grown out of it. A neighbour of mine told me that people can grow out of these things. She knows a lot about it because she had an uncle who had fits, and she hadn't seen him have one for years. She said the medicine did not do any good, anyway."

Lewin gave a sigh. Did human doctors have the same problems that vets do, that patients did not listen to the doctors instructions and either stopped the medication or used the syrup or tablets in the way they felt was better? How would the doctor really know?

"Which doctor was treating him?" asked Lewin.

"A doctor in Ireland, Dr. Kaplan. He is in Belfast. He was there three years ago. I presume he is there still. But can this be a fit? It can't be a fit."

"This is more than a fit now. It is status," said Lewin.

"Intravenous Valium... they give it in our hospital," said Tracy helpfully.

"Do you have any of that?" asked Lewin, turning towards the paramedic.

"I think it is one of the things we are required to keep," said the paramedic. "But we need a prescription and he is not a, uh... a... horse or something like that."

Lewin laughed. "We must try to get his doctor, Dr Kaplan in Ireland. Can you arrange that? We could use someone else, but his own doctor who knows him will be infinitely better. We need your son's full name, address in Ireland, etcetera."

He indicated for the father to go with the paramedic, which he did a little reluctantly, leaving his wife and child. They walked quickly in the direction of the cockpit.

It was ten minutes later that he was back, during which time Lewin and Tracy had the boy lying over three seats using a fresh oxygen mask from another seat. Lewin was patting him and stroking him saying, "Don't worry, there have been dogs that have had this, and I have even treated a horse in status, and today he is frisking around his field. Don't worry, they all got better."

Tracy stifled a smile. "Epilepsy in animals?" she queried.

"Oh yes," said Lewin, "and there can be all kinds of reasons for this, such as a lack of vitamins or worms. We even treat them on similar medicines." He looked at the boy's veins. "I am sure this will be the same to giving an intravenous injection to an animal; easier, in fact."

"I am a nursing sister," said Tracy, reminding him.

"Oh yes, of course," said Lewin. "Of course, you should give it to him, but first we have to make contact with that doctor."

It was at least ten minutes later that a flight attendant came rushing along the isle to call Lewin to the phone.

Tracy took his place and realised with horror that she was patting and stroking the boy as if he was a dog, just as Lewin had been doing. He came back with an injection of Valium, which Tracy gave intravenously and, over the next few minutes, the boy's face changed as he roused briefly and fell into a deep, natural sleep.

"Thank heavens," said Lewin. "That is better. I spoke to his doctor from Ireland. The boy definitely has epilepsy, and he was very disturbed about the status. He wants to see him as soon as he gets to Ireland if it in the next day or so; otherwise, they have to find the nearest neurologist for an emergency appointment."

The mother was smiling with relief. "What was that?" she asked Lewin.

"It is a kind of seizure or fit," said Lewin. "It is like having many fits, but it seems like a very long one, because it can go on for hours and you usually have to have medical attention to stop it."

"But he is better from the fits," said his mother.

"He most definitely isn't," said Lewin. "And you need to see that doctor as soon as you arrive. Are you going to Ireland? Where are you going to be staying?"

"Lisburn," said the father. "Near Belfast."

"Lisburn," said Lewin slowly. "Isn't that in Portugal?" His heart was starting to beat faster.

"Oh, there is a Lisbon in Portugal. This is Lisburn, a suburb of Belfast, Northern Ireland."

"That is funny," said Tracy. "That is exactly where we are going. We can speak to your doctor for you if you like."

The man looked very excited. "Dr. Green," he said. "You will do us the greatest honour if you would come and stay with us for a few days. We would only be delighted, and feel far safer for Kidon's welfare."

Tracy and Andrew looked at each other and nodded. Things were definitely falling into place, but the immediate problem was Sky, but Northern Island would be as good a place to start from.

"Tell us about Ireland," said Lewin to Mr. O'Hare, trying to make him feel better. He, now more than his wife, was still looking distinctly shocked.

"Well, it is Northern Island, of course," he said, already

looking a little better, "which is very beautiful, especially by the sea, the mountains and the old castles. We even have a castle in Belfast called the Carrickfergus Castle. And, as a vet, you might be interested in birds, and we have many of these, especially by Strangford Lough, which is a haven for migratory birds and others. Of course, we have our problems, the constant hatred between Protestants and Catholics." He went on to describe this until Tracy suddenly had a realisation.

"Sky did tell me where she was," she said. "She is in Northern Island. She told me about the trouble between these religions, and I think this is the place for it."

"It sure is," said Mr. O'Hare. "Famous for that, we most definitely are."

They had been invited to the O'Hare's home, but declined, saying that they would like to stay in a hotel close by. Exhausted, they were soon asleep.

It was about midnight when they received a call from a very agitated Mr. O'Hare. "Sorry to wake you," he said, "but there is a child, Sky Sheldon, missing from a school picnic. Could that be the child you are looking for?"

Feeling an icy lump in his chest Lewin asked for the number of the local police, arranging for someone to come over.

Within minutes, Tracy and Lewin were answering the door to the local police who were looking extremely concerned. "The child has been missing since mid-morning," they informed them.

"What about the father, Mr. Sheldon?" asked Lewin after some discussion, at the same time remembering that Sky said her father would be away.

"He is away on business. Sky always stayed with the O'Brien family when he was away, which was quite often. Perhaps you should meet them first thing in the morning." The inspector looked at his watch. "It is a little late now, nearly 2 a.m. We will wait till at least 7 a.m."

It was exactly 7 a.m. when the inspector arrived to take them to the O'Brien home. Neither Lewin nor Tracy had slept well, and it was discovered at the O'Brien house that no one had slept there either. Mrs. O'Brien had made some breakfast for the Greens and they sat around the table, the anxiety about Sky quite palpable.

When she met Colleen, Tracy mentioned that Sky had written about her.

"Oh, are you Sky's mother?" asked Colleen. "She so looked forward to getting your emails and, in class, she kept telling us about the South African penguins, Pamela, Peter and Percy. Every time she heard more news, she would tell us. The whole class was following their travels. Awfully clever birds, those were," she said.

"Well, children," said Mrs. O'Brian. "I think it is important for you to tell your story before you go to school. Dad will take you there by car instead of you having to catch the school bus, but you can't miss too much of the morning, That would not be good at all."

With a groan, the children sat down and soon the O'Brien's and the Lewin's were given a detailed picture of what had happened.

CHAPTER 12

The rain lashed against the school bus window, making it difficult to see the road ahead, despite the valiant efforts of the overworked windscreen wipers.

Mr. Donaldson, the driver, shifted in this driver's seat to try to ease the ache in his back caused by the strain of leaning forward at an uncomfortable angle in an attempt to see more clearly. If only the rain would let up to give him time to make some mileage! They had been due at their destination half an hour ago, but in this rain it could take them another hour.

In actual mileage, they were, in fact, fairly close to their picnic site, but who knew when they would get there, and who would enjoy a picnic in this weather? Maybe they should just turn back.

He looked at the petrol gauge. Yes, he would need to fuel up again; fairly soon, in fact. However, according to his calculation, they should be close to Bentley, the last town they would pass on their way.

Where was Bentley, though?

The children in the bus had stopped their singing some time ago. Most of them had their noses pinned tightly up to the windows, having to constantly wipe the glass with their hands to prevent it from completely fogging over.

In fact, the bus was surprisingly quiet for the presence of thirty-five children.

Two of them were asleep. Four of them were half heartedly trying to play Monopoly.

Four girls on the bus were having a long discussion, seemingly oblivious to the weather outside.

The rain started to come down even harder. Oh, when would it ever stop!

The bus was now almost crawling along the road, which seemed to be getting more and more slippery and, therefore, more dangerous.

Oh, how far was Bentley? It couldn't be far now.

He would stop the bus there, even if it was for half an hour and he would be in touch with the organisers of the picnic and see if they would rather be headed for home. It was useless driving along this road, and what kind of picnic would the children have in this weather?

He looked in the rear-view mirror. He wasn't the only one who was having trouble. A large, panelled truck had been following him for at least ten minutes, keeping the same speed as he was doing. He had several times pulled over to the side of the road to let him pass, but the truck kept behind him.

For a good few minutes it had given him an uneasy feeling, being followed by a truck like that, but he quickly put it out of his mind. After all, who would want to stalk a bus full of school children going on a mid-term, picnic? He even laughed at himself.

The wind howled and raged around him. It seemed that the bus would not hold the road.

"Bentley, Bentley, Bentley," he heard himself murmuring. The place seemed like a haven, and it was so close.

Crunch... crack... snap!

The windscreen wiper in front of him tore away from the window. Now he could hardly see at all! He had no option but to stop, and stop he did.

The truck stopped behind him and then overtook him, making its laborious way into the distance.

Now what was he to do? He couldn't drive without a windscreen wiper.

The children in the bus had come up to him.

"What's the matter, Mr. Donaldson?"

"Are we stuck?"

"Are we out of petrol?"

"Can't we go through the rain?"

"Are we at the picnic site?"

He explained to them that the windscreen wiper had broken and that they would have to wait till the rain stopped a little.

"But it might rain all day," said a boy with red hair by the name of Tony.

Mr. Donaldson was irritated.

"If you can come up with another windscreen wiper, I will carry on driving. We are nearly at Bentley and we can stop there. But, with no wipers, I can't see anything. With the wipers, I can hardly see anything."

"You have a wiper that's working on the other window," said the boy.

"That's right," said the man, "but the driver's seat is opposite this one. I can't drive and look out of that one!"

"But," said the boy, "can't you take it from that side and put it on this window?"

Mr. Donaldson stared at him in amazement.

"My boy, you might have something there. There is probably a brain underneath that carrot top of yours. You might, indeed, have something there!"

He went to the door of the bus, shuddered a little as he went out into the driving rain and, within a few minutes, had a working windscreen wiper in front of him.

"Now we can go," he announced, feeling some fresh energy despite his dripping hair and clothes. At least something about this journey was going right.

The rain slackened a little and he was able to increase his pace to a faster crawl.

He went on, singing a little to himself. The children once more wiped the windows and pressed their noses against the glass.

Everyone was looking out for Bentley. Maybe he could use his cell phone there.

The bus crawled on and on, the rain lashing into its side and bouncing back with an injured fury.

Suddenly everyone lurched as the bus screeched to a halt.

"We all had to get off the bus," continued Colleen O'Brien, a girl who must have been Sky's age. "It was dangerous to be on it, because, with one of the wheels missing, although there were double wheels, we could not stay inside the bus. Also, Mr. Donaldson had to try his best to put on the spare wheel, and we had to go out. But it was raining badly, so we were in a kind of dilemma. So we all went outside in that terrible storm. People stopped their cars and asked if we would like to go with them, and we refused. We would rather be together. The people just said they would call for help for us. Sky had been with her friends at the back of the bus, but she also had friends at the front, so each had thought she was with the other ones, so they did not notice she wasn't with them. We were standing there for at least ten minutes in the rain before a van came and took many of us to Bentley. Meanwhile, Mr. Donaldson changed the tyre and the rest of us went to Bentley, too. As I said, we thought Sky had gone with the van. They thought Sky was with us. We don't know where she went. We are sure she would not have gone with one of the cars."

"Unless she would have known the person," said Tracy slowly, "knew and trusted that person".

"But she knew not to take lifts from strange men," recited Colleen. "We all know that."

"Perhaps this was a strange woman. Does the rule apply there, too?"

"I suppose not," said Colleen slowly. "But she would have told us if she was leaving. She would have told somebody."

"Do you remember anything about the cars that stopped?"

"Well, a few stopped for quite a long time, just to give some of the children shelter until the van came. There were about four or five of these."

"And you are sure there was no way she could have remained at that place?"

"Police have searched and searched."

"She must have been offered shelter and driven off with," said Lewin.

"I suppose that figures," said Tracy. "They would just say they wanted to move the car out of the way and they would be gone. But someone must have seen it."

"The rain was very heavy, and you could hardly see anything," said Colleen, her eyes wide.

"But someone just might remember," said Tracy.

"I wish we could find Sky's father," said Lewin.

"Oh, he can be away for a long time. He has very secret work to do. We suspect for the government. He can be away for a month at a time, even longer."

"But who looks after Sky?" asked Tracy indignantly.

"Oh, we do," said Colleen. "He has a kind of arrangement with my parents. She boards with us sometimes, even when he is home, because he is often out till very late at night. But you know about that, don't you, Mrs. Green? I mean, Sky has been writing to you for a long time now and she told you everything, I think."

"Not everything," said Tracy. "She never, ever told me how to find her or even which country she lived in."

"So how did you find her here?" asked Colleen incredulously.

"By the bird population in this area. Sky went on holiday with her father and described everything. My husband, Lewin, is a vet, and also a bird lover and expert, and he pinpointed the area as soon as I showed him the email from Sky. Then we found a 'Sky' and found you."

"My father would be very interested to talk to you," said Ian, looking at his dad. "He took a special interest in everything the penguins were doing. You were writing to Sky about it. I know that pigeons go by air and penguins by sea, but it is also amazing the way they find their way."

"I would love to see how your pigeons operate," said Lewin.

"Maybe we could take you out some place with one of the birds, and we can let him go, and you can see if he comes back."

"Of course he will," said Colleen. "They always do. They don't have any problem finding their way."

"Have you a pigeon loft?" asked Lewin.

"Oh yes," said Mr. O'Brian. "In fact, as soon as the children go to school, we can show you the loft and everything."

"That would be great," said Lewin. "I would appreciate that."

When the children finally left and Mr. O'Brien returned from taking them to school, they settled down to make definite plans as to what could be done.

Mr. O'Brien and Lewin found themselves to be kindred spirits. They could sense the intense animal lover in each other and they began to swap anecdotes and stories of the animals and birds they had known.

"We are actually missing one bird," said Richard O'Brien. "He somehow got lost at the picnic. Something must have happened to him in the storm. We have no idea."

They spent the next three days trying to do more detective work, spending a lot of time with the police and with the O'Brien's and with various other people connected with the school.

It must have been 2 a.m. on the fourth night when the phone rang and they heard Mr. O'Brien's voice sounding both excited and agitated.

"Listen, Lewin, Ryder, the bird who was lost at the picnic, has just come back in. He was hurt, so he has taken a long time to get here. There was a note with him from Sky. I don't know if it is good or bad news. She seems to have gone to Scotland with two people, a man and a woman who have virtually kidnapped her. She obviously wrote the note when they were about to cross the ferry, but she also attached part of a train ticket and the words 'silk' and 'head' on the back of it. I am not quite sure what it means. They must have drugged her, because she sounds very vague as to the time."

Tracy woke up and would not listen to any of Lewin's reasoning. They were both going over to read that note and to see it urgently. Mr. O'Brien did not seem at all surprised by this request.

Within minutes, both were at the O'Brien's loft.

"Let me show you the note," said Richard O'Brien, meeting him at the gate.

"I would like to see Ryder first," said Lewin, who had brought some of his medical equipment. "You said the bird had been hurt."

"Yes, of course," said the man with relief. "I forgot you are a vet."

Ryder had a deep gash in his side possibly made by a squashing instrument. It was a miracle that the bird had managed to take the message home. He had lost a great deal of blood and was very weak and shocked.

Richard took Tracy to see the note and the ticket whilst Lewin gently worked and dressed the wound and gave the bird an injection.

"He needs to sleep for several hours," said Lewin. "He is still very agitated, and he must be at complete rest."

The bird, instinctively having faith in him, let him do as he wanted, but his heartbeat was still fast and his breathing shallow.

"Now let me see the note," said Lewin when the bird was

settled.

"Dr. Green, I must say, I am very impressed with your touch," said Richard, clearly struck with Lewin's handling of the bird.

"I love these little chaps," said Lewin, "and pigeons are amazing birds. And this one struggled to bring this message home. If you hadn't had a vet on hand, I might say that he had given his life for it."

Sky's message was written in shaky printing. Obviously the child was terrified. She seemed to have crossed from Larne into Stranraer in Scotland and had been in the train that met the ferry. The ticket she had sent was running from Glasgow to Stranraer so it was obviously not hers. It must have been picked up in the train carriage somewhere. How did she keep the bird for so long and how had she managed to let him go? How had Ryder hurt himself? Suddenly, he knew, he had not been wounded with a sharp instrument. Someone had tried to pull the window closed on him, and he had been caught on the latch.

"And there is another word torn here; could it be Lee?"

"And where do we go from here?" asked Lewin. "That train line goes on for many miles. How do we know where to look?"

Richard turned over the ticket. "Well, the word 'silk' is written here, and then the word, it seems, 'HEAD', in capital letters. I wonder what that was about. And it seems to be Sky who wrote it. We have to work from that."

"In the meanwhile, we have to alert the police about this"

"But her captors must have seen that there was a pigeon. I mean, they must have shut the window on him. They must have been afraid that he would return to us."

"They probably did not realise he was a homing pigeon or that the bird had not been killed. I am sure they thought it was the end. Sky would have been very careful, surely."

Lewin went over to see the bird but found it was sleeping peacefully, its respiration and heart rate sounding far more healthy.

Tracy was busy studying the map especially the route of the railway line. She stopped at Selkirk and pointed it out to Lewin.

"Okay," he said. "Tomorrow to Scotland. We have to come back here to continue our search for Andy. In the meanwhile, we have to put everything else aside and find Sky."

* * *

Sky had been sitting somewhat dreamily on the bus looking out of the window at the pouring rain. Sitting on her lap was Ryder, the pigeon. It was her turn to hold him as Colleen and Ian had taken their turns and had handed Ryder, tissues and all, over to her.

It was incredible, she thought, how birds could find their way back from all kinds of places. She remembered what

Tracy had told her about the bird that had flown home from Boston back to Wales.

The children had decided to release the bird just before they left the picnic spot to see who would return home first. They were all sure it would be the bird.

They had even attached a message ring so that they could write a letter to themselves, a thing they had often done and then saved the notes.

She was actually sitting almost on top of the wheel that seemed to explode with a load roar. The bus jerked and swerved and landed in a strange, tilted position. The wheel's partner on that side had fortunately averted any real disaster or calamity, but it still placed the bus in a position it couldn't be driven. It also meant that, whilst it was being fixed, none them could stay in the bus, so all the children had to make their way out of the bus into the driving rain.

She was glad she had taken a waterproof half jacket with her, and she put the bird into the front of it and zipped it up on both of them. The bird was very quiet as if he knew that this was necessary to be protected from the rain. Anyway, he was not very fond of rain. She put on the hood and joined the other children who had covered themselves with groundsheets and whatever else they could find that seemed to be waterproof in order to shield themselves from the raging storm.

Mr. Donaldson, apologising profusely as he went to change the tyre looked very harassed but refused any help from the children except that he allowed two of the boys to hold things for him.

Sky found that the rain was beginning to seep through her jacket in certain areas so she took shelter under a large tree. Now that really was much dryer and she signalled to the other children to join her. But they muttered something about lightning striking trees and remained with their eyes glued to the tyre that Mr. Donaldson was trying to remove from the bus.

Sky was relieved that she could actually take off her hood, so well did the tree protect her from the rain. Her long fair curls hung about her shoulders, becoming a little scraggly at the ends as they absorbed the wetness of her jacket. She did not like wearing the hood as she could only really see in front of her.

She was vaguely aware of a car stopping behind the bus and then moving slowly towards where she was standing. A man and a woman were in the car and the woman, who she vaguely recognised, leant across the driver's seat and asked what the problem was.

Sky told them about the burst tyre reassuring them that the driver was fixing it.

"But to have you all in the rain!" she said in a concerned way. "And can the driver do it all by himself? Perhaps you should come with us and we can call for help for him."

That did sound like a good idea and the people were vaguely familiar and after reassuring her that they would drop her back to the bus, she climbed into the car. As she did so she remembered all the warnings she had heard about taking lifts from strangers. But this was different. They were in trouble on the road.

"Would you like some warm coffee?" the woman asked. "You are looking very chilled."

Sky had been worried that she might get quite sick from this and she accepted the mug gratefully.

"Sorry, it is not really hot, but it is the thermos flask that we drive with, and we have been out for a couple of hours already and the weather has been cold."

Shy looked outside at the rain and the mist, and gulped down her coffee. In less than ten minutes, she was lying in the back seat of the car in a drugged sleep.

It was several hours later that she awoke, her body aching and tense with the awareness of danger. A movement inside her jacket made her aware that the pigeon was still there, and this somehow comforted her.

The man and the woman, unaware that she was awake, were talking.

"I doubt if anyone has missed her yet. There was so much chaos with the bus. I am sure that some other children would also have been given rides and they won't realise Sky is not with them."

Sky gave a shudder when she realised that they knew her name. She had been thinking before her coffee that she had actually not introduced herself. The coffee... That must have been drugged. But why? However, she had known before that she could be in danger. Why had she accepted this ride? Oh why? Oh why? She had been warned she was in danger. Why had she done this?

The car was parked but she could see no one around. But why could she not just open the door and jump out? But they would probably taken the precaution to use the child safety lock so she would not be able to open it.

She would only alert their attention that she was awake and she would prefer not to do this. She tried to ascertain where she was but could not. There was nothing she could recognise.

"The ferry is only due in another forty minutes. How do we get her onto it?" asked the woman.

"Well, she will still be very sleepy, and we will somehow get her onto it. People won't really notice a child and we will make sure she does not speak. They would not have put out any kind of search for her and, by the time they are aware of it, we will be far away. I wish the ferry would be sooner, but we just have to wait here for it. Maybe just before we go to it we can give her a tranquillising injection, just a light one that will keep her asleep."

"But Head," began the woman, "Head, Lee."

"Don't worry, it will be all right with Head," he said, irritated.

Ferry. Where were they? Where were they going? Afterwards, where would they be going to? She purposely let out a sigh and turned over, making it seem as if she was fast asleep. In this position she could reach her pocket where there was a pen and some scraps of coloured paper. Plus, what or who was 'Head'?

Ryder was a homing pigeon and it was a matter of time till he would be noticed. She had to give him a note to take back with him where she would explain that she was being taken out of Northern Ireland, perhaps into Scotland. She wondered how far they had driven and in which direction.

She wrote the note quickly, using the floor of the car as a base, and she folded it several times, making some more sleep noises as she attached the note to the bird. Sleep was, actually, beginning to overtake her especially as she later felt a pinprick and she had only snippets of knowledge of getting onto a ferry and eventually on to a train.

Again she woke properly, aware that the bird was still inside her jacket, almost as if he was aware that he should keep still. She realised however, that she could not push her luck too far with Ryder. She would have to let him go soon. She was lying on the top bunk with the man and the woman sitting on the seat beneath her.

As she looked around her, she saw a scrap of a train ticket and she somehow fixed this, too, to the bird. But there was no way she could release him at this point. There was no way she could suddenly open a window. She and Ryder were well and truly trapped.

She had been too drugged to feel really frightened but she

realised that somewhere she was afraid. This was the culmination of the conversations she had heard with her father, the threats he had so often received.

If only she had told Tracy how to find her, she was sure she and Lewin would have come to help her. She longed to see them so much. Why had she never told them to come to her, or even sent them a photo? She had been afraid, hadn't she? She had even been afraid for them, and, of course, there were other reasons.

This time, somehow, the man and woman sensed she was awake, and the man nudged the woman to speak to her.

"Sky," she said, in a voice of almost forced kindness. "Sky, you are with us and we are not going to hurt you, but, at this time, we cannot let you go."

Sky answered in a way that was sleepier than she was feeling. "Why, where are we? Is this a train? Where are we going?"

"We are not going to hurt you," said the man, in a silky voice that she was sure she had heard before. "We are not going to hurt you. We have been instructed not to. But we must warn you that if you don't co-operate..."

"Not necessary," said the woman with irritation. "I am sure she is sensible enough to cooperate with us. She is not a fool."

The pigeon gave a faint peep and Sky started coughing to drown out the noise.

"Oh, please, could I have some water in a cup and

saucer?" she asked, noting that they had been brought their teas.

"Saucer?" questioned the man.

"Oh, I am afraid I might spill it up here. I am kind of shaky. I am not really sure why." She was glad that they had not seen that she had put the bird on the top bunk on the side nearest the wall beside her.

"Perhaps you would like some tea," suggested the woman.

"Oh no," she said. "That coffee you gave me in the car made me feel a bit sick. I would like some of the rolls you have there and some water in a cup and saucer."

She was given both and she gave the pigeon some water in the saucer and a fair amount of breadcrumbs. Ryder ate hungrily. All the time she made sure that she was chattering quite loudly so that no one would notice the bird.

"We are getting off soon," said the man, "so don't be too long with the water."

"Where are we getting off?" Sky asked.

"Silk…" began the woman.

"No," interrupted the man. "That is not necessary, not necessary at all." His face flushed red with anger, and Sky retreated to eat the rest of her bread and drink some of the water. The pigeon had had his fill and, once more, agreed to go inside Sky's jacket. How long could she keep him?

What if she went straight from the train, into a car, into a house with closed windows? She had to be prepared at any moment. She wrote the word 'Silk' and then the again word 'Head' and what else had she said before? 'Lee', so she wrote it on the back of the ticket and attached it, once more, to the bird. She folded the ticket as tightly as she could and attached it more securely to the bird.

Just then the man opened the window to throw out some wrappers and Sky pushed the bird through the window just as he was shutting it again. The window caught and almost squashed Ryder and Sky watched disconsolately as the bird fell like a dead weight next to the railway line.

"What was that?" the man almost screeched.

"Oh, just some kind of mouse that was up here," she said. "It was dead and I threw it through the window when you opened it. Maybe it was just a toy." She had added the last bit upon realising that they had not really seen it.

"Dead mouse, indeed," said the woman, "on the Scottish Railway. Obviously, it was some dirty toy that a child left. But there is no time now, because we have to go. Please hurry up."

Sky, still devastated, started to get down from the bunk.

* * *

It was barely 5 a.m. the next morning when the police came to wake Tracy and Lewin.

"We have an idea what the two words might mean, and we might have a link to the third. We have been in touch with the Scottish Police, Scotland Yard, and, in fact, the South African Police and they have suggested that we search a certain part of Selkirk in Scotland."

Tracy and Lewin nodded. Well, they had thought of Selkirk, hadn't they? They were disappointed that they would not be part of it, but the next few words shattered that illusion.

"We wondered if you would be prepared to help us. It would be a natural thing for you to do, and would be our best cover. The Headley Society is a well-respected organisation, but we have always been suspicious of them. Some people seem to fear them. On the other hand, they do a lot of charity work. We would rather not go to them directly." The inspector continued to outline a brilliant plan where they would be the main players. They seemed to have a very good idea of what was actually happening and who they were dealing with.

"But I also want to search for Andy, Andrea Sneddon, my daughter, my real daughter," said Tracy.

The inspector shot Tracy a strange look, seemed to be about to say something, and then stopped. It would not be necessary.

"First thing's first," said Lewin. "When Sky is safe, we will look for Andy..."

The information they would have would be very limited as the inspector explained. "We have to brief you both on what to do, but we cannot tell you anything about what we are looking for. You will just have to trust us, and we cannot guarantee that it will be without danger. But we will protect you as much as we can." They were to leave for Scotland within the day.

As the day wore on, Lewin became progressively more uncomfortable. "Tracy, is there any way I can persuade you not to come with me? I mean, there could be a lot of danger and... I know they asked both of us to go, but it could be that I can go by myself." He had been talking further with the police and had not liked what he was hearing.

From the expression on her face, he realised that it was useless to continue. She was obviously determined to come.

"I am coming," she said flatly. "What exactly are we going to do?"

"Well, we will tour Selkirk," he said. "We have been given a Mr. McPherson, who will take us in his car. We need a driver to show us where we would be going to; otherwise, we might take a lot of time by ourselves. He knows the area extremely well. I have also been in touch, of course, with the police in the area, who have been very well briefed on the case and, in turn, briefed me. In fact, Mr. McPherson is one of their top plain-clothes detectives, but we cannot make that obvious."

"But won't that make it more dangerous for Sky?" asked Tracy. "I mean, it should not be obvious that we are taking a policeman with us."

"As I was saying, it is not obvious at all. As far as anyone who checks is concerned, he is a driver who works for a car hire place. He actually does work there, as it provides an excellent cover for whoever he wants to be. No one on Earth will know he is more than just our driver and a bit of a tour guide," said Lewin.

"Maybe it is better then," said Tracy a little hesitantly. "I see this is a very big area. How are we going to find her?"

"Well, we at least have an area to search," said Lewin. "At least we have the message from the bird and the police seem to know much more than we do. We are going to a large country house mansion that takes in guests at a fairly high price. We have been asked to keep our eyes and ears open there. It may have links to this Headley Society. This afternoon, as you know, we take the ferry and then the train. That is how Sky went."

They did the trip in stormy rainy weather and were relieved when the got close to their destination.

"Do they ever have good weather in these parts?" asked Tracy as she and Lewin got off the train in Selkirk. The skies were grey and there was a steady drizzle that seemed to be permanently in place.

"This is not South Africa," said Lewin, "and the grey skies are responsible for the green grass and trees. You have to choose, bright blue or bright green."

They stood on the platform, which, though partially covered, seemed to let in the rain at all angles. A man of about sixty came up to them and introduced himself as Mr.

McPherson. "You would like a taxi, a car, a tour guide or a hotel?" he asked with a smile.

"Yes, we would, actually, all of these," said Lewin, marvelling at the casual request when everything had been prearranged. "But we would like to be in the country, but not too far from the city."

The man thought for a few minutes. "I think I know just the place for you," he said as he helped them put their cases in the car.

They got into the car, glad to be out of the rain. The car sped its way out the city.

After about a mile and a half the car turned into a side road.

This time the car reduced its speed as the road became a muddy dirt road, full of potholes and bumps.

They followed that road for a long time.

"We should soon be there," muttered Mr. McPherson. "In fact, even the sky is clearing. We shall be seeing some blue sky if we are lucky."

Anyone looking at the magnificent wrought iron gates and the high thick walls with at least three rows of evil-looking spikes on them might imagine all kinds of luxurious living behind them. What they would not imagine, however, was that the large stone mansion with its extensive grounds, known because of its size as the 'Country Palace' probably held a terrible secret.

Carved into the gate was a large thistle together with a

sword and a wine goblet.

On further investigation one might see armed gardeners working in the grounds, some not having the slightest talent for gardening.

There were many cars nestling comfortably in the large garages amongst the Mercedes, BMWs and the Vintage Rolls Royces. If one searched extra well, one could notice a helicopter hidden carefully in one of the massive sheds.

Between the garages and the house, one would see magnificent water fountains, some of them set in mirrors, which allowed the water to catch the sparkle of the sun. By night, these would be lighted by various coloured lights.

The fountains themselves would constantly change shape, at some points dying down only to be reawakened in a crystal cascade. These fountains were situated at various levels, running together by clear streams and bursting forth in sparkling waterfalls. Between them were borders of violets and pansies turning towards the sun to absorb its filtered rays.

Part of the house had been turned into a hotel, as Mr. McPherson had said, but this was a small, separate part of it. The house itself was large enough for a person to get lost in its labyrinth of rooms. Indeed, at this point it looked as if it had once been something like a luxury palace.

From the moment they had passed through the massive gates, it had seemed as if they were in a kind of wonderland. The fountains were lighted up with green, blue and red lights alternately shining on the spray. On the grounds were lanterns, lighting up fairy tale alcoves and caves.

They had stopped outside the magnificent, massive building and had been escorted very politely by a group of male and female servants who had carried their suitcases in for them.

They were welcomed at reception by a rather sombre looking gentleman who agreed to accommodate them at a price, a very considerable price.

They said goodbye to Mr. McPherson who returned to the city, arranging to meet them the next morning.

They were led across thick, luxurious carpets up a wide, winding, carpeted staircase to a corridor with about twenty suites leading off it. They surely must have crossed several floors Each of the suites was comfortable and magnificent.

They had hardly closed the door when one of the servants came in and announced that lunch would be served in half an hour. Would the couple like to get ready?

Tracy gave a gasp as they were led into the enormous dining room. It was unlike any hotel dining room they had ever seen. There was a long table, perhaps fifty metres long, laden with every delicacy they could imagine. It was definitely more like the banquet hall in a palace.

The chairs were beautifully carved with dark leather seats and high backs. As they walked towards their seats they were aware of their feet sinking into the rich Chinese carpet. What they were more aware of and what disturbed them a little was that there were only six other guests and these were seated at the other end of the table.

Of the food, there was no room for complaint, either, with regards to its presentation, its quality or its abundance. Were the really in a quiet village in Scotland or had they stumbled on the palace of a prince or a count, somewhere in Europe?

When they had eaten their meal they decided to look around and they were soon walking towards the steps and up and up and then down their corridor towards the landing along which they had come when they arrived. Their feet again sank deep into the soft pile of the carpet. As they went towards their room to rest, alongside the walls were pictures, many of them lighted from beneath to bring out their true beauty, and all of them classic originals.

"I am so tired," said Tracy. "To think we came so far to miss Sky. She has gone, and who knows if we can find her?" She was enveloped in a wave of helplessness.

"Sleep, Tracy," said Lewin. "It is important you get some rest. You can sleep till dinner time. Maybe after that you will be able to see things in a more positive way."

She needed little persuasion and the bed was particularly comfortable as she lay back into the luxurious pillows. Within a few minutes she was fast asleep. In the meanwhile, he would keep his eyes and ears open, and, what had they said, 'familiarise himself' with the place as much as he could. That was actually quite difficult because they had already seen that the hotel was quite cut off from the massive house. There was definitely something very strange about the place, and even about the staff.

Lewin, too, lay on the bed, and was about to tell himself that he, too, needed rest, when he heard a strange, eerie, whispering sound coming from the pipes around the washbasin.

The whispering stopped, only to be repeated a few seconds later. He was straining his ears to make out words. Eventually it stopped completely.

"It seemed like whispering from far away, from another world," said Lewin to himself. He had never believed in ghosts, but he had to admit it gave him a creepy feeling.

He listened for a long time, but nothing happened, and he, too, fell asleep.

Whine, whine, whine, humph.

Lewin came rushing over to the basin where the noises were coming from. He listened intently for several minutes as the noises came and went.

He started to blow down the basin plug hole, making all kinds of weird noises.

"Lewin what is that?" asked Tracy, waking up alarmed.

Lewin looked a little embarrassed that Tracy had heard.

"Nothing, Tracy," said Lewin. "I think it is just the pipes."

"Maybe we should bang on the pipe," said Tracy. "Then it might stop. This is a good hotel. We can't have wailing pipes."

"That's good idea, but where are the pipes?"

"Maybe in this sort of cupboard underneath the basin,"

said Tracy.

Lewin bent and opened the double doors. It was pitch dark, and he felt around for the pipes.

"Nothing here," he said. "There are no pipes at all." He shut the cupboard in disgust. "It isn't even a proper cupboard."

"But there must be pipes," said Tracy. "There are always pipes in these sorts of cupboards. That's what they are there for, to cover over all the plumbing." She was now completely awake.

She got out of bed and pulled the doors open to reveal, as Lewin had discovered, a black hole. Except for the base, she could not even feel the shelves.

"That's strange," said Lewin, searching his medical bag for a torch. He shone the light into the cupboard, and then all around it.

The cupboard led directly into the wall between themselves and the room next door. There was a small ledge at the base to give the impression of a cupboard, but this seemed to lead simply onto nothing. There was an opposing wall made of rough spider-webbed bricks about two feet away. However, he at last found the pipes that were running, neatly, to the right of the far wall.

There were no sides or roof to the strange cupboard. In fact, when Lewin shone his torch upwards, it seemed that they were not far beneath the vast roof of the building.

Lewin leaned over the edge of the base and shone his

torch downwards. It was definitely leading into a space between the two walls, but it seemed to run down, down, down towards the bottom of the building.

"Amazing," he said, bringing his head back into the room and allowing Tracy to look around. "I think we should find out if all the cupboards lead into a space like this. I think I saw an empty room next door. I mean, there are hardly any guests in this place."

He went inside and immediately realised that the basin was on the opposite side of the room. There was no way it could lead into theirs.

Lewin went back to their room and slumped back onto the bed. He lay, half dozing, thinking of the position they were in. How would they ever find Sky? Plus, after that, how would they ever find Andy? Why were they placed specifically here? Why did they have to keep their eyes and ears open? There was hardly anyone here. At the rate they were charged, he could somehow understand this. He began to doze off...

Whimper, whine whine humph, whirr.

There were the noises again! Lewin ran over to the basin. The noises were definitely coming from that direction.

He opened the cupboard doors. The noises became significantly louder, perhaps three times as loud.

He fetched the torch again and leant his chest on the base of the cupboard, leaning over on the sides. The noises seemed to be coming from the bowels of the house, somewhere on his left, away from the wing that was their luxury accommodation. The noises had stopped but he decided to respond, producing a series of realistic animal noises, some of which he had practised since he was a child.

"I see you have learnt several languages from your patients," said Tracy, in a sleepy voice.

Lewin was just busy meowing like a pitiful cat when he heard someone far beneath him on the other side.

"Kitty, kitty, time for supper, come kitty."

He started to purr and the voice, a very normal-sounding woman's voice, came again.

"Kitty, kitty, nice kitty, come here kitty."

Well, he would try to speak to her.

"Excuse me," he said, as politely as he could whilst he was shouting. "Excuse me, can you help me?"

He heard something drop. He had certainly startled her. He wondered who she was. Was she one of the servants? Would she report that she had heard a 'cat' speaking to her?

He started to laugh and, as he pulled his head back into the room and closed the door, he was laughing so much he could hardly control himself.

"Hey, what's the joke?" asked Tracy, a little indignantly. "Are you laughing at yourself from all the strange noises you have been making?"

"No, oh no," said Lewin. "Someone was calling the cat, and then I called the person. It was a lady."

"You did what?" asked Tracy.

Lewin told her what had happened.

"I want to look downstairs," said Tracy. "One feels so cut off over here. At least we have some contact with the rest of the house that way. Maybe if we get there, we can find something out here."

"Maybe," said Lewin. He had already switched on the torch and was looking down, down into the base of the house.

"That's interesting," he said. "That's really interesting."

"What is?" asked Tracy, curious.

"Well," said Lewin. "I have spent a lot of time looking out of the windows and, unless I am really mistaken, this passage or opening or shaft or whatever it is, goes way below ground level. We really must be looking into the cellar, or maybe even the dungeons." He shuddered. "I want to go down there. I want to go down and investigate. I will take you down the normal stairs later, but I will go down this way now."

"Are you crazy?" asked Tracy. "What do you think you will find down there?"

"I don't know," said Lewin, "but I feel we are doing nothing over here. That way, we will at least be doing something."

"But it's a sheer drop," said Tracy.

Lewin once more shone the torch down the shaft. "Hey, wait a minute," he said. "We could go down there. There are sort of metal spikes along the wall. Do you think they would hold me?"

Tracy peered over his shoulder at them.

"I hope so," she said, "and it isn't a sheer drop; there are all kinds of places you could get stuck on, lots of wood, planks, pipes and things. You wouldn't drop straight down."

Lewin liked the idea more and more. The purpose, he was not sure about, but they had been asked to explore, and they might be able to find out all kinds of things.

Within minutes, Lewin was balancing on three spikes just below the level of the bathroom cupboard. He seemed to be perfectly at ease as he began to descend slowly towards the basement of the house.

Tracy leaned over and watched him as he felt with his foot each time for the spikes beneath him.

Everything was an eerie quiet around them, everything, that is, except for the sound of running water far, far beneath them.

"Do you think there is a moat?" asked Tracy uneasily. "I mean, will you land up in some water?"

"No, I don't," said Lewin. "This isn't a castle. It sounds more like someone running a bath, or, rather, a swimming pool. Tracy, if I take a long time, don't worry. If there is anywhere to go way below ground. If I can find doors leading to anywhere, I am going through."

"But Lewin..."

"We were told to find out as much as we could. I love you," he added.

"I love you, too. Please be careful," she said.

He climbed as quietly as he could, down, down, down. The sound of running water became louder and more definite.

Yes, it was from a tap, from a few taps. They seemed to be fairly close to Lewin. He had passed several places where there seemed to be exits or entrances into the shaft through cupboard doors such as theirs, but he had ignored these, choosing to descend as far as possible. Perhaps these could be explored later.

Lewin was beginning to wonder if he would arrive anywhere at all, when he saw a door with a fanlight that he peeped through. The sound of running water was becoming louder and louder. He could not see through it very well as it was caked with dust.

Lewin moved carefully, eventually being able to see through the ventilation slats.

From here he could see into an enormous kitchen, a strange mixture of the old and the modern. There was a massive, solid oven, probably run on coal. Not far away from it were three large microwave ovens, almost commercial size.

It was now obvious where the running water was coming from. There were two large sinks and at each a man was washing a mass of dishes. How many guests and servants *did* live in this house? They had been convinced there were not many guests at this time.

He watched, fascinated, as the men rinsed one dish after another. They were both whistling different tunes, but these could hardly be heard over the sound of the water running into the steel sink.

Lewin suddenly noticed a door further beneath them and

to their right. He was about to go to it when it opened and a woman came out, wiping her hands on her turquoise floral apron.

She looked around her, and Lewin had a few anxious moments until she found what she was looking for, a large broom, standing next to the door she had opened, which was then hidden by the door.

She pulled it in and slammed the door shut. Possibly, she thought, the whole thing was a broom cupboard, nobody having ever realised there was a whole shaft above.

That's interesting, thought Lewin. *It shut, but it doesn't sound as though it was locked.*

Though there were people there the water was making such a loud noise, no one would hear him moving around and he was here, anyway. He just wanted to see basically if there was a way of moving around the house more freely.

He did a few contortions and was soon beside the door. He pushed it slowly. It was not locked. He pushed it a little further. He had to be careful. Well, he was being careful, but he wanted just one look. He pushed the door further and slowly pushed it open.

From the below ground level, the kitchen looked even larger. The water was still running and the two men were busy washing the dishes.

From somewhere a woman's voice was calling. Perhaps it was the woman with the turquoise flowered apron.

At that moment one of the servants who was washing

dishes switched off the tap and started to flick the water from his hands. This was the time to leave, before he turned around. He went through the door and it closed quietly behind him. He would have to try during the night when these people were no longer working.

Lewin remained at this level of the shaft for a few more seconds, waiting to hear if anyone was coming after him, and then he started to climb up towards their room. He hoped he would find the right one. Hopefully, Tracy would be waiting for him and would make some indication for him. He started to ascend the shaft and, halfway through, called softly to her. She did not answer, and he proceeded to go higher until he noticed another entrance right opposite him. He noticed that the wood of the small door was of an excellent quality and was highly polished. He opened it slowly and found himself in an elegantly furnished room with many books surrounding the walls.

It was obviously a library or a study or something, but he saw that the room was locked and the dust around the door frame seemed to indicate that no one had come this way for several months. He was quite sure they would not use his way of entry. He looked around at the books and was surprised to find several books in Afrikaans, a language only spoken in South Africa. Most of them were law or accounting books. Had a South African guest been here and left his study books here? It was a very strange find in a fairly deserted region of Scotland.

He continued to walk around the enormous study, inspecting the beautifully bound books and works of art and the antique furniture. Some of the books were in another foreign language, probably Spanish or Portuguese.

"Not bad," said Lewin to himself as he wondered if the library was open to the guests.

He went back through the magnificent small door, which was on the other side part of a book cupboard and started to climb up.

He saw Tracy leaning over somewhat anxiously and shortly afterwards they were back in the room, lying on the bed.

What an exhausting but interesting adventure he felt, as he shared the experience with Tracy. However, he realised that he had not really found out anything, not that he knew what he was really looking for.

"This is so odd," said Tracy when he got back. "I mean, why are we here? What is here? Why do they just tell us to keep our eyes and ears open and not give any indication at all as to what we are supposed to look for? It is so strange. I mean, Mr. McPherson speaks a lot to us, but he never really says anything. I keep thinking the police know what they are doing, but we are just players in a large performance. They even said as such."

"Well, what I did now… I feel like a real player. In fact, I am quite stiff."

"Do you think the police have an idea where Sky actually

is?" asked Tracy.

"Well, the words 'Silk' and 'Head' definitely had a strong meaning to the police, especially after they had consulted with other departments. They seemed to understand immediately and get into action. It was not that much later that they arranged for us to come here as guests. This is not a real hotel. It can't be. There is something very strange over here, and I think that maybe we are preparing for the grand finale. As long as the play has a happy ending," said Lewin fervently.

Sometime during the night, a violent storm came up, which woke Tracy.

She looked out of the window. All that could be seen was the rain lashing against it. Vaguely she could make out large, angry shadows of trees being hurled around by the wind, trying desperately, as it were, to cling to the security of the ground.

"I am going down there," said Lewin, waking as he heard her. "No one will hear me in this storm."

"No," said Tracy. "No, how can you?"

"Tracy, we have to find Sky, and this place has something to do with her disappearance. We know that for certain. The police brought us here. Though we have had wonderful food and accommodation, the police brought us here for a purpose."

"All right," she said." I can't come with you?"

"Definitely not," he said. "I will be operating in the dark, mostly just so as not to be seen. Two of us would make the risks twice or probably four times as much."

"How long will you be?" she asked.

"This is Mr. McPherson's emergency number. If I am not back in three hours, call it somehow. But he is coming early in the morning, anyway, to continue our tour of this area, so you can tell him then. But, Tracy," said Lewin, as he saw her anxious expression. "I will be back. Don't worry. But, again, give me time, because I have to wait till the coast is clear."

At that moment, there was a brighter than usual flash of lightning.

"At least you will have some light," she said.

"That kitchen is well below ground level," he said. "I don't there is any way the lightning will make a difference."

"How far?" she asked.

"Well, like a second or third basement of a building. Don't worry. It is just seen as a broom cupboard. The woman down there has no idea the ceiling of that cupboard virtually goes on forever. If they find me, I will have hidden in the broom cupboard, and I am a legal guest. Maybe I got very hungry at 2:30 a.m. and made my way to the kitchen."

"All right," she said. "If I don't find you, I can wake someone up and say you went to the kitchen to see if you could get a sandwich, and you had not come back."

"Good," he said. "Please get some sleep. Don't wait up for me. You need your sleep for tomorrow."

Despite her resolutions to the contrary she quickly fell

back to sleep, hardly conscious of the heavy storm outside.

Lewin shone the torch downwards and then switched it onto a setting where he could put it on with a light touch of his finger. It clipped on to his top pocket, which made it easy to carry. He needed both hands and both feet to be able to carry on down the shaft. Thank goodness he had checked before that all the iron 'steps' were there. Nevertheless he got a fright when his foot suddenly slipped. He must concentrate on what he was doing. He did not want to land in the far distant broom cupboard,

He stopped beside the library entrance and could feel the wood panelling. There was no light there and no real need to go there.

He went down steadily, noting from his position that he had no idea what was happening or what had happened with the storm.

As he felt he was nearing the bottom of the shaft he switched on the torch glad that he had done so because there was a commercial size vacuum cleaner blocking most of the 'broom cupboard'. He was glad that there was enough space for him to stand on the ground at a tight squeeze and he saw with a bit of manoeuvring with the vacuum cleaner and the brooms he could be by the door. He hoped it was not locked, but then, who would lock a broom cupboard?

Wow! There was less space than he had thought but soon he was out of the cupboard and in the large kitchen. There was, as he expected, no one there, but there was a fire on in the large stove and this gave him some kind of minimum light, so that he did not have to use his torch as much as he had expected to.

However, the kitchen was not his real destination. The staff obviously did not work at this hour, but he began to wonder what time they started in the morning. He knew that bakers back home often started at 4 a.m., or even 3 a.m. He would have to be careful.

There was no one in the large kitchen and he flashed his torch around the walls, seeing a large closed door. As he went over to it he saw that it was locked; bolted, in fact, but then the bolt was on his side of the door so obviously it was the kitchen that was locked. Quickly he realised that there must then be another door because who could bolt something from the inside and how would they then get out.

He found a double door, which, to his surprise, was actually unlocked. Then perhaps the other door somehow led outside. But that was not important at the moment. He was in the actual mansion, right at the basement.

However, it did not look like a basement. As he walked through the door, he saw that there was a small lantern-like light burning, which helped a lot in his search.

He gave a gasp. If the rooms upstairs had been luxurious, these rooms were the epitome of luxury.

He walked into a hall-like room again dimly lighted by two electric lanterns and here was a large table, similar to the one above surrounded by ornate priceless luxurious chairs that were built both for comfort and efficiency. This table was not only for eating. To the side of each place at the table was a small deep drawer with all kinds of sophisticated equipment, mostly recording and possibly translation equipment. There was also a small compact computer screens of the size used in aeroplanes. When replaced in the drawer, you would not really be aware that anything was there as all this was in a compartment at the back. At the front compartment of each drawer was a serviette ring with a few beautifully designed serviettes. There was also a menu and a small notebook and expensive Swiss pen. In fact, Lewin realised. You would not notice the electronic equipment unless you pulled the draw out quite far. The draw opened easily up to one point and then had to be manoeuvred slightly to see the rest of it. By some chance he had pulled it open all the way at one go. However, if he had been sitting at the table he would definitely done this more gently, and possibly missed it.

He went to the head of the table and noticed a larger drawer, which was locked. Well, he could do nothing about that, but he did discover that, indeed, several of the drawers were actually locked. He wondered what this was all about.

There was a strange coat of arms magnificently decorating the wall. However, as he looked at it he realised it had something very sinister about it, almost something evil, yet magnificent. He put the torch on it for several minutes trying to work out what it was about it that was both regal and terrifying, but he gave up holding the memory of the image in his mind. He shuddered as he continued his way around the room. There were ornate cupboards similar to sideboards, several of them around the room. He wondered what they held. He tried all the doors but without success.

There seemed to be nothing more of interest in this room that he could actually get to and he went through a door, noting he had entered some sort of computer room with at least ten very modern computers placed conveniently in front of chairs for anyone who might want to use them. He wondered if they were for the guests, but quickly dismissed the thought.

There was something about the computer that put across a strong sense of a successful business and the room he had just emerged from would be the board room. However, why was the business several floors beneath the mansion?

He was struck by the presence of the Coat of Arms he had seen in the boardroom, which seemed to cover the whole wall. It had been beautifully carved. He noticed that the computers had, in the corner of the box, a tiny, similar crest to the one in the boardroom. He wondered about the significance and if it had any reference to a Headley Society.

As he approached the computer, he suddenly had a daring idea. Knowing that it could be an extremely unwise thing to do, he switched it on.

He gave a gasp as it sprang to life and he was looking at active screen. His hopes were dashed, however, by a request for a password. He knew that some of the Windows programmes could bypass a password but he found this to be impossible. Well he had better forget about it and switch off the machine.

He typed in a few jumbled letters, but the computer would not let him in. Well, he shouldn't really be looking, should he?

He used all kinds of combinations of passwords and then typed in 'Headley'. It did not work. Then again, all these people would not have the same passwords. He experimented with various numbers after the Headley and was about to give up when the 'Headley 77' suddenly opened up the computer. He was startled and a little nervous. Suddenly, there was a flash from somewhere above him.

The screen became black and, almost relieved, he slipped out of the room. He was somewhat disappointed and then elated as he realised that he had just somehow proved that the Headley Society was real and that it did have connections with the mansion.

Knowing that the kitchen staff would be coming right away for their early shift, he quickly ascended the stairs.

CHAPTER 13

Mr. McPherson fetched them the next morning arriving at the mansion at about 10 a.m. as arranged. Lewin and Tracy had been treated to a magnificent breakfast and at this stage realised that there were at least twenty other guests living in the hotel part of the mansion, probably on a different floor. As soon as they got outside, they realised that the weather had become quite treacherous. They were able to get into the car without getting wet, however, as it could drive into a covered area.

"Have you anything to tell me?" he asked, as they got into the car.

Lewin proceeded to tell him what he could, and he nodded giving no indication of the importance or otherwise of these discoveries.

Mr. McPherson had with him a map that listed all the houses in the area, including a rough idea of their sizes. "We are here, down this road over here."

"Hey, this is such an interesting map; it tells you all about the houses on the way. I never even knew such a map existed!" said Lewin, looking at it closely.

"Police," said Mr. McPherson quietly. "It's from the council records."

"I think we are coming to something," he said.

Tracy and Lewin looked at him in surprise, because the gates they drove up to were broken and discoloured. The paths were overgrown, the fountains rusted, and their stones fallen. It was first Lewin and then Tracy who saw that there was something extremely familiar about the gates and later the garden and the house. Everything was exactly similar to the house they had been staying in, even the pattern on the gates.

"We will all look around here," said Mr. McPherson, who seemed to be very aware of where he was. "This is another house associated with the Headley Society, but this one is a mystery. It seems to be totally deserted, yet there are comings and goings that we have been trying to monitor and have not been able to fathom. Perhaps you can help us here. Tell me if there is anything familiar about it."

"It is the same as the other one," said both Tracy and Lewin together.

Mr. McPherson simply smiled.

They arrived at the house and this, too, had a deserted look. Some of the panes of glass were broken and in disrepair.

The door was the same, solid oak, but that too, was not shiny as they remembered the other one and there was varnish peeling off from the bottom of it.

It opened easily without a key and both Lewin and Tracy gave a gasp. This house had not been lived in for several years, of that they could be sure, yet here were the steps leading up to the bedrooms. Here was the magnificent dining room with the long massive table and the tall, high-backed velvet chairs. However, the velvet had spoilt with the years of dust and the chairs themselves were caked with dust and dirt.

Lewin could even write his name in the thick dust on the table. It was as though they had gone back or even forward half a century or more in time. What was this all about?

This was not from a few days. It was from a few years, perhaps many years, confirmed by two large spider webs stretching from broken light fittings to the dust coated sideboard. Spiders did not do that in a matter of days especially as there was no spider to be seen and the web itself was filled with dust.

By no stretch of imagination could anyone have presumed that people had been living there in the last few years. Yet, Mr. McPherson spoke about strange movements in the grounds.

Totally confused, they climbed the stairs, stairs, which were caked with dirt and grime. The stairs in their hotel had been carpeted, hadn't they? They looked around for evidence of the carpeting being removed but there was none. These stairs had never been carpeted, Tracy was sure.

The upper floors of the house were in an even worse condition. The cobwebs were enormous. However, there was the rooms with the same brass door handles, but, whereas, they had been gleaming and shiny, they were green with age. The rooms were entirely empty of furniture and here too, there were no carpets and no signs that there had ever been carpets.

They went from room to room recognising things, yet, at the same time, being aware that many years had passed since anyone had been there.

"I feel that maybe we are back in our hotel and we slept for a hundred years without noticing it," said Lewin quietly.

The policeman looked at him seriously.

"This is definitely a duplicate of the place," said Lewin, "but the other was new, luxurious, sparkling and alive."

"I must admit it is very similar, but it is not the same." said Mr. McPherson as they walked around.

"But it is," said Lewin. "I remember the passages, the furniture, and the curtains. This is just like the other place. I am sure that the same person designed the two places and made them exactly alike. I remembered exactly where we had to go to the dining room. I remembered the chandelier in the hallway. There was that little alcove that we moved to when the men were coming to fetch us for supper. This is not just chance. This is an older version of exactly the same house. Or the other one was renovated and this one just left alone. I wonder why. And, though I am a vet, I know a little bit about architecture, and I see that the new house has been renovated very recently and, up till six months ago, must have looked very much like the first one. If we had time, we could probably look up the history of these houses. They are identical and fairly close to each other. They must have, at one time, been built by the same person and belonged to the same family. There is a chance they might have been sold together and belonged to the same person or group of persons."

"The records are known to us. Two different private people own them, but then maybe they are both members of this group."

"The Headley Society," said Tracy. She was not sure she really understood, but she was willing to follow Lewin's logic. They did not comment on her observation.

.They entered the room that seemed to be in the same position as the one they had occupied in the luxurious mansion hotel and at this point they realised that Mr. McPherson was no longer with them and this increased their sense of the eeriness of the place The room was empty but there was the washbasin with the cupboard beneath it that Lewin had found. Lewin slowly opened the cupboard door and, even as he opened it, he was aware that this was the same cupboard with the same gaping hole behind, except for the pipes; whereas the others had been had been bright and shiny, these were rusted and discoloured.

"I am going down here," whispered Lewin, making sure he was speaking far from the cavity.

"Lewin," she said in alarm. "Lewin, you can't do that. Lewin, please don't leave me here. This isn't the same. This place is frightening. Please don't go there."

"Let me try it out," said Lewin. "If there is anything alive in this house, apart from rats and spiders," he said, noting her look of horror. "If there is anything alive in this house, this is the only way to get to it."

He started to climb down, thankful that the rails were holding out. After some time he realised that his feet were near the end of the tunnel where the ancient kitchen should be. He entered expectantly and to his disappointment he saw immediately that no one could have been here for many years. He looked around further. He went out into a courtyard, but this, too, was derelict with age He realised that this was, of course, at ground level and not, as in the first house, quite far below. He should also look at ground level for a stairway or even a trap door to the extensive cellars that must be there. He searched for some kind of door, some kind of entrance, which would lead him to another part of the house without any success. He looked at his watch, noting rather guiltily that he had been away for over an hour. He hoped Tracy was all right.

He climbed back to the room they had been in, only to find to his horror that Tracy was not there. Perhaps she had felt claustrophobic and gone down stairs, but there was no sign of her at all.

Feeling very uneasy, he decided to investigate if there was any chance that she had gone down the pipes behind him and was somehow downstairs in the kitchen.

Oh why had he left her? She had not been happy to be left behind, and she had been afraid, very afraid to be all alone in a room with absolutely nothing in it except some cobwebs and layers of dust and grime.

She must have gone somewhere else, somewhere more comfortable. But then nowhere in this deserted mansion was there any area of comfort, at least, not that he had seen.

What would he have done in a similar position? Well, he would not have stood in the room for an hour. He would have at least done some kind of investigation of his own, even minor ones. Surely she must be in one of the other rooms, gaining information about the place, and the mansion certainly did have many rooms, as did the duplicate hotel.

True, the mansion was what might call 'scary' but it was in fact seemingly no more than an old, deserted, dilapidated country mansion. Why should anyone be afraid?

He made his way quietly into the other rooms, becoming confused as to whether he had actually started off in the correct room. Was that room really the one that corresponded to the room they had stayed in in the modern, luxurious duplicate mansion hotel?

As he went from room to room and from floor to floor, he had a sense of not being alone. But he was alone, and there was no reason for him to feel this way.

He stopped and strained his ears listening for some sign of life.

No, it wasn't any sound that made him uneasy and as if he was not alone. He felt as if he was being watched, as if someone's eyes were following his every move.

Shaking off this feeling as best he could, he went systematically from room to room checking to see that Tracy was not there.

One room in particular made him feel that someone was watching him and he found himself exiting rather quickly, grateful that there was, in fact, no one to witness his moment of fear.

He shook his head as if to take away the unwelcome thoughts and thought he heard a footstep somewhere along the passage.

Telling himself that the mansion could not possibly be haunted and that anyway he did not believe in ghosts, he continued his search of the rooms. Obviously the footstep he had heard had been an echo of his own, taken on by some nearby loose floorboard.

From the grimy cracked windows he could see that the weather was deteriorating again and tall trees swayed in the wind starting to brush and beat against the windows. He felt grateful for this noise which had a normal explanation. At least he would not imagine he was hearing footsteps.

He went speedily past the rest of the rooms , opening the doors as he went. There was nothing inside any of them.

Perhaps Tracy had gone downstairs. Once more he was in the magnificent dining room with the long massive table and the high tall backed tattered velvet chairs.

There was no sign of Tracy anywhere. He spent some time on this floor, searching for her, realizing that he was becoming very anxious and uneasy.

This wasn't just an abandoned, deserted mansion. It had been made quite clear to both of them that this was a dangerous and evil place.

He shuddered, fear for what had happened to Tracy suddenly overwhelming him. The spider webs stretching across the broken light fittings somehow made everything more sinister. But wait, perhaps she had followed him down the shaft behind the sink. Yes, that would have been her most obvious move.

He ran up the broken staircase and looked down the shaft. Where was Tracy? Had she really gone down there?

He descended the shaft as fast as he could finding himself once more on ground level. There must be something here, or rather someone here. He thought that Tracy must have been here but there was no sign of her. Perhaps she had gone outside. Perhaps she had needed fresh air and had gone outside into the gardens, but no one could have stayed outside in such a storm, which was, in fact beginning to abate. Tracy would have come inside again as soon as it started.

He walked frantically around the deserted kitchens and then the dripping gardens. No, she could not be there.

He went back to the cupboard and looked up at the shaft, searching high above towards the room he had left her in, and from where he had come.

He was staring up the shaft almost as if in a dream when he suddenly became aware of a tiny shaft of light. But then it disappeared again. It was surely his imagination. But then everything had to be followed up. He was not a person to panic easily but he realized he was close to desperation. But there, again was the tiny shaft of light which as quickly disappeared. But now he had climbed up to the spot where he had seen it and his pulse quickened.

He saw the tiny crack of light, which he had noticed before, shining from a panel in the wall. As he put his ear onto it he could hear voices, the voices of two women and a young girl. He recognised Tracy's voice and breathed a sigh of relief and quietly he knocked at the panel. It was quickly opened for him and he looked through in amazement as he saw a golden haired child who just had to be Sky, Tracy, was with a woman lying on the floor who was looking decidedly ill. She was obviously trying to help her.

He gave Sky a delighted smile, and she returned it. Without delay, he was put into the picture. The inside of the deserted house had, fixed in the centre, a sturdy, invincible structure, unnoticeable from the outside.

Sky had been held prisoner under the care of the woman on the floor, who seemed to have suffered some kind of cardiac emergency. The woman had been terrified when she had seen Tracy, but quickly mollified when Sky explained she was a nurse as she realised she needed urgent medical help. With only a brief but intense hug for her adopted daughter,

Tracy had attended to the woman who seemed to be recovering, but was in terrible pain. Lewin bent down to help, between them stabilising her as much as possible.

"You need to go to a hospital as soon as possible," said Lewin.

The woman could hardly speak, but indicated that Mr. Eastway would not allow it.

"Who is Mr. Eastway?" asked Lewin.

She glanced nervously at the door, and Lewin followed her glance. He had also noticed some steps going upwards, and he nodded to Tracy and Sky.

"I don't think this is very safe," said Lewin quietly. "I mean, if anyone had to come along now, we might be in an awful lot of trouble."

As if in response, there was the sound of a door opening and of footsteps walking swiftly in their direction.

Tracy, Lewin and Sky seemed to have the same idea at once and they fled silently towards the staircase.

Tracy and Sky went straight up to the next floor, but Lewin ran up a few steps and stopped to wait and watch what the man would do. He walked straight past the stairs not even glancing upwards. Lewin got a good look at his face and a shudder went through him. Never in his life had he seen a face so evil. Ugly? No, definitely not. In fact, the man by any usual standards was so-called good looking. It was his eyes that seemed to host dark shadows, and his mouth, which had a rigidity that was terrifying.

Lewin shuddered, instinctively knowing that, if this was the kind of person they were up against, they would have to be extremely cautious.

He saw that the woman was ill and that Sky had disappeared and with a growl he noticed that the panel was open. Swiftly he climbed up the pipes to find the child.

Meanwhile Tracy, Lewin and Sky had found refuge in a small room far to one corner of the house. Judging by the layers of dust no one seemed ever to go there and they sat down on the dusty floor, whispering to each other.

It was the wrong choice however, and within ten minutes the man had found them. He had a gun, a sub-machine gun in his hand. Again, Lewin felt the deadly power of his eyes as he heard Tracy speak.

"You were driving a red car," she said. "I will never forget your eyes. It was you who pushed me off the road!"

The man gave a short laugh. "I must say that you are worse than a cat. A cat has nine lives. You have had far more. Our organisation has had you on our hit list for years. Then, of course, you disappeared. But here you are; what a surprise!" he ended sarcastically. "Your ex-husband betrayed us, and for that he must die, you must die, and the girl must die. And you, Doctor, you will have to think about things and, eventually, you will die, too. But I will leave you together a little longer. I am sure there are many things you want to say to each other, a united family in their last moments."

With that, he locked the door, leaving them together.

"Tracy, Mum, I have to tell you something," said Sky, raising her light blue eyes towards her. She had a strange expression. She, too, obviously realised how close to death they all were. "Tracy, please don't be cross with me. I have to tell you something. I know that this is dangerous and that we might never get out of here, and I feel you must know the truth." Her eyes seemed to reflect pools of hidden emotion, and... was it fear?

"The truth about what?" asked Tracy gently.

"About Andy," said Sky. "I didn't tell you the truth about Andy."

Both Lewin and Tracy were silent as they nodded for her to go on. Tracy's heart began to beat fast. Sky looked so much like...

"You see, we don't have to look for Andy. I mean..."

Slowly, Sky uncovered her forearm to reveal a triangular birthmark, and then she pushed her sleeve up a little further. There, just below her elbow was the tell-tale burn mark where the iron had scalded her.

"I am Andy," she said simply. "I could not believe that I had a mother out there, so I gave you my name, Sky. People call me Sky because of the colour of my eyes. I thought you had died. Dad told me you had died. But you described me exactly. You had the marks. You even had my correct birthday. I had to keep contact with you because maybe my mother hadn't died. Maybe you were my mother. I wanted to write to you, to be close to you, whilst I made my own investigation. I started to ask more and more questions, and my father kept insisting you were dead. But, one day, my father let slip something that made me realise that you were not dead, but that you had been so badly injured that you were in a coma and would never wake up, and that, as far as he knew, maybe you were dead by now. I asked if there was any chance you would be able to talk, and he said 'definitely not. She would never know or recognise you. She probably isn't even alive'.

"I tried to find out how to get in touch with the family, but he wouldn't tell me. But I knew, didn't I? I had been writing to you all along. But, on principle, I kept on asking. One day, after I had asked for about the tenth time, he mentioned that you..."

However, she could not complete her sentence as Tracy swept her into her arms and covered her hair with kisses. "Somewhere, I must have known this. How could I not have seen this? The way you wrote, how could I not have recognised that it was my own daughter?"

Tracy was flabbergasted. All this time, she had been listening to and corresponding with... her own child. Sky had known all along who she was, or, at least, after some time she had become convinced who she was, but she had never told her.

"And you look so much like my beautiful little Andy looked. Though your hair has lost some if it's curl, I must admit." Half laughing, half crying, she held the child close to herself. "My darling, I am just so happy, happier than I have ever been. I have found you, my darling."

"Mum," said Andy. "Mum, I thought you were dead."

Lewin was finding it hard to keep back the tears and he, too, was both laughing and crying. "This is a great day," he said, "a very great day for all of us. Here we are a united family. And," he continued soberly, "if we don't think of something, we are all, heaven forbid, about to leave this planet as a united family."

"No!" exclaimed Sky and Tracy together.

It was obviously getting darker outside. The light no longer penetrated the cracks in the blinds and the distant noises were changing.

"Sky, would you like to tell us what happened? After all, we have many years to catch up," said Tracy. "And, also, shall I call you Sky or Andy?"

"My name is Andrea, as, of course, you know, but I have always loved the name Sky. It was a sort of fairytale name that someone called me because of my eyes, and I would call myself that in my dreams. You know everything about me, Mum. We have been corresponding for ages, and I know all about you and Lewin, and about Pamela, Peter, Percy, Dassen, Priscilla and Peggy. I have never seen a penguin. We don't get penguins here."

"When did you know you were in danger, that something was wrong?" asked Tracy.

"How did it start?" echoed Lewin, who, up to this point,

had been very quiet.

"Well, I suppose it was when Dad met Melissa. I think she and her family were all mixed up in this. I think they used to fight about it. I would hear them. They were into some money scheme that Dad had been involved with in South Africa. But this seemed to be almost criminal. The family would also come to visit and have their meetings in the study. I could hear what they were talking about. One day, her brother caught me listening behind the door. I know I shouldn't have been listening, but then he tested it himself to see if I could hear anything and realised I had heard a whole lot. But I didn't realise then that it was dangerous. My father had bought me a computer, a really nice one, not anything like his, but a strong one, and he got me a connection to the Internet. I had a nanny at the time who was a part-time student at a university. She was the best nanny I ever had. She taught me a lot about all the programmes, email and downloading stuff, and, at night, I used to spend time on the computer I used to email all my friends who had computers. My father didn't mind, because, in this way, I was out of his hair and I didn't get involved in what all his friends were doing, at least, not at that point. And, that way, I was able to surf the internet as I wanted. I eventually got into Towermail and joined them. She helped me get it from my pocket money with her credit card. She put in a lot so I would not have a problem trying to get money into it later, and then, one day, I saw your message. My, father, as I said, had told me all about you and shown me photographs, and I had thought you were dead. He had said so, very often."

"Heaven forbid," said Lewin. "Then what would I have done?"

"But," continued Sky, "the nanny left before her exams were due, and the next nanny knew nothing about computers. And now... Mummy, are we all going to die?" Sky put her arms around her. "At least we can all die together."

"Heaven forbid," said Lewin again.

"My father is also here somewhere," said Sky, looking at her mother a little uncertainly. "I mean, I think he is in danger. They are holding him and trying to make him talk, but he won't do that, I know. But maybe he will because they have been threatening to hurt me."

"He is here, Andrew?" asked Lewin.

"He is known in Ireland as Anthony Sheldon, but his name is Andrew, I think," said Sky. "I think I know where to find him, but I wasn't allowed to go to him at all."

"Where is he, Sky?" asked Lewin. "Where would I find him?"

"Well, it is a few floors below us," said Sky.

"How are we going to get there?" asked Tracy.

"There are stairs," she said. "They lead into a sort of lounge."

"How do we find them?" asked Lewin.

Sky frowned. "You know, I was there, but I am not sure exactly how I got there. I was taken there to see my father, but

I remember being very sleepy and not really watching or aware of where I was going. After I spoke to him I was taken up here again. I suppose I just went down, and then upstairs back here."

Lewin had begun to look more carefully around the room, trying to find an entrance through the floor or behind the walls. He put his head in his hands and tried to think.

Well, he had come into the room in an unusual way so he would do the same thing again and get out that way.

"See you soon," he said. "I have to go. I have to follow this through. Besides finding Andrew, we actually need to get out of here. Sky, you obviously did not come in this way. You would definitely have remembered it." He showed her the shaft, and she gasped.

"No, but can I come with you?" she asked.

"As soon as I know how it all works, you and your mother can come with me, but I have to find out where I am exactly. Andy, Sky, tell me first, though. Do you think that your father is on ground floor or below ground floor?"

"Below ground floor," she said. "Definitely."

"Thank you," he said, and waved to her as he went up.

"It is downwards, not up," she said.

"I know, Sky," he said. "But I have to go up first and find another way down, further down." With that, he was gone.

The woman with them was terrified.

"We are all going to die," she said, "all going to die. I know Mr. Headley Eastway, and we are all going to die. He won't tolerate this. He never tolerates anything. No one dares oppose him, and I did nothing, did I? I just obeyed him. I don't know where you people came from. I just had to get the girl. Where did you people come from? What are you doing here?" She continued to wail, forgetting that Tracy and Lewin had probably saved her life.

Lewin climbed up the shaft, aware that he was breathing in an unacceptable amount of dust. This shaft had obviously not been used often, probably not for years, even for decades.

He climbed up until he came back to the room, which matched his bedroom in the hotel. But did it match? That was something he had to find out about.

As he reached the top and got into the dirty dusty room he tried to imagine their luxurious accommodation and put it in this context.

No, he would have to go to the top of the ancient stairways and go on from there. He tried to imagine that he was walking on the plush carpet, his feet sinking into the generous pile.

In doing this, he nearly tripped over a loose tile in the present house, and quickly pulled himself back. Now, how did they reach their bedroom?

He had noted the room he had just come out of but on further thinking he realised that the suite they enjoyed in the hotel was, in fact, two along from this one. They had just not realised it when they were contrasting the two homes.

He went into the room and went over to the basin opening

the cupboard beneath it.

He shone his torch down and shuddered. Whereas the other shaft in the first room was filled with dust, this shaft was obviously well used with shiny bars on the sides. This meant that he had to be extra careful.

He climbed down, very aware that he was now in a longer shaft, one that was the equivalent of the kitchen area in the other house, which was reaching way below ground.

He was interested in that it actually ended in a broom cupboard and he was not surprised to see a well-equipped kitchen with staff and the smell of cooking.

On the previous day he had avoided going into this situation but this time he was desperate and he somehow slipped through the door into the room that he knew would have the long table with the high-backed chairs and the electronic equipment with all the luxury of the mansion, He looked for the crest gracing one large wall and he went over it to see if there were any steps hidden behind the passage there. The crest was exactly the same as the other one except that without shame or secret there was 'The Headley Society'.

He did not want to spend too much time here. He knew the big man was somewhere around and he needed to bring his family downstairs to speak to Andrew.

There had to be another way up. It could not be that Sky would have forgotten if they had come up a cramped shaft.

He walked over to what should have been the computer room in duplicate, but stopped when he heard voices.

Finding a small secluded alcove that would hide him from the entrance, he went in, just in time. The door opened and a man emerged and from his hiding place and he again caught sight of his eyes. No wonder Tracy had nightmares about them. They were strong and piercing and incredibly evil, even more evil than they had appeared before.

The man went over to what looked like a bookcase and, as if it had been a light door, slid it backwards to reveal an entrance.

He looked up and then returned. Lewin hoped he was not going to the room where Sky and Tracy were. But as he followed him from a distance he saw not only a fairly good staircase going upwards but also several well-lighted corridors he could have turned into.

Wasting no more time he quietly climbed the stairs, realising as he reached ground floor that he had been in at least a second basement.

He had to climb five short flights to actually get to the room where his family was. He emerged into the room through a loose panel in the wall, which even had a small handle on his side. He left it slightly ajar knowing that they would be going through it to see Andrew.

The older woman was asleep and they had to try not to wake her as Sky and Tracy followed him down the steps. He was relieved that there was no trace of Head himself.

They went down the stars fairly quickly until they came into the conference room with the long table and shield.

"My father is through this door," said Sky, recognising her surroundings. "I knew he was underground somewhere, but not how to get there."

Carefully, Lewin put his ear to the door to make sure Andrew was alone.

At a nod from Lewin, they all went through the door, Sky going over to her father and giving him a hug.

* * *

The man turned around to face them, and Tracy gave a gasp. The man, too, seemed puzzled, then shocked, and then flustered as he saw Tracy. For a moment, they both looked uncertain, and then their eyes locked. Lewin felt himself grow cold.

"Andrew!" said Tracy, who seemed to be the first to recover herself a little; after all, Sky had warned her that her father was here.

"Tracy!" he said. "But you can't be Tracy. I left Tracy more dead than alive. The doctors told me there was no chance, no chance at all that you would ever recover to the point of being more than... more than..."

"More than a vegetable," finished Tracy quietly.

Andrew had become very pale, which made his blush at these words stand out as two isolated spots on his cheeks and jagged blotches on his neck.

"I wouldn't put it that way," he said.

"Never mind," she said. "The doctors did."

He looked incredibly vulnerable standing there. He was still fairly handsome in a classic way but there were lines around his mouth, which showed dissatisfaction with life. He had also lost an incredible amount of weight, which made his features a little too sharp.

He was no longer the devastatingly good-looking man she had married so many years ago.

She found herself feeling sorry for him. She wondered what he had done with his life.

Lewin had already assessed the situation and he quickly introduced himself.

"Green? I never would have thought that Tracy was Mrs. Green. Congratulations. When did this happen? How long have you been... alive again?"

Andrew was clearly embarrassed.

"It took three years to recover completely" said Tracy, "and Lewin and I have only been married for three months."

"Congratulations," said Andrew quietly. "I am very happy for you." He seemed at a loss for words. "I never would have dreamt... You cannot imagine how happy I am for you. Can I speak to you alone?" Andrew looked at Tracy. "No, I think it is better I speak in front of Lewin, and Sky. After all, he is your husband, isn't he? And I made the mistake of... believing the doctors. It is surely something you don't blame me for. If I had had the slightest hope, which, in fact, no one ever gave me; if I had had the slightest idea, I would never have done it. Now I am the loser and Lewin... you are the winner. I cannot begrudge you. I can only feel that I was too hasty in getting a divorce, but the doctors told me there would never be any hope. I would have to forget about you and live my life with Andy as best I could. And there were other things..." His voice trailed off.

"You never married again?" she asked.

"Actually, not," he said. "If only I had known. I never dreamt this could have happened. But I am so happy you are well."

However, Tracy needed other answers. "I found out much later that you owed everybody money and had skipped the country," said Tracy. She tried to bite back her words. She had not meant to be so blunt.

Andrew had blushed crimson. "I have been paying it back steadily," he said. "I don't owe so much anymore. But it is more than that, far more than that."

"I know that," said Tracy. "Duncan told me."

"You saw Duncan!" he exclaimed. "How is he? Did they get married?"

"Yes, and they have a baby," said Tracy.

"I am so happy for them," said Andrew. "I never heard from them."

"When you pay someone regularly from a numbered Swiss bank account with no hope of an address, I would think that you would not hear from them."

"But, Andrew," said Lewin, "we would like to know

something else. Who could want to harm or injure, or even kill, Tracy?"

Andrew's face became a deathly white. "They went for you?" he asked.

"Who?" asked Lewin and Tracy together.

Andrew slumped forward in his chair and put his head in his hands. "The accident," he said. "The accident... the red car!"

The terrifying connection forced its way into his mind as he remembered the day of the accident, Yes, someone had phoned before. He had almost forgotten that. Yes, someone had phoned before the police and told him about the accident. Why had he not really remembered that?

He looked at Lewin, as if awakening from a dream. "The red car," he whispered.

"That," said Lewin slowly, "and other things."

"More things?" asked Andrew. His eyes had widened with panic. He was no longer white but a clammy red, and his breath was coming in short bursts.

"It must have been after you left," said Lewin. "When Tracy went down to the Cape."

"Tracy went down to the Cape?" asked Andrew wonderingly. His voice was dull, with a slight tremor.

"Who was it?" asked Lewin. "What is the story? We need to understand it. At least that will give us some lead."

"Yes, perhaps," said Andrew. He shut his eyes for a few moments, letting out a deep sigh. "Whilst I was married to

Tracy, I had a good job in a firm of accountants. I also had a strong share in my father's business. We were well off, more than well off, and we wanted for nothing. Then, a year or so before Tracy's accident, I was approached by a colleague of mine who told me that he had joined a scheme and had a guaranteed return on his money. What is more, he had already been paid out way above what he had originally been promised. I was not interested. I always avoided such schemes. But I began to see that what he was saying was true. He had sold his house and replaced it with a mansion that must have cost ten times the price. He and his wife were suddenly driving the most expensive cars and going on regular short holidays and trips overseas. As I say, we were not poor by any means, but this seemed to be too good to be true, and I invested some of my money in it. The returns were immediate and far beyond my expectations. I found myself receiving money that took very little effort to come by. I invested more and more, selling some of the shares in the business to do this. I influenced my clients to become interested in the scheme, and they entrusted their money to me to do the best I could for them and to make them rich quickly. I promise you that I never invested their money without their permission like the press would have liked everyone to believe. I have been paying back to them as much as I can."

"Was someone so upset and angry about this that they wanted to kill us?" asked Tracy. Something still did not add up.

Andrew looked at her. "No, Tracy," he said. "I found out afterwards that the whole scheme was a dishonest one. It was more than dishonest. It was actively involved in serious criminal activities. The friend who introduced me to it, when I confronted him, said he had no idea what they were really into and apologised. I said that I thought the whole thing should be exposed, and he became angry in a way that I had never seen before. Then he became very cold and said that I was free to do what I wanted as long as I was prepared to take the consequences. I did report them and the police arrested several of them. They were not able to catch the top men, though. And then, your accident happened. At first I did not connect it, except for the occasional doubt. I went through a terrible time feeling that you might have tried to take your own life because that was what people were saying. But then there was no earthly reason that I could think of for you to want to do that. And then they started talking about the red car. And you were not getting better, and the doctors said that your mind had gone and would never come back. And then the death threats on myself, and then on Andy. I divorced you, left what money I could with you, and you had a lot of insurance paying you and ran away with her to safety, leaving no trace of where we had gone. I so want Andy to be with her mother now. She needs you. She needs you both. Though I must have contact with her and see her sometimes, please."

The room had become darker and long shadows threw themselves across the carpet. Had the lights been dimmed?

A door above them opened and a voice to match the evil eyes seemed to snarl at them all. "What a wonderful little party I have here. Why, a whole family reunion... All the Sneddons, though, of course, one of the Sneddons has become a Green. Don't think you have any hope at all of eluding me. I have had many people killed, and you will join them. Yes, I know you brought police officers with you, but they are well taken care of. We have deactivated their communication system. We are not that ignorant, you know. Now I can kill you all, slowly but surely. Andrew Sneddon, did you really think the name Anthony Sheldon could protect you from us? You have lost everything, all of you. Did you really think you could disturb my kingdom? I am the master, the head, the kingpin. I have murderers, drug dealers, kidnappers and hijackers in my employ and completely under my control. Andrew Sneddon opposed me, betrayed me."

The door was shut with a bang as the voice disappeared.

Five minutes later another panel opened to reveal Mr. McPherson.

Lewin gave a sigh of relief asking how on earth he had got there and did he realise what a dangerous situation they were in.

"Oh yes, we know that," said Mr. McPherson, "but the police helicopters should be here any minute. I called them on my cell phone at least ten minutes ago after I heard what that guy with the creepy eyes said to you."

"You heard all that?" asked Lewin. "Where have you been all the time? You disappeared back there. We thought you had left."

"Well, I just about followed you and, of course, there were others of us. After all, we set this up very carefully, and you just had to play your part, which, I must say, you did excellently. At the same time, we were concerned about you and more or less knew what you were going to do and, when we got up to the room and started to go down the pipes under the sink, we heard the voices. We heard it all. Don't worry, we heard it all.

"We have been waiting for this moment for many, many months; years, in fact. We have been watching and waiting. We knew they were after you, Mrs. Green, and after Sky, or, rather, should I say, Andrea, and, of course, Andrew. But Sky and Andrew were missing, and we knew that, if you went after them, they would somehow not be able to resist going after you. We found out a few months ago that they had contact with the Headley Society and that the chief, named 'Head', was deeply into something terribly evil, but we were not sure what. We needed to be sure. We knew the hotel you stayed at had something to do with that, and we knew there was an identical house somewhere... The council property map seemed to indicate this one, but we needed confirmation, which you gave."

"Will we get out of here?" asked Andrew. "Will we be

safe?"

"Oh yes, definitely," said Mr. McPherson.

Almost at that minute, they heard another welcome sound, as the first police helicopter arrived.

CHAPTER 14

It was early morning when Benzie got off the plane at Kennedy Airport and went through passport control with his American passport responding with a nod to the official's comment welcoming him home.

He found a taxi and gave his family's address. As he did so he felt a sense of panic as to how he would be received. Perhaps, in fact, his family would have moved. Perhaps they would have taken on an apartment, especially as there would now only be the two of them. In that case, how would he find them?

A sudden panic overtook him as he looked out of the window at the familiar streets. What if they had moved? What if everyone had moved; although, there would obviously be a forwarding address? He would just have to find them. If Pamela, Percy and Peter penguin had found their homes on Dassen and Robin Islands, then he could find his family.

What if they did not want him? However, he had been through that with Lewin and Tracy, and they had made him fairly certain that they would want him.

They were approaching Long Island. He had known that it was not far from the airport. He wished he was living further away so that he would have a chance to think. But he had been thinking all the time in the endless night of the plane ride. He had left Johannesburg Airport before 8 p.m. the night before and had arrived early morning, but there had been a whole six hours of time difference that had been added on to the night; plenty of time for reflection.

He realised that it was still early and that he would probably have to wake up his parents, but he had no option. He was not going to wait outside especially as the spring morning had a cold nip in the air. The beginning of April, he remembered, could be quite cold. He remembered it had always been fairly cold at this time.

He had arrived at the door of the house, and could see that the same familiar curtains were shut behind the windows and that the nameplate of his family was on the door. They had not moved! For that, he felt a relief.

He paid off the taxi, suppressing the impulse to beg him to wait for him in case he needed to go back.

He placed his luggage on the lawn and quietly knocked at the door. There was no answer so he knocked again a little louder.

A twelve-year-old boy answered the door and, for a moment, both brothers stared at each other. Benzie did not dare ask him his name. He knew his name. He could not be making a mistake.

"Benzie!" said his younger brother, flinging his arms around him. "Benzie, you are back. I didn't die, but we could not find you to tell you that."

"Craig," whispered Benzie, tears running down his cheeks. "Craig, where did you come from? Craig, they were switching off the machines. You were going to die that day."

"Well, they did switch off the machines and I carried on breathing, so they switched them all on again, and I eventually got better. But you had gone."

"I had killed you," said Benzie hardly able to speak.

"No, you didn't. You just took me for a ride in Dad's car. You didn't kill me at all. You didn't even know if I had died."

"Where are Mum and Dad?" asked Benzie.

"They are still fast asleep," said Craig. "I don't want to wake them up yet, because it is their thirty-fifth wedding anniversary party tonight, and we will all be up late, and Mum has been up most of the night cooking."

Craig suddenly looked up at him with an impish smile. "Benzie, will you do something for me, just to act out a daydream I have been having for at least two years about your coming home? I will give you some coffee and some cereal, and we can hide your cases in my room, but can I take you to Mike's house...? He used to be your best friend, didn't he? You can be there for the day. Benzie please can we do that?"

"What about Mum and Dad?" asked Benzie.

"Benzie, tonight all the family will be here. You know David and Martin are married, and David and Sheila even have a baby girl. And Jimmy is engaged, so we will have them all here."

Benzie was amazed to hear this.

"Benzie," he said, beaming. "Benzie, just imagine this. I have imagined it for two years already. Please, Benzie, just think...It was the night of the wedding anniversary... The family was having a guest. Little did they know that that extra guest was..."

He looked so excited and so pleased to see him that Benzie had to agree. His own intense joy and relief at seeing Craig alive and well and enthusiastic and up to mischief as usual was almost too much happiness to cope with.

Also it would be quite fun to surprise everyone. Another thing was that he had not really slept on the plane and was extremely tired. Several hours of sleep would do him good...

It was the night of the wedding anniversary. The Sands family were putting the finishing touches to the table, making things perfect before their guests would arrive.

Mr. Bernard Sands would be back from the city in another twenty minutes together with several guests who would be coming to the party.

Craig had asked permission to bring two extra older friends of his and the family had agreed. Visitors were always welcome. In some strange way, thought Mr. Sands, it made up, a little, for Benzie's absence. However, he did not want to think about his son who three years ago had left home condemning himself as a murderer. He had not been able to understand that the family loved him completely whatever had happened.

Mr. Sands had not believed that Benzie would do this. He had seemed to be the one who was closest to the family. On the other hand he understood how sensitive he was, and that he could not bear to be the one to cause any hurt to the family. Had he not known how much he had hurt them by going away? It had been extremely traumatic to believe they were going to lose their youngest son, but the joy of his recovery was marred by the disappearance of their second youngest son. They had not been able to find him whatever they had done.

At first, his family knew where he was, though he never visited.

He started to travel and from his last postcard seemed to be somewhere in South Africa saving oiled penguins. but that had been several months ago. They had heard nothing since and he never let them have a return address.

However, he had made it obvious that he had broken forever with them.

Bernard Sands gave a sigh as he picked up a photograph of his five sons. Yes, five sons, yet only four at the celebration. His wife caught his look, and her eyes filled with tears. Yes, it was a hard thing, perhaps the hardest thing to have a son that had all but disappeared.

However, they could not dwell on the aching of both of their hearts. There were still the last minute preparations, which their two daughters-in-law were working on. They needed help. And there were still the guests to look after. Some of them had arrived already. There was an elderly couple whose children had got married and gone to live far away. There was a family who had just moved into the area.

There were also two widows who were regular visitors to the Sands family.

However, they could not start yet. The two young men were not here yet. At that moment, he heard them knock at the door and he felt his heart break within him when he saw that one of them had been, for many years, his son Benzie's best friend.

He did not recognise the other young man, possibly because he had a cap pulled quite far down over his face and he was looking at the floor. Perhaps the young man was very shy.

His son's friend, Mike, indicated that they would like to speak to him privately.

Not thinking too much about this he welcomed them into his private study. It was only when the door was closed that the second young man looked at him.

Mr. Sands felt his heart give a jump as he whispered, "Benzie! Benzie! I don't believe it. It's my Benzie!"

Father and son held onto each other, tears rolling down their cheeks. "Benzie, Benzie," said his father. "I am so glad to see you again. We have been so worried about you."

"I'm sorry, Dad," said Benzie, his voice choked with

emotion. "I'm sorry, Dad. I could not bear the thought that I had killed Craig. I could not be with you knowing I had caused you all so much pain."

The realisation seemed to strike Bernard Sands and he drew back and looked at his son for several seconds. "Benzie, you look so well. Benzie, you are back with us. Oh, my Benzie!"

Once more, he hugged his son, the tears flowing even faster.

"Mum," said Benzie. "Mike, please ask Mum to come in here."

He realised that Mike, watching this, had been crying, too, but he was able to dry his eyes, sniff a couple of times, and call Anne Sands.

She came in looking a little anxious as to why the young men were upset and hoping it would not delay the party.

She recognised her son immediately and her face lighted up as she held him. "Benzie, my Benzie. You have no idea how much we prayed for you to come back." She spoke between her tears. "We knew that you would come back one day."

"But what happened, Benzie?" asked his father later as they were all seated around the table. "The last time we heard from you, you were cleaning oiled penguins somewhere on the coast of South Africa. Because you were there, we actually followed the news broadcasts."

"Yes," said Craig, who had not stopped alternately

smiling and crying since he realised his big brother had returned. "There was Peter, Pamela and Percy Penguin. They swam hundreds of kilometres until they came home, right to the places they had left, to those islands right in the ocean over there. When I used to think about you, I used to think that, if they can find their way home and if there is something so deep and strong in them to find their way home, you would somehow find yours."

Benzie smiled. "That is what started me off on my journey back home. Of course, there were other people there. There was Dr. Lewin Green, and Tracy, his wife, and their daughter, Andy, who was also lost for a long time, but is with them again. All of them, and I mean the penguins, too, taught me so many things about life. So you have your fifth son with you. Just as those penguins felt their homes on Robben Island and Dassen Island calling to them, which gave them the strength to swim for days through the ocean, something must have been calling to me, something stronger than we can ever imagine. We all still hear it calling."

It was several months later that his mother handed him some mail that had come for him. One of the letters from SANCCOB told him that Ben, flipper band A5738, had been sighted together with Priscilla, flipper band A8329… Tracy's bird and that they were in their nest with two downy, fluffy chicks. The other letter was from Lewin telling him that Tracy had given birth to a son and that Andy now had a little brother.

Published with Create Space Independent
Publishing Platform   2013

Made in the USA
Middletown, DE
07 May 2021